CW00418825

Wooing the Farmer

What Reviewers Say
About Jenny Frame's Work

Unexpected

"[Jenny Frame] has this beautiful way of writing a phenomenally hot scene while incorporating the love and tenderness between the couple."—*Les Rêveur*

"If you enjoy contemporary romances, Unexpected is a great choice. The character work is excellent, the plotting and pacing are well done, and it's a just a sweet, warm read. ...Definitely pick this book up when you're looking for your next comfort read, because it's sure to put a smile on your face by the time you get to that happy ending."—*Curve*

"*Unexpected* by Jenny Frame is a charming butch/femme romance that is perfect for anyone who wants to feel the magic of overcoming adversity and finding true love. I love the way Jenny Frame writes. I have yet to discover an author who writes like her. Her voice is strong and unique and gives a freshness to the lesbian fiction sector."—*Lesbian Review*

Royal Rebel

"Frame's stories are easy to follow and really engaging. She stands head and shoulders above a number of the romance authors and it's easy to see why she is quickly making a name for herself in lesfic romance."—*The Lesbian Review*

Courting the Countess

"I love Frame's romances. They are well paced, filled with beautiful character moments and a wonderful set of side characters who ultimately end up winning your heart. ...I love Jenny Frame's butch/femme dynamic she gets it so right for a romance." —*The Lesbian Review*

"I loved loved loved this book. I didn't expect to get so involved in the story but I couldn't help but fall in love with Annie and Harry. ...The love scenes were beautifully written and very sexy. I found the whole book romantic and ultimately joyful and I had a lump in my throat on more than one occasion. A wonderful book that certainly stirred my emotions..."—*KittyKat Book Reviews*

"*Courting The Countess* has an historical feel in a present day world, a thought provoking tale filled with raw emotions throughout. [Frame] has a magical way of pulling you in, making you feel every emotion her characters experience."—*Lunar Rainbow Reviewz*

"I didn't want to put the book down and I didn't. Harry and Annie are two amazingly written characters that bring life to the pages as they find love and adventures in Harry's home. This is a great read, and you will enjoy it immensely if you give it a try!"—*Fantastic Book Reviews*

A Royal Romance

"*A Royal Romance* was a guilty pleasure read for me. It was just fun to see the relationship develop between George and Bea, to see George's life as queen and Bea's as a commoner. It was also refreshing to see that both of their families were encouraging, even when Bea doubted that things could work between them because of their class differences. ...*A Royal Romance* left me wanting a sequel, and romances don't usually do that to me."—*Leeanna.ME Mostly a Book Blog*

Charming the Vicar

"The sex scenes were some of the sexiest, most intimate and quite frankly, sensual I have read in a while. Jenny Frame had me hooked and I re-read a few scenes because I felt like I needed to experience the intense intimacy between Finn and Bridget again. The devotion they showed to one another during these sex scenes but also in the intimate moments was gripping and for lack of a better word, carnal."—*Les Rêveur*

The sexual chemistry between [Finn and Bridge] is unbelievably hot. It is sexy, lustful and with more than a hint of kink. Bridge has an overpowering effect on Finn as her long-hidden sexuality comes to the fore. The scenes between them are highly erotic— and not just the sex scenes. The tension is ramped up so well that I felt the characters would explode if they did not get relief! ...An excellent book set in the most wonderful village—a place I hope to return to very soon!"—*Kitty Kat's Book Review Blog*

Heart of the Pack

"A really well written love story that incidentally involves changers as well as humans."—*Inked Rainbow Reads*

Hunger for You

"[Byron and Amelia] are guaranteed to get the reader all hot and bothered. Jenny Frame writes brilliant love scenes in all of her books and makes me believe the characters crave each other."
—*Kitty Kat's Book Review Blog*

"I loved this book. Paranormal stuff like vampires and werewolves are my go-to sins. This book had literally everything I needed: chemistry between the leads, hot love scenes (phew), drama, angst, romance (oh my, the romance) and strong supporting characters."—*The Reading Doc*

Visit us at www.boldstrokesbooks.com

By the Author

A Royal Romance

Heart of the Pack

Courting the Countess

Royal Rebel

Dapper

Unexpected

Charming the Vicar

Hunger for You

Soul of the Pack

Wooing the Farmer

WOOING THE FARMER

by
Jenny Frame

2019

WOOING THE FARMER

© 2019 BY JENNY FRAME. ALL RIGHTS RESERVED.

ISBN 13: 978-1-63555-381-9

THIS TRADE PAPERBACK ORIGINAL IS PUBLISHED BY
BOLD STROKES BOOKS, INC.
P.O. BOX 249
VALLEY FALLS, NY 12185

FIRST EDITION: MARCH 2019

THIS IS A WORK OF FICTION. NAMES, CHARACTERS, PLACES, AND
INCIDENTS ARE THE PRODUCT OF THE AUTHOR'S IMAGINATION OR
ARE USED FICTITIOUSLY. ANY RESEMBLANCE TO ACTUAL PERSONS,
LIVING OR DEAD, BUSINESS ESTABLISHMENTS, EVENTS, OR LOCALES
IS ENTIRELY COINCIDENTAL.

THIS BOOK, OR PARTS THEREOF, MAY NOT BE REPRODUCED IN ANY
FORM WITHOUT PERMISSION.

CREDITS
EDITOR: RUTH STERNGLANTZ
PRODUCTION DESIGN: SUSAN RAMUNDO
COVER DESIGN BY SHERI (HINDSIGHTGRAPHICS@GMAIL.COM)

Acknowledgments

Thanks to Rad, Sandy, and all the BSB team for all their hard work behind the scenes. Big thanks to Ruth Sternglantz for her endless encouragement and always making the editing process fun.

As always, thanks to my family for their continuing support and encouragement.

Lou, thank you for your unshakable loyalty and belief in me. Thank you for taking care of me and always doing more than you should. To my other true love, my dog Barney, thank you for keeping me company while I write. You are the bestest boy!

xx

Dedication

To Lou.
My inspiration and my love.
xx

CHAPTER ONE

"Your car's here, Little Pen."

Penelope zipped up the last bag on her bed and shouted, "I'll be down soon, Mummy."

She looked around her bedroom in her parents' Victorian mansion in Mayfair and let out a sigh of relief. As much as she adored her parents, she'd had enough of being Little Pen. Once she got outside their door, she wasn't Little Pen, the baby—she was Penny Huntingdon-Stewart, successful businesswoman and social media personality. Penny knew more than anyone the power of names, both on herself and others. The Huntingdon-Stewart name had been like a weight around her neck all her life.

A bark from her little dog brought her attention back to the bed. Princess Baby Bear, to give the dog its full name, was Penny's brown toy poodle, and her baby. She co-starred on Penny's YouTube channel, her Instagram account, and in the books and TV series she did, not to mention being the love of Penny's life. They were a team and Penny didn't go anywhere without her. She groomed her like a cute teddy bear and not like a traditional poodle, but Princess was never seen without the cutest little clothes that complemented Penny's style.

"What is it?" Penny said to Princess. "You want to go and see Grandpa?"

Princess adored her father and enjoyed nothing more than lying on his lap by the fire. "Wait, I just need one photo and you can go."

As if understanding what Penny needed, Princess sat on the suitcase on the bed while Penny gathered a few things to set up the picture she wanted for social media.

"Okay, we got the cute, the hint of new beginnings, and now..."

Penny grasped the copy of *Lady Chatterley's Lover* she had borrowed from her parents' library and placed it on the case.

"For the hint of sex."

Penny held up her phone and, happy with the set-up, said, "Smile, Princess."

After the click, Princess barked again excitedly. The photo was exactly what she needed so she said, "Off you go then. I'll meet you downstairs in a few minutes."

There was a knock on her door as Princess rushed out, and her big brother Hugo came into her room. "Are you ready, Pen? Let me take your bags."

"Thanks Go-Go. It's these last two." Penny had found it difficult to pronounce Hugo when she began to talk as a child, and so Hugo became Go-Go, and it stuck.

She checked one of the bags for the hundredth time it seemed, to make sure her large stock of medication was all there. The medication that ruled her life, that she couldn't *have* a life without.

Everything was there, so she put her book in her holdall and zipped it.

Hugo picked them up and said, "Are you sure you don't want me to come with you, just to help with the bags and boxes?"

Penny loved her big brother and her big sister very much, but she needed space. She needed space after living back with her parents for the past six months. Penny was fiercely independent, ran her own business, and she had not expected to be back in her old bedroom at age thirty, but her health problems had forced her to be.

"I'll be fine with the boxes. I've got my two drivers. I'm more worried about the mud and muck than the heavy boxes."

Hugo laughed. "I'm sorry, I just can't imagine my little sister as a country girl. You live for shopping, art galleries, lunch with the girls at the best restaurants. I don't know how you'll survive."

Penny frowned and looked down at her Gucci pumps and despaired at the thought of getting them dirty.

"It's not my idea of a good time, Go-Go. The mud, the strange smells. Yuck. It's Olivia's idea, and she's never steered me wrong yet…well, hardly."

Olivia, Penny's friend from school and business partner, had helped build *Penny's Kitchen* from a small YouTube cookery show and vlog, to TV shows, branded food in supermarkets, and a social media sensation.

But since Penny collapsed on live TV and was taken to hospital with an epilepsy attack, she had withdrawn from her social media empire, and rumours and lies had spread about her health. So now Penny was ready to get back out there after recuperating with her mother and father.

Olivia suggested a country cooking web series to shoot while Penny wrote her own country cookbook.

Penny added, "It's only for a few months, and it looks good to the public. Penny Huntingdon-Stewart, city girl, going back to basics and living in the country to renew myself and the brand. I'll do anything to drive the business on."

Hugo sighed. "When will it be enough? You don't have to keep proving yourself all the time, Pen. Stress isn't good for you, and your drive to build this business has taken its toll on you."

Penny picked up her last Louis Vuitton bag. "So says the youngest ever maths professor at Cambridge. We all have to strive in this family, Go-Go. You know what the Huntingdon-Stewart name means. Besides, you know me—I'll make the country fabulous," Penny said with a wink.

Hugo walked over and kissed her on the cheek. "As long as you're happy, Pen. Just look after yourself. Let's get your bags downstairs."

Penny nodded and double-checked she had her mobile in her bag. Her phone was the nerve centre of her and her business, and it was rarely out of her hand. She then had a quick look in the large mirror in the corner to make sure her long golden-blond hair wasn't out of place.

It was early June, and the weather was warming up, so she'd decided a light duck egg wrap-around dress with pink flowers and a plunging neckline would be appropriate for the country.

As they walked down the big oak staircase, Penny was faced with the portrait of the man who made the Huntingdon-Stewart name the most famous, and who they all tried to aspire to—their great-great-grandfather, Horatio Huntingdon-Stewart, who was prime minister and one of the greatest statesmen the country had ever produced. He lived over one hundred years ago, but his legacy burned brightly.

A war hero, a great reformer, and an advocate for the poor—when people heard Penny's surname they thought of Horatio. It was a difficult reputation to live up to when you were dyslexic, suffered from epilepsy, and left school without any qualifications. That feeling of inadequacy fuelled Penny to constantly strive and prove she was worthy of the name she bore, and now it was time to get back in the saddle.

Quade took the last bite of her bacon sandwich and lifted the local newspaper. She had finished all her early morning chores on the farm and was now eating breakfast before she went back out. Sitting across the breakfast table in her farmhouse kitchen was her black and white collie dog Dougal.

Dougal sat up on a chair just like her, eating bacon scraps Quade had given her. Apart from the rustle of the newspaper, the only other noises were the crackle of fire from the wood burning oven, and news playing on the radio in the background.

Quade wasn't even listening. The radio was just on so there wasn't silence in the room. She hated silence and being alone. She read through all the local news, from jumble sale notices to charity evenings at the local pub, The Witch's Tavern. The pub was the hub of her social life, not because she was a big drinker—she wasn't—but apart from church and special village events, the pub was the only time she got to socialize in this small village.

Quade got to the adverts page of the paper, and she said to Dougal, "Mr. Jones is selling an antique writing desk." She looked over the top of her paper at Dougal. "Do we need a writing desk?"

Dougal cocked his head to the side as if trying to understand what Quade was saying.

Quade folded her newspaper up quickly and lifted her cup of tea. "If I keep talking to my dog, one day you're going to reply and I'm going to shit myself."

Talking to her dog was just another reminder of how empty this cottage was. Since her uncle died, she had thrown herself into making the farm a success, but as things settled down, she had more free time, and more time to realize she was alone, apart from Dougal. Quade had good friends in the village, friends who would do anything for each other, but when she met her best friends at the pub—Harry and Annie, Bridge and Finn—they each went home with a partner, while she went home to an empty cottage and Dougal.

She needed a change in her life, some kind of fresh start. Quade looked around her kitchen and wondered if she should decorate, do something a bit different. She always kept the cottage in good order and freshly painted but never strayed from the style her aunt had. It was outdated, she knew, but Quade wouldn't know where to start choosing a new style for her home.

That was the thing. Since her aunt and uncle died, it didn't feel like a home. A home needed two or more loving people. Since ever Quade could remember, all she wanted was a wife and a simple life working the farm, but partners were thin on the ground in a tiny English village.

This had become even more evident to her since her good friend Bridget had found her partner Finn and fallen in love. She put down her tea and sighed. Time for dinner with her ladyship tonight. Quade enjoyed dining with her friends, and Annie's cooking was amazing, but she felt awkward being the only one not in a couple. Dougal, though, always enjoyed the company.

"Dougal? We're going to see Riley tonight for dinner." Dougal barked and looked at her with a happy bright-eyed look. "It's all right for you—you get to eat and play with Riley and her puppy."

Puppy was a bit of an understatement. Caesar was only six months old and huge already. When Harry had told her stepdaughter Riley she could get any dog she wanted, both Annie and Harry were greatly surprised when she had chosen a blue Great Dane. Although large, he was a daft, goofy dog, and a good companion for Riley.

Would Quade ever meet anyone who would be more than a companion or friend to her? She looked at the picture of her aunt and uncle on the dresser and said, "Aunt Julia, if there's anyone in the world out there for me, help me find them."

She shook her head. "What am I doing? First my dog and then a picture."

Quade stood and drank the last of her tea. "Come on, Dougal, let's get back out to the fields. There's fence to mend."

"Mummy, I'll be fine," Penny said as her mother Lavinia squeezed the life out of her at the bottom of the stairs.

"You'll be all alone in the country, with no one to check on you." Her mother's overprotectiveness wasn't meant to be overbearing. She meant well, as did her father and all her family. Ever since her first epileptic attack at school, they had been constantly protective and vigilant.

But she couldn't live like that twenty-four hours a day any longer, like the last few months.

"I'll be around people all the time. It's a small village," Penny said.

Hugo added, "Mum, Harry lives there. She'll watch out for Pen."

Lavinia brushed Penny's hair from her eyes. "Just promise me you'll keep in touch all the time and take it easy. No stress. I don't want you in hospital again."

Penny kissed her mother on the cheek and smiled. No one would believe that a woman as accomplished and dedicated to her career as a Lavinia Huntingdon-Stewart, who had a long career in politics as a campaigner for women's rights, and now sat in the House of Lords, found the time to be such a devoted mother. All her children adored her, as did her husband, and Penny felt guilty for pushing her away sometimes.

"I promise I'll take care of myself." Penny looked at Hugo. "I don't need anyone to look in on me, but I promise I'll call you all the time. Now let me say goodbye to Daddy."

They walked into the drawing room, and she saw Princess sitting on her father's lap by the fire. Her father, Guy, wasn't in the best of health, having suffered with heart problems for the past year.

"Little Pen, come here, my darling." Her father beckoned her over.

She went over and knelt by his armchair and stroked her dog. "Has this little rascal been keeping you company, Daddy?"

"Yes, she's a good girl. Are you leaving now, Pen?" Guy said.

"Yes, all set. I'm going to miss you." Penny took his hand and smiled.

"I wish you didn't have to go. Your mother is going to worry terribly, and me. I don't like the thought of you staying alone."

"I promise you, I'll take care of myself, but I have to get back out there. Into the business world, on social media, make videos, concentrate on my career and build it back up."

Social media had always baffled her father and trying to explain to him how you could make money and run a business on it was hopeless, despite the fact he was the cleverest person she knew. Up until he retired from his professorship at Cambridge, he was one of the world's top quantum physicists.

Guy took her hand and kissed it. "I'll never understand what you do, but I'll always defend your right to do it, my Little Pen."

Pen stood and hugged her father. "Thank you, Daddy. I love you and I'm going to miss you."

"I love you. Take care of yourself," Guy said.

If Penny didn't make tracks soon, she would never leave her loving family. She felt guilty for pushing them away. All they did was give, and she pushed.

She took a breath and found her steely resolve. "I better get going."

Penny opened her Louis Vuitton dog bag and patted the floor. "Come on, Princess Baby Bear. Time to go."

Princess jumped off her father's lap and ran over to Penny. She sat nicely beside the bag, panting with excitement. Already wearing a white polka dotted pink jumper, Princess sat patiently while Penny slipped four shiny pink boots on her paws.

Once they were on Penny leaned down and said, "Kiss." Princess gave her a kiss, then followed her instruction to jump into the bag. "We're all set to go."

One last kiss to her father and she was walking with her mother out to the car. Her brother was putting the last of her bags into the minivan in front of her white sports car.

Penny shouted to the driver of the minivan, "Just go ahead, Martin. I'll be leaving in a few minutes."

Her regular driver Tom opened up the door to her pride and joy, her white Ferrari. She climbed into the passenger seat and placed Princess on her lap.

Penny's parents always thought it strange that she bought a car, and such an extravagant and powerful car, when she wasn't allowed to drive because of her condition. But to Penny it was a symbol of what she'd achieved in business. She'd bought it with her own money and not her trust fund.

The minivan pulled away, and she said to her mother and brother, "You two go in. I need to shoot some video before I go."

Lavinia rolled her eyes. "All right, well, phone me as soon as you get there."

"And tell Harry we all miss her at Cambridge," Hugo added.

Penny gave them a bright smile. "I will."

Once they walked back inside, Penny said to Tom, "I just need to shoot some video before we leave."

"No problem," Tom said.

Penny stroked Princess's head. "Mummy's just got to make a quick video, and we'll go to have fun in the country—well, as much fun as mud and cows can be," she said with a sigh.

On her dashboard was an elaborate set-up of video camera and microphone. She set her phone in a holder beside it and checked her appearance in the mirror.

"Oh God, look at my lippy," Penny said. She quickly pulled her handbag from the back seat and got out her make-up bag. She quickly reapplied her lipstick and looked to her dog. "How do I look?"

Princess barked happily in response, and Penny smiled. "Fabulous? Just like I thought."

She put her things away and lifted Princess onto her lap before pressing the button on her video camera.

"Hello, friends!" Penny lifted Princess's paw and waved it at the camera. "Say hi to Penny's friends, Princess."

She imitated a baby voice for her dog and said, "Hi, Penny's friends."

Then she kissed the dog's snout and addressed the camera. "This is just a quick video to tell you about the start of life's next great adventure for Princess and me. We are just about to drive to a little village in Kent—yes, that's right, we're bringing *Penny's Kitchen* to the country. Let the fun begin!"

Penny shut off the camera and posted the video, as well as the photo she took earlier, and turned to Princess. "Let's make this fabulous, Princess." Then to her driver, "Let's go, Tom."

Quade left her farmhands to finish the fence without her. She was due up at the estate manager's office for a planning meeting with Mr. Stevens. Since Harry had appointed Quade assistant estate manager, much of her farm work had to be delegated to her farmhands. It certainly kept her busy, and Quade liked to keep busy.

"Come on, Dougal," she called to her dog, and he ran after her. She was just coming out of her field when she heard a sports car roaring up the road. They didn't see many sports cars in Axedale.

Lady Harry had a couple, but nowadays a Land Rover was more her style.

She stopped and watched a white Ferrari slow as it approached her. The blacked out window lowered halfway and revealed a woman with long blond hair, sunglasses, and glittery bright pink nails. There was a man driving and a little dog barking on the seat with the woman, making Dougal bark back excitedly. "Quiet, Dougal."

The woman still hadn't looked up and was animatedly engaged in a phone conversation.

"Hang on a sec, Olivia. We need to ask directions."

She looked up and Quade saw the woman's lips were the same luscious pink colour as her nails.

"Excuse me? Could you tell me where Northwood Cottage is?"

"Northwood?" Quade said with surprise. No one had lived in Northwood Cottage for years. "It's just a mile up the road and to the right—"

Before Quade could say any more, the woman said, "Thanks. Got that, Tom?" The woman put something in Quade's hand and zoomed off.

Quade looked down at her hand and saw she had given her a five pound coin. "She tipped me? What am I, a bloody waiter?" City people. "Come on, Dougal. We need to make a quick call before we head up to Axedale."

CHAPTER TWO

Penny walked around the living room of Northwood Cottage while talking to Olivia on speakerphone. "I know I said traditional cottage, but there's traditional and too traditional. It looks like it hasn't been redecorated in a hundred years."

Penny's suitcases were sitting at the bottom of the stairs, and her camera and editing equipment was piled on the sofa and chairs in front of the fireplace.

"It's rustic, Pen. That was the brief. I sent cleaners, people to set up your internet connection, and filled your freezer, fridge, and cupboards with all the supplies you'll need to start with. What more do you need?"

Penny sighed and looked at the fireplace. It was empty and desolate just like the rest of the house. How on earth was she meant to make a fire?

"I thought it would be cosy and warm at least. This place hasn't been lived in for a long time. I've got to make it look warm and inviting for the viewers and set up the camera and sound equipment"—Penny threw her hands up in the air—"and write the book. I don't know how I'll ever get it all done."

She walked into the kitchen and laid her phone down on the kitchen table, then held her face in her hands. It was all so overwhelming.

Olivia was quiet for a few seconds then said, "Do you want me to send down a production team for you? You know that's what I wanted for you."

"No," Penny said quickly. "You know I do this on my own, Olivia."

She heard Olivia sigh. "You're so stubborn. If that's what you want. Besides, stumbling and learning new things is part of the charm of your show. This could be big for you, Pen. I've got some American networks sniffing around."

Penny, who was looking in the Aga and trying to figure out how it worked, stood up suddenly. "What do you mean sniffing around?"

"They're interested in bringing you to American TV. They love the idea of the upper-middle-class socialite with a cooking show. They love your YouTube channel, and this new little English village vibe just adds to the charm."

Penny started to feel the buzz of excitement that success in business gave her. It was everything she wanted, for *Penny's Kitchen* to be a household name on both sides of the pond.

Suddenly the cottage was now a challenge, a means to an end for success. "I can do this, Olivia—just keep them interested. If we want to launch a Penny's Kitchen range in America, a TV show could be a perfect vehicle. Only, no live shows. You did tell them that?"

"Of course. I promised you I would never ask you to do that again after…" Olivia hesitated.

Penny remembered the fear and dread of being on one of the biggest live daytime shows and feeling the telltale signs of a fit coming on. The video of her fitting had gone viral and embarrassed her to her core.

When she woke up in hospital, she thought her business and career, her way to succeed, had been ruined, but this idea of Olivia's was her chance to give a shot in the arm to her company.

"I'm going to make it fabulous." Penny smiled.

"That's my girl. I'll talk to you soon. Bye."

Once Penny hung up, her dog started to bark at the front door. "What is it, Princess?"

She walked over and opened the front door just in time to see a Land Rover driving away. She looked down on the doorstep and saw a box of chocolates with a note sitting there. Penny lifted them up and read the note.

Dear Miss,
   I don't need a tip for giving directions. I own the farm next door. I used your money and bought these chocolates for you. Enjoy them.
   Yours faithfully,
   Sam McQuade

Penny laughed. "Oh my God, how old-fashioned. *Dear Miss* and *Yours faithfully?*" She hadn't really noticed who had given her directions, and it was just second nature to tip anyone who helped her in her social circles.

Penny looked down at Princess and said, "Someone's feathers are ruffled. We better smooth them over. We don't want to make enemies this quickly."

Princess barked and followed her inside.

A few hours later Penny got a box of her signature muffins she had brought from London to give to Harry and changed into a short pink floral-print dress. She popped Princess into her bag and walked down to where she had asked for directions. There was a small dirt road which led up to a farmhouse just over the brow of the hill.

Penny looked down at her heels, then back to the dirt road. "Princess? Do we really walk up there?"

It was a tough choice, but she didn't need any enemies already, so she said to Princess, "Looks like we're walking. Let's hope this grumpy farmer appreciates my sacrifice."

Gingerly Penny began to walk up the dirt road. She swayed as her heel stuck in the mud, nearly toppling. "Bloody Olivia. City girl in the country will be great. Yes, funny for everyone else that sees me falling on my backside at every turn."

She finally got to the top of the hill and lifted her head. Penny stopped breathing when she saw the most delicious, tall, sturdy, well-made butch chopping wood at the front door of the farmhouse.

"How very Lady Chatterley," Penny said smiling.

That must have been the woman on the road. She never noticed how gorgeous she was when she stopped to ask for the directions.

Penny stood silently, gazing at her swinging the axe. The butch was wearing just a white sleeveless T-shirt, and every time she swung the axe, Penny could see the play of her solid muscles and broad shoulders. Her jeans hung perfectly on her hips, and she wore heavy work boots that just added to her sexy ruggedness. Penny had never really seen anything like her. No one she had ever been out with in London had been quite like this rural farmer.

Maybe the country would have its compensations.

Just then a black and white collie dog came out of the house barking excitedly, and the farmer looked up. Penny took a step forward, tripped, and came crashing to the ground.

Princess was barking, and suddenly Penny had a flashback of falling as she fitted on live TV. Panic and embarrassment spread through her.

Quade ran over and lifted the woman's head off the ground, supporting it gently. Dougal was barking, and a little poodle dog the woman was carrying was barking, making the scene all the more chaotic.

"Are you all right, miss?"

"Let me up," the woman said angrily.

Quade held her there. "Take it easy. You could have broken something. I'll check you over."

"No." The woman pushed against her, and Quade had no choice but to help her to her feet but took care to take her weight.

"What's your name?"

"Penelope Huntingdon-Stewart."

Quade wasn't expecting that accent or that name. She sounded just like Harry and Bridge, and there wasn't a person in the country who was taught history at school that didn't know the name Huntingdon-Stewart.

"Okay, Penny, I've got you. Just be careful."

Penny put her right foot down and cried out in pain. Quade scooped her up in her arms without a second thought and started for the farmhouse.

"What the bloody hell do you think you're doing?"

Quade ignored her and said to Dougal, "Watch out for the little dog, Dougal. I'll come back for it in a minute."

She looked down at the beautiful woman in her arms, and her heart skipped a beat, despite the scowl on Penny's face. When she had looked up and saw what Dougal was barking at, she nearly dropped the axe on her foot. The vision of Penelope Huntingdon-Stewart looked so out of place in her driveway. She appeared as if she had just stepped out of a designer store in London and had a chauffeur-driven car waiting for her. Was she dreaming? Penelope was like some kind of vision she had concocted in her mind of everything she found attractive in a woman. A tumble of long wavy blond hair, a beautiful figure, and with her luscious pink lips and nails, so utterly female.

"You better put me down, right now," Penny demanded.

"I will in a second—I'm just trying to help you," Quade said. Why was she being so difficult?

Quade kicked open the living room door and carried Penny over to a leather armchair in front of the fire. She got her seated and brought over a footstool.

"Okay, let's put your foot up here, and I'll go and get your dog." Penny grimaced as Quade lifted her leg onto the stool. "What's his name?"

"It's a she. Princess Baby Bear," Penny said while she shifted about trying to get comfortable.

Quade burst out laughing. "Princess Baby Bear? You're having me on."

Penny looked up at her with indignation. "Her name is Princess Baby Bear."

Quade held up her hands, "Okay, okay, touchy. I'll get *Princess Baby Bear*."

When Quade walked away, Penny brought her hands to her face. Her ankle was throbbing, she'd just made a complete fool of herself, in front of the stud farmer, and had to be carried in like a child. Like an object of ridicule.

More than the pain of hurting her leg, she felt the remembered humiliation of all the other pupils laughing at her and imitating her epileptic fit. Children were so cruel. And not just children. Even as she grew up, Penny always seemed to find herself on the ground, and feeling stupid.

Although she had to admit being carried in the sexy farmer's strong arms was nice, she'd laughed at her. People always laughed.

Quade walked back in with Princess licking and kissing Quade's face relentlessly.

Little traitor, Penny thought.

Quade handed the bag over to Penny and she took Princess out of it and let her jump down to the floor. She immediately went over to Quade's dog, who wagged his tail and made a fuss over her.

"I called the doctor. He'll be out in ten minutes," Quade said.

"You did what?" Penny said angrily. "I don't want a doctor."

"You could have broken your ankle. It needs to be checked over," Quade insisted.

Penny had enough of this. Who did this farmer think she was? She carefully took her leg from the footrest and tried to stand, but she cried out at the intense pain that shot from her ankle up her leg.

"What are you doing?" Quade knelt and cradled her ankle gently in her hands. "Don't be daft. Sit back and rest your leg before you do more injury to yourself."

Penny had no choice but to sit back. It was so frustrating. Her first day here and she was already relying on someone else because of her clumsiness.

"I'm not *daft*. I just don't need people fussing around me. I can take care of myself."

Quade put her leg back on the footstool and stood up. "Well, you can't do much about it now. The doctor won't be long. Are you just passing through the village?"

"No, I'm staying at Northwood Cottage," Penny said more sharply than she meant to.

Quade stuffed her hands in her pockets and let out a breath. "I'll go and get us some tea, and some ice for your ankle."

Penny felt bad but was soon more annoyed when Princess went running after Quade and her dog. "Bloody turncoat."

❖

Quade stirred the tea in the pot, then turned her attention to the little dog trying to get her attention by her leg. Dougal, far from being jealous, was sitting happily at her side, seemingly pleased by the dog's company.

Quade knelt down and ruffled the dog's curly fur. "Hi, pal. So you're Princess Baby Bear? A bit fluffy for a dog, isn't it?" Princess lapped up her attention. "Although going by these silly pink clothes, you are a perfect match for your owner, apart from your personality."

She lifted one of Princess's booted paws and said, "What on God's green earth is this? Shoes on a dog? Bloody hell."

Quade shook her head and sighed. She never thought her day would go like this. One of the famous Huntingdon-Stewarts in her front room. Aunt Mabel would be so proud.

She got up to get some biscuits for her guest as well as some dog treats for Dougal and Princess, then carried the tea tray through to the front room.

The sight of Penny made Quade catch her breath and stop in the doorway. She focused on the manicured pink fingernails that seemed to sum up the perfect picture of femininity that Penny was.

Quade wished she could have had a wash and brush up before meeting her. Strangely, Penny was holding her phone up and taking a picture of her leg.

She carried over the tray and laid it on the coffee table. "Why are you taking a picture of your leg?"

Penny looked at her as if that was the most stupid question she'd ever been asked.

"So I can post it on my social media, and let my followers know what's happened to me," Penny said slowly as if Quade was an idiot for asking.

Quade was not on social media and didn't pretend to understand it. She'd heard Riley talk about it, and the only time she really used the internet was at the Axedale estate office or for her own business—ordering farm supplies, the cattle market website, things like that.

She gave the dogs their biscuits and sat across from Penny. "Why would you share something so personal on the internet?" Quade asked as she poured out the tea.

Penny rolled her eyes. "Have I stepped back into the eighteenth century or something? Because I run a business on a social media platform, and my followers follow my life events."

Quade didn't understand what Penny was talking about but decided to leave it for the moment.

"Milk and sugar?" Quade asked.

"No sugar, and do you have any dairy-free milk?" Penny said.

Quade looked up at her quizzically. "Dairy-free milk? What do you mean?"

"You know, almond, hazelnut, any nut milk?"

"Nut milk," Quade said as if she was talking a foreign language. She tried the words again. "You want nut milk? How do you milk a nut?"

Penny smacked her hand on her forehead. "Where have you sent me, Olivia? Hicksville? Black tea will be fine."

Quade handed her the cup, still somewhat confused. "Biscuit?"

"No, thank you. Listen, could I ask you to drive me home? I'll be okay tomorrow, I'm sure."

"No, you have to see a doctor," Quade repeated. Penny looked really angry. What was wrong with this woman?

"People don't tell Penelope Huntingdon-Stewart no."

"Well, I just did, so get comfortable. The doctor won't be long, and then I'll take you home," Quade said.

Penny drank her tea but didn't look happy. A beautiful face like that shouldn't be angry, Quade thought.

A silence hung between them, and Quade felt compelled to fill it. "I'm sorry you caught me so underdressed. I was just chopping wood and then was going to have a shower." Penny looked at her bare arms and then looked away quickly. Penny had no reply, but her dog jumped into Quade's lap and started to kiss her face. "Hey, at least your dog likes me. She's very sweet." That actually got her a ghost of smile from her guest.

"She's friendly," Penny said.

Unlike her owner, Quade thought. "Can I ask you something?"

Penny sighed. "If you like."

"Why does your dog wear shoes?"

Again Penny looked at her like she was crazy to ask the question. "To protect her little paws from the dirt and stones, from anything that could harm her."

"But that's what paws are for—dogs are meant to get muddy and run through water, and have fun. You need to let a dog be a dog."

"Clearly city dogs have different needs to country dogs, but Princess doesn't like her paws to get dirty," Penny said sharply.

On cue Dougal went to Penny and laid his head on the armrest of Penny's chair. She smiled and started to stroke his head. Good old Dougal could make anyone smile.

There was a knock at the door. "That'll be the doctor." Thank God.

CHAPTER THREE

The Axedale kitchen was filled with the beautiful smell of Annie's delicious food. Harry was meant to be getting the wine, but she found herself gazing over at her wife as she dished their dinner into serving bowls. Harry would have laughed if someone had told her five years ago that she'd be a happily married woman with a stepchild, and not only that but blissfully happy.

And that's what Annie had done for her and Axedale—she had brought bliss and happiness. It was strange. She wasn't a believer in anything spiritual or supernatural, but she had always felt Axedale had a gloomy cloud of darkness hanging over it as she grew up, but now she would swear the house itself felt different, as if love had chased away the blackness and brought peace.

"What are you gazing at so intently, your ladyship?" Annie said pulling Harry from her thoughts.

She smiled and walked over, taking Annie in her arms. "You and the happiness you have brought to me and Axedale."

Annie smiled and traced her fingertips down Harry's cheek. "I'm glad to hear it. Kiss me."

Harry did and started to deepen the kiss, but Annie pushed her back. "Oh no, we have guests. You know where deep kisses lead."

Harry grinned and lifted Annie onto the kitchen table. "That was my plan. Let's cancel dinner and go to bed."

Annie gave her a mock glare and smacked her lightly on the bottom. "Now, now, your ladyship. We have the vicar upstairs."

She gave light kisses to Annie's neck. "It's Finn's last night before she leaves on tour. I'm sure Bridge would be glad of the excuse to go home and get her whip out."

Annie laughed. "Come on, the food's ready to go. I promise you'll have my full attention later."

"You promise?"

"Cross my heart and hope to get—well, you know the rest. Come on." She slipped off the table and began to put the serving dishes onto trays. "Can you take this heavy one, sweetheart?"

"Of course." Harry looked at her watch. "I wonder where Quade's got to. She's not usually late."

Annie took the last dish out of the oven and then looked at the kitchen clock. "Yes, it's not like her. I hope everything's all right."

Harry started to walk up the kitchen stairs. "I'll give her a call once I get this to the dining room."

Quade was flustered as she jogged from her Land Rover up to the doors of Axedale Hall. Being flustered was not a usual state of being for Quade. She was calm, diligent, and usually laid-back, but that had changed this afternoon when Penelope Huntingdon-Stewart came walking up to her farmhouse.

Dr. McTavish had arrived and confirmed that Penny had a sprained ankle, not a broken bone. Penny had made everything such a fuss. Despite her bad attitude, Quade had offered to take her home and sleep on the couch to make sure she could get around, and help with anything she needed, but of course she refused. She had at least taken her aunt's old walking stick, when offered. That would help her move around.

Quade stopped inside to catch her breath. "Bloody stubborn woman."

She heard the thunder of running footsteps coming down the huge staircase. Quade looked up and smiled when she saw Riley, her best friend Sophie, and the gigantic puppy, Caesar.

Dougal ran off excitedly to meet them at the bottom of the stairs. "Hi, Quade," both kids said, and then began to make a fuss over Dougal.

"Hello, Riley, Sophie," Quade replied and stroked Caesar's large head after he came to greet her. "Hey, pal. You get bigger every time I see you."

Riley came over and gave her a hug. "Sophie is staying for a sleepover."

Quade smiled. "That's great."

It was lovely to see Riley happy and settled. When she had arrived in Axedale with Annie, she had found it hard to fit in to the small village school, but the pretty Sophie arrived in the village with her parents a few months later and the pair had been inseparable since.

"Can we take Dougal with us, Quade?" Sophie asked.

Riley added, "Yeah, we're going to look for treasure on the grounds with my metal detector."

"Sure, but aren't you coming for dinner first?" Quade asked.

Riley shook her head. "We had pizza earlier. Come on, Dougal."

The two dogs and two kids went running off out the front door. Quade looked up at the ceiling and let out a long breath.

Fantastic. Two couples and just me.

Usually Riley would eat with them and it wasn't quite as awkward. Tonight would be awkward and remind her how alone she was.

She hurried along the corridor and walked into the dining room to find what she feared. The two couples sitting across from one another, and intimately close.

"Quade. We thought you'd never get here." Harry stood and took her jacket.

"Sorry, I got held up." Quade sat down at the end of the table and said hello to Bridge and Finn.

This was Finn's last night in Axedale before going on a national tour for two weeks. With Bridge's encouragement, Finn had gone back to magic and her touring shows, although Finn only booked dates for a few weeks at a time so she wasn't away from her lover for long, especially now they were engaged. Bridge and Finn's wedding was due to take place at Axedale when Finn got back from her tour.

Quade envied the bond both couples had, and her loneliness felt worse when she was in their company.

Annie placed her hand over hers and smiled. "Well, you're here now. That's the main thing. Let me get you some dinner."

"Is there anything wrong, Quade?" Finn asked.

"Nothing wrong. I just had an unexpected afternoon," Quade said.

Bridge said with a smile, "Oh, do tell."

Harry handed Quade a beer. "Thanks, mate." She poured her beer into her glass and took a drink. "This woman—"

"Woman, a good start," Bridge joked.

Annie raised an eyebrow to her friend. "Carry on, Quade."

Harry sat down and suddenly there were four pairs of eyes staring at her, making her feel a little uncomfortable. Quade didn't like being the centre of attention.

She stared at her glass and cleared her throat. "It's nothing very exciting."

Quade explained how the woman had asked for directions and gave her a tip.

"I bet that went down like a lead balloon," Harry said.

"I know, like I was some hotel porter. Anyway, I bought her chocolates with the money and left them at her door. Then this afternoon she comes marching up to my cottage, up the muddy driveway in heels higher than Bridge's, with a little dog."

"I like her already," Finn joked, and got a swat on the arm from Bridge.

"Is she staying in the village?" Annie asked.

Quade nodded. "She looks like she's walked out of a fashion magazine. Anyway, I look up to talk to her and she fell on her ar—backside."

"What's her name?" Bridge asked. "She sounds quite the dish."

"Penelope Huntingdon-Stewart," Quade said.

"Pen's here already? I wasn't expecting her for a few days," Harry said.

"Pen?" Bridge said. "You didn't tell me she was coming."

Quade was quite confused. "You all know her?"

"Her parents are friends with my mother," Harry explained. "She's younger than Bridge and I, but we saw her and the family often as we grew up."

Annie frowned. "You said she fell. Is she okay?"

"As far as I could tell," Quade said.

"What are you not saying?" Annie said.

Quade couldn't say what she really thought of her. "I can't. You know her."

"Spit it out, Quade," Harry said.

"She's a bloody stubborn woman who complained the whole time I tried to help her," Quade said quickly, getting her frustrations off her chest.

Both Harry and Bridge laughed.

"What?" Quade asked.

Bridge replied, "Stubborn is Little Pen's middle name. She's well known for it."

"So what happened?" Annie said.

Quade explained everything, how her help was rebuffed at every turn, how she insisted on the doctor examining her, how her offer to stay on the couch this evening was rebuffed.

"Her little dog was friendly, but Penny...I mean, she asked me if I had nut milk. Can you believe that?"

They all chuckled, and Harry said, "Oh capital offence in the countryside."

Bridge leaned across the table and patted Quade's hand. "I know she seems prickly, Quade, but she has her share of problems that make her self-sufficient and stubborn."

"Really? What?" Quade asked.

Bridge looked over at Harry, and Harry said, "Her brother Hugo was a colleague and friend at Cambridge, so I know she had a difficult time growing up. Pen suffers from epilepsy, and it's been quite severe over the years."

"Poor thing," Annie said, "we'll need to make sure she's well looked after."

"She's a lesbian and just your type too," Bridge said.

"She is?" Quade almost squeaked as she said that. She just never expected Penny to be gay.

"We'll need to set you up, Quade," Bridget said with a grin.

"Bridge, she's a city girl and a Huntingdon-Stewart. I'm a farmer."

"Oh, don't talk such nonsense." Bridge snorted. "Annie fell in love with a countess, and I fell in love with a magician, a bloody dishy one at that. Don't create barriers where there are none."

Quade nodded but inside she knew that she just didn't have that kind of luck. She pictured Penny with someone in a suit, suave and sophisticated. Quade didn't think herself sophisticated in the slightest.

The evening ended after a good meal, and Quade drove back to the farmhouse. She sat in her car for a few minutes, thinking about Penny. She had been too hard on her, especially with the challenges she faced, and guilt twisted inside her.

She knew how debilitating epilepsy could be. Her aunt had suffered with it her whole life.

Harry said she'd had the cottage checked and set up for Penny, but it was a big change for someone coming from city life, and her little dog wouldn't get a walk either with Penny's ankle the way it was. She resolved to go around to the cottage tomorrow with some firewood and offer to take her dog out with Dougal. Hopefully she wouldn't get rebuffed this time.

❖

The next morning Quade put some firewood in the back of her Land Rover and drove to Northwood Cottage. She stopped outside and sat for a few moments, looking for any signs of life. Quade turned to Dougal who was sitting in the passenger seat and said, "Everything looks quiet. Maybe she's not up yet."

She looked at the time, and then tapped her fingers on the steering wheel. "Half past nine. Maybe I should just leave the wood by the door with a note."

Dougal just looked at her quizzically. Quade was looking for excuses. She could feel a nervousness creep into her stomach as she drove over there. She didn't know why. Penny had been rude, ungrateful, and standoffish, but yet she held herself with such grace, elegance, and femininity that Quade couldn't help but admire her beauty, and feel somewhat in awe of her. Not to mention the fact that she was a Huntingdon-Stewart.

Quade let out a breath and looked into the driver's mirror. She tried to smooth down her choppy sandy-blond hair, but really she was never going to look smart after spending the morning feeding cattle and mucking out.

"Okay, Dougal. Ms. Independence will just have to take us as we are. Come on."

When they got out of the car she heard Penny's little dog barking. "Your little pal is awake, anyway."

Quade walked up to the door, took a breath and lifted her hand to knock. Before she did Quade heard a cry of pain and a bang.

She knocked quickly. "Penny? It's Quade. Are you okay?"

Quade heard shuffling and then the door opened. She tried to speak but she was too transfixed by Penny. She was wearing a pink unicorn onesie with the hood pulled up. The hood had a yellow horn and two eyes, while Penny's gorgeous hair tumbled out the sides of the hood.

Quade had never seen anything like it, or anything like Penny. She would have imagined the woman she met yesterday to wear silky designer nightwear, not this. Penny obviously had a playful side.

As Quade stared, Penny said, "Have you never seen anyone in a unicorn onesie or something?"

"Honestly, no I haven't."

"Well, I'm glad I have broadened your horizons." Penny gave her the smallest of smiles and Quade's mouth went dry.

"So, how can I help you, Quade?" Penny said.

Quade shook herself from her thoughts. "Oh yes. Sorry, I thought I would bring you over some firewood, and then I heard you shout. Is everything okay?"

Penny was cradling her hand. "I was trying to light the wretched fire and burned my hand."

Quade immediately wanted to react, to take control of the situation and help, but she remembered her conversation with her friends last night, and the problems that coloured Penny's reactions.

She took a moment and then said carefully, "Would you allow me to help you?"

Penny narrowed her eyes and gazed at her. She clearly wasn't expecting that question. After a few seconds she said, "Yes, I could use the help. Come in."

When Penny turned, Quade saw there was a tail swishing at the back of her humorous onesie, but instead of smiling, the sight and the sway of Penny's hips and the cute tail made her stomach flip, which caught her by surprise.

She didn't get long to think about that as Princess ran at her and Dougal excitedly. Quade reached down and stroked the dog's head as Dougal greeted her too. "Hi, Princess."

Princess was dressed in little pink pyjamas, and Quade shook her head disapprovingly. She wasn't going to say anything and get on Penny's bad side when she had just got in the door.

When she looked up, she saw that Penny was walking with difficulty on her sprained ankle and again had to stop her instinct of going to her aid.

"How's the ankle?" Quade asked.

"Painful, but I can move around, which is the main thing," Penny said as she led Quade into the cottage front room.

The room was chaos. All sorts of what looked like photography and video equipment was strewn over the table by the window, across the coffee table, and throughout the room. By the fireplace there was a small video camera set up, pointing directly at the fire, for some reason.

Penny sat on the couch and held out her hand. "I burnt my hand on the bloody fire. It's so cold in this old place."

"Do you have ice?" Quade asked.

"I suppose. My assistant had the place stocked up before I got here."

Penny cradled her hand and watched Quade stride off into the kitchen, and of course Princess ran after her. "What is she, the Pied Piper of dogs or something?"

Penny was secretly pleased Quade came back today. It gave her the chance to apologize for yesterday. Last night as she lay awake, in pain and quite alone in this empty cottage, all she could do was think and replay the memories of falling and making a fool of herself.

Quade had only tried to help. She never laughed or made Penny feel silly, but Penny realized she'd been in one of her moods and taken it out on her new neighbour.

When something like that happened, the shutters of protection came down, and she knew she could be defensive and prickly.

Quade came back with some ice wrapped in a tea towel. Instead of handing it to her, Quade knelt in front of her and said, "Give me your hand."

Unusually for Penny, she did as she was told and held out her hand. Quade wrapped the towel around her hand, and she hissed with pain.

Quade covered her hand with hers and looked up at Penny with what she could only describe as dreamy blue eyes. Oh my goodness.

Quade held her gaze and her hand silently, affording Penny the time to study the chiselled features in front of her.

When she first saw Quade yesterday, before she made a fool of herself and everything got out of hand, she had taken her breath away. In her social circle, *butch* had almost become a bad word, and those women who tended towards the masculine end of the scale did not look like the woman before her.

Quade looked like the butch characters whom she had read about in the romance novels she so adored. The kind of butch who strode on to the scene with extreme confidence, swept the girl off her feet while defeating the bad guys, and made lesbians hearts flutter.

Quade was this. She was authentic and, Penny suspected, lived authentically.

"What's wrong?" Quade said.

Penny looked down and Quade was still holding her hand. "I've never met anyone like you before."

Quade gave her a smile that made her stomach loop the loop. "Well, I can honestly say I've never met anyone like you, Penny, so that's makes two of us." She pointed to the fireplace where the two logs that refused to light sat. "Would you let me show you how to make a fire?"

There was the question again, just like at the door. *Would you let me? Would you allow me?* Why the change from yesterday? Yesterday Quade just steamed in and took charge. She had definitely changed her attitude for some reason.

"Yes, please. I was freezing last night."

Quade started to roll up the sleeves of her checked shirt and said, "How could you be cold in that fluffy unicorn get-up?"

"It's freezing here. Mind you, I'm always cold," Penny admitted.

Quade went onto all fours and crawled a few paces in front of the fire. Penny forgot about the pain in her hand and her ankle instantly. Wow! Just look at that muscled bum. Talk about eye candy.

Penny was used to observing and being generally sexually frustrated. She was always seen with the right people at social events—actresses, singers, businesswomen—but that was as far as she got with anyone. Her carefully constructed image meant everyone assumed her sex life was full and one to be envied. No one, not even her family, knew the truth.

"Penny? Penny?" she finally heard Quade say.

She'd been caught looking, and looking was all she ever could do. "Sorry, what did you say?"

"Why have you got a camera set up here?" Quade asked.

"So I could film myself lighting my first fire. To share on social media."

"I don't understand. I thought you were into cooking," Quade said.

Penny rolled her eyes. She forgot she was in Axedale, where the wonders of the internet age had yet to penetrate, it seemed. "Cooking and lifestyle. My followers want to see my life," Penny said.

Quade narrowed her eyes and said slowly, "Okay."

Penny watched as Quade cleared out the mess she had made trying to light the fire. Maybe now was a good time to make peace.

"Quade? I wanted to say sorry for being so bad tempered yesterday. I felt a fool and—"

"That's all right," Quade said generously and gave her a big smile.

"Oh, I…" Penny wasn't expecting to be let off that easily. No one was that easy-going and nice, were they? "Thanks. I was actually bringing you a box of muffins to make up for the tip misunderstanding."

"Don't worry about it, really. Let's get you warmed up, eh?"

Penny was already warming up in Quade's company without the fire. Princess and Dougal were sitting by Quade's side, as good as gold. They made such a sweet picture.

"Oh, can I film you? I'll remember how to do it then."

Quade raised her eyebrow. "If you like."

Penny reached over to the camera and pressed record. "Go."

"To begin, you have to start out with a clean grate. So I'll brush this out. It hasn't been lit in a long time," Quade said, picking up the hard brush sitting amongst the fire tools at the side.

A billow of dust puffed up into the air as she brushed out the fireplace. Penny felt even worse about yesterday, considering how kind Quade was being.

"Thank you for this. Once I've seen you do it, then I'll be able to do it myself." Penny was reassuring herself as well as telling Quade. She hated to get help for anything, but after this she would be self-sufficient.

"You're welcome. It's what we do in the country. Help each other." Quade gave her that disarming smile again. The kind that made her heart beat extra fast.

She decided to change the subject. "Tell me about your job. Is it your farm, or do you work for someone?"

"No, it's mine. It's been in my family for generations."

"Dairy or—"

"Beef," Quade said.

Penny could just imagine what kind of cattle. If social media and the internet hadn't penetrated in Axedale, she doubted organic farming had.

Quade finished cleaning and picked up some sticks of wood from a holder by the side of the fire and broke them into various lengths. "Okay, the two most important things about making a fire are fuel and air. These little bits of wood are your fuel, called kindling."

Penny watched as Quade piled small sticks on the grate. "The other thing a fire needs is air, so space between the kindling is essential. Fuel and air make fire, okay?"

"Fuel and air make fire." Penny imitated Quade's deeper voice and laughed gently.

"Exactly. Now you put the logs on top, facing lengthways so they don't roll onto the carpet."

Penny was just fascinated watching Quade teach her, and she could watch and listen to her all day. Of course it helped that

Quade was so good looking. Penny was really surprised not to see a wedding ring on her finger.

Quade continued, "Next, you add paper."

There was a pile of old newspapers by the side of the fire, and Penny had wondered what they were for. Quade ripped them into strips and piled them under the grate.

"More fuel to get the fire going. And lastly, you light the paper." She used a fire lighter, and in seconds the fire was consuming the paper, and then spread to the pile of kindling on the grate, and finally to the logs.

"That's beautiful," Penny said. The fire danced, crackled, and popped, and already the cottage felt cosier. "Thank you, Quade."

Quade felt her chest puff up with pride. Penny was actually being nice to her, and it made Quade happy to help the damsel in distress.

"No problem. A fire makes all the difference in a home."

She prodded the fire with a poker a few times. Quade saw a flash and looked up. Penny was pointing her phone at her, taking her picture.

"Great picture." Penny smiled and turned the phone to show Quade what she'd taken. "Would you mind if I shared this picture?"

"Shared it with who?" Quade didn't quite understand.

"Shared it online with my followers."

Quade narrowed her eyes. "Why would they want to see me?"

Penny rolled her eyes. "Because I share my life, I document my life. My followers want to see what I do with my day."

"Why?"

Penny sighed in frustration. "Is that all you can ask?

Quade went back to tending the fire. Clearly Penny was quick to anger, and from experience she knew not to antagonize someone like that. Her aunt had been similarly temperamental, a fiery Irishwoman, but the most loving you could find. Her uncle was very laid-back and he took it all in his stride. Luckily Quade took after him. Nothing much fazed Sam McQuade.

"Sorry, I don't understand all this social media stuff. I heard you were a cook, but can you explain how you do that online?"

Penny looked as if she had been ready to say something pithy, but the wind had been taken from her sails by Quade's open, non-confrontational question.

"Well…"

Quade looked up and smiled. It appeared to make Penny falter.

"I run my own company, Penny's Kitchen, a cooking and lifestyle company. It's a multimedia platform. I have a website, a blog, a YouTube channel, and Facebook, Twitter, all that kind of thing."

"And people watch your cooking demonstrations on YouTube?"

Penny nodded. "Sometimes Facebook too. I'm a lifestyle brand—the videos and pictures are part of that."

Quade stopped prodding the fire. "You're a brand? How can a person be a brand?"

"Dear God," Penny said with a sigh, "I'm a brand because my followers buy into the way I live, my philosophies of life."

Quade couldn't help but laugh. "Your philosophies?"

Penny's face went red with anger. "Don't laugh at me. My philosophies are clean eating, intuitive eating, non-processed foods. Only eating meat from quality organically fed sources."

"Okay." Quade hadn't a clue what clean eating or intuitive eating was, but she wasn't going to ask and appear stupid again. She placed the fire poker in its holder and stood up quickly. "Do you want me to make the fire in your bedroom?"

Penny sat up sharply. "No, no one goes in my bedroom."

That was a strange thing to say. No one goes in her bedroom?

"Okay. How's your hand?" Quade asked.

Penny pulled off the ice and waggled her fingers. "I think it's less stingy. Let me get you those muffins before you go. To say thanks."

Penny started to get up gingerly, and Quade offered her hand. "Let me help."

"No, I'm fine," Penny said.

Bridge and Harry were so right about Penny. She was the most stubborn woman she had ever come across, even when they were being nice to each other.

Penny walked towards the kitchen, and Dougal and Princess ran ahead, followed by Quade.

The cottage kitchen had more equipment spread out, and there didn't seem to be much room for what Penny had in mind. It was a lot smaller than her farmhouse kitchen.

Penny picked up a box of muffins and handed them to her. The label showed a picture of Penny holding a mixing bowl and spoon, with a dazzling smile. Something Quade hadn't seen in real life yet, but wished she had.

"I hope you'll like these, Quade. They're made from non-dairy products, all organic and gluten free," Penny said.

Quade read out the quote printed on the box. "*Clean, healthy, and delicious.*"

"Yes, that's my catchphrase. That's my brand identity."

Finally, Quade saw the beaming smile in real life, and her heart skipped a beat. Penny seemed to come alive when talking about her business.

"And you can buy these in the big supermarkets?" Quade asked.

"Yes." Penny's eyes appeared to sparkle with enthusiasm. "I have a range of foods in the supermarket now. Including these." Penny reached behind her and picked up a second box. "This is for Dougal."

Quade's eyes went wide when she saw it was a box of dog treats with a picture of Princess on the front. "Dog biscuits too?"

Penny reached down and picked up Princess. "Not just any dog biscuits. Quality organic dog biscuits. Isn't that right, Princess?" Penny kissed her dog's little nose.

"You really are a big businesswoman," Quade said.

She remembered her conversation with Bridget last night.

She's a lesbian and just your type too. We'll need to set you up, Quade.

Bridge, she's a city girl, and a Huntingdon-Stewart. I'm a farmer.

Add to that successful businesswoman, and it created yet another barrier between them. Not that she had ever taken Bridge's suggestion seriously, but seeing Penny this morning in her unicorn PJs had only amplified her attraction. She could tell there was a sweet, beautiful girl in there, underneath that stubborn shell.

"Thanks. I'm sure Dougal will love them."

Penny put Princess down and said, "Come here a second."

Quade was confused when Penny reached out to touch her cheek. "You have a smudge of ash from the fire."

She held her breath while Penny rubbed her cheekbone with her thumb. Penny looked into her eyes, and a warmth spread from Penny's fingers onto her cheek and throughout her body.

Penny's rubbing thumb became a caress, and Penny's lips parted. They looked silently at each other, Quade seeing everything she had ever dreamed about in Penny's eyes.

When Penny's fingernails gently scratched the short hairs above her ear, Quade shivered, and Penny snatched her hand away.

Quade felt an awkwardness between them now. She looked down at Dougal playing with Princess and her ball.

"Looks like they're getting on well," Quade said, trying to make conversation.

Penny was cradling her injured hand, with her arms crossed defensively across her body. Something had changed.

"So it seems," Penny said flatly.

Great. Miss Attitude is back. Time to go, Quade thought.

"Do you want me to take Princess for a walk for you since your ankle is in a bad way?"

"What? No, Princess doesn't like to walk."

"Of course she likes to walk. She's a dog—she was made for walking. I can call for her tonight, if you like?"

"If she needs to be walked, I can walk her. I don't need anyone's help."

"Maybe if you didn't dress her like a doll and put shoes on her, then maybe she'd remember she was a dog."

Penny's face was like thunder. She walked back into the living room and said, "Thank you for your help with the fire, but I mustn't keep you."

Quade let out a breath and said to Dougal. "Come on, pal. We're going."

When they got outside, Penny slammed the door shut. Quade looked up at the sky. "Why did I say that."

It wasn't like Quade to react in anger, but Penny was making her hot, in more ways than one.

Chapter Four

L ater that evening, Penny decided to go to bed early. She sat on the side of the bed and took out her large pillbox. Taking these meds three times a day was depressing. Every one she swallowed reminded her of her limitations, and her deep-seated fear. Fear was her constant companion. Would she wake up in the morning normally, or would she wake up fitting, and paralyzed with fear.

It wasn't only at night. She had to fear every little thing she did and assess if it was safe or not, like using knives. If she had an attack while using a sharp chef's knife, it could be dangerous, and so she was the only cook she knew that used a machine for chopping.

It angered her that she had to do these little things differently, but at the same time she wouldn't let it beat her—Penny always found a way. The medications were the same—they were a symbol of her curse, as she called it as a child, a condition that she wouldn't let beat her, and the medications allowed her some semblance of control over her life.

Penny snuggled under the duvet and Princess curled up at her side. She had spent the evening making plans for videos and writing some little scripts. She felt a twinge from her ankle and sighed. It had really kept her back today. She'd hoped to have all her equipment ready and prepared for shooting some film.

Her mobility had improved over the course of today, and she hoped that the anti-inflammatory pills the doctor had given her would enable her to get started tomorrow. Harry had called her this afternoon to ask if she needed anything, and she promised she would be okay and would try to see her and Bridget tomorrow.

She had to get out in the morning, or else she'd have everyone descend on her and try to be so helpful. Not that she was ungrateful, but it made her feel uneasy.

Penny was reminded of Quade. Why she had let her help, she didn't know. It wasn't something she would normally do. She stroked Princess's head and sighed. "You like Quade, don't you?"

Princess's eyes popped opened and she looked around, apparently looking for Quade.

"She's not here just now, poppet," Penny said.

She thought about the video she had taken of Quade and wanted to see her again. The smile Quade had shown her was an image that stayed in her head all day, and she wanted to check if her memory was embellishing it or if it was really as she remembered.

Penny picked up her iPad and found countless notifications from her followers at something she had posted. She was used to a lot of online attention but something she had posted had obviously hit a nerve.

Her notifications took her straight to her Instagram account, and the picture of Quade she had posted earlier. Penny hadn't said much about the picture or used Quade's name. She just captioned it, *Sexy Farmer teaching me to make fire.*

The likes and comments were flying in. She scanned down the comments and some of them were downright naughty.

"Wow. The girls are going mad for your friend, Princess."

Penny reached for her video camera that was sitting on her bedside table and started to play the video. She could see exactly why everyone was salivating over Quade. Quade was something that she didn't think existed any more. An old school butch who was completely at ease with her butchness. Tough, strong, but—going by their interactions so far—kind and gentle.

Penny traced her finger over Quade's chiselled face as she watched the video, and her stomach clenched with excitement. She quickly dropped the camera onto the bed and reminded herself that attraction was a waste of time.

Going out with the right people to book launches and parties was one thing, but the thought of anyone getting past her bedroom door worried her. Not to say she hadn't had dreams about the perfect partner.

When she closed her eyes at night she imagined having someone to hold her, someone to make her feel safe when a frightening epileptic episode took over her body, but never in Penny's wildest dreams had she ever imagined someone as good looking as Quade, with gorgeous eyes.

"I have to find the flaw," Penny said as she put the camera back on her bedside table.

Whenever she met someone attractive, and interesting enough that she couldn't forget them easily, she found a flaw that made a closer relationship impossible. It was always easy enough, but this time it might be more difficult. Quade was helpful, kind, forgiving, and gentle, as demonstrated by her kindness to Princess. Penny would find that flaw—she always did.

As she reached for her book, she saw the notifications on Quade's picture still popping up on her iPad. "Sexy Farmer has set the internet alight, Princess," Penny said.

She looked at *Lady Chatterley's Lover,* and the image of Quade chopping wood yesterday burned in her mind, and her body.

"Get a grip, Pen."

She put down her book and switched the light off quickly.

Quade was sitting at her computer desk in her office, which was really her spare bedroom. She was trying to order some farm supplies, but her ancient desktop was making everything more difficult as usual. She wasn't the best with computers, and neither had her uncle been. They were forced to buy a computer when their suppliers went online, and this was the same computer she'd had since then.

"Bloody thing," Quade snapped, as the curser on the computer spun. It usually worked in the end—it just took its own time—but it was frustrating.

Quade looked down at Dougal, who was lying by her feet, and said, "How about a snack?"

Dougal jumped up excitedly at the word *snack*. Maybe by the time they came back, her purchase would have actually gone through. She led Dougal down to the kitchen and spotted the muffins and dog biscuits Penny had given them.

Quade opened the dog biscuits and gave Dougal a handful. He started to snaffle them up straight away. Then she picked up the muffins with trepidation.

"I don't know which I'd rather, Dougal. Yours or mine. No dairy, no gluten, no sugar, no anything?"

She opened the box and the sweet smell of blueberry hit her. "Hmm, they look the part but…" Quade brought the muffin to her lips. "Here goes, Dougal."

She took a bite and was immediately surprised by the taste. It was sweet, with a light and fluffy texture. "How does she get it to taste nice without dairy and sugar? Penny must be a good cook."

Dougal whined and raised his paw. His signal to beg for food. "Okay, here you go, pal."

Quade tore some muffin off and handed it to Dougal, who swallowed it up in one gulp. "You can chew, you know."

She got another few dog biscuits and took the muffin upstairs. Thankfully the computer had done its thing and completed her order. Quade gave Dougal the rest of the dog biscuits and set her muffin on the computer desk.

Quade had an urge to find out more about Penny. She didn't normally use the computer for things like this, but she typed her name into the search engine. The computer made a sound like it was a plane taking off, and again the curser spun.

She sighed and sat back to eat her muffin while she waited. Quade had never met anyone like Penny. She looked as if she had a cook and a whole household staff, not that she cooked for herself. Quade chuckled, thinking of her in that unicorn onesie. It was both adorable and sexy at the same time—was that even possible? Perhaps for someone like Penelope Huntingdon-Stewart.

Quade enjoyed her last bite of muffin just in time for her search engine to return the results for Penny. She was astonished at the number of news stories, website links, and videos it returned. Her computer would take a week to play a video, so she clicked on Penny's *Wikipedia* page.

She read through the history of the family, some of which she had learned at school, but when it got to her parents and siblings, she was astonished to learn about them.

"A serious, clever family," Quade said.

Then she read about Penny's background and the private school she went to. So posh.

She read on:

Penelope Huntingdon-Stewart, age twenty-seven, has built her brand of clean and intuitive eating from a small weekly blog to one of the brightest and most successful British food brands in just a few years. Penny's Kitchen products can now be seen in supermarkets up and down the country.

"What is intuitive eating?" Quade wondered.

In the last year she has suffered—

Just as she was about to get some information on Penny's problems, the computer crashed and switched itself off.

Quade smacked the side of the old-style monitor. "Bloody thing. Ask it to do one more thing than order supplies, and it blows a gasket."

She looked at her watch. "It's well past our bedtime anyway. Let's turn in, Dougal."

Quade walked through to her bedroom and started to undress. As tired as she was, Quade felt a restlessness in her body, an energy that she hadn't encountered before. Normally after a hard day's work, she fell into bed and fell straight asleep. But tonight, as she set her alarm clock, she sensed that when she shut her eyes, she would see a beautiful girl in a unicorn onesie.

The next morning Penny's ankle was slightly better, and she was going to venture out to her first day of country living. She wanted to get the vibe of village life before she started scripting her vlogs and making her cooking videos.

She stood in front of her full-length mirror and smoothed down her floral summer dress. She might be in the muddy country, but that wasn't going to change her style. Her hair was pulled back into an elegant bun, with strands of hair hanging loosely to frame her face.

She *was* going to have to concede her high heels. There was no way she could walk in them with her ankle the way it was, so she decided today was the time to break out one fashion item she had planned for country living—wellington boots. Not just any wellington boots, but designer ones that had been matched with the outfits she had brought.

This first pair were highly polished pink boots with a floral pattern to match her dress. She slipped them on with some discomfort to her ankle and looked in the mirror. Penny smiled at her reflection.

"It's certainly a fashion statement. What do you think, Princess?" Penny turned to her dog who was lying on the bed dressed in a pink floral sweater, similar to her dress design.

"You like it, poppet?"

Princess barked in response and Penny smiled. "I knew you would. Penny and Princess are going to make this village fabulous."

She picked up the selfie stick from the bed to take a picture of them both and saw she was still getting notifications about Sexy Farmer. Quade. She wondered if she'd see more of her today and was slightly frightened by the fact that she was excited by the prospect.

"No, no. Don't even think about it, Pen. Hunky farmers are best left in the imagination."

She swiped the notifications away and picked up Princess. "Ready to smile, poppet?"

Penny made sure she got her whole outfit in the shot and clicked to take the picture. She edited and posted it quickly to Instagram, put on Princess's little shoes, and made her way downstairs gingerly. Her ankle was painful, but she was determined it wasn't going to hold her back. She had spent enough time being held back by her own body.

At the dining table downstairs, Penny put Princess into her handbag and checked that her small video camera was working okay, and that her phone was tucked beside Princess. Bridget had phoned this morning and asked if she would like to join her for tea with Harry and her wife at Axedale. She was looking forward to seeing Harry again, so she said she would meet Bridget at the church, and then Bridget could drive them the rest of the way. Her ankle wouldn't cope with walking far.

Now with all her things together, she walked outside the door. She noticed a pile of small logs stacked by the side of the door, with a loaf of bread and a box of teabags, and a note.

Penny,

I thought you might need some more logs for your fires, and some essentials you might not have yet. The muffins were delicious, by the way. If you need any more logs, just give me a shout.

Penny let out an exasperated sigh. "Why does she have to be so bloody sweet? I need to find that flaw."

❖

Bridget stood outside the church gates and chuckled to herself as she watched Penny walking down the road towards her. Bridget had been a shock to the people of Axedale when she arrived. A woman vicar in a biker jacket was always going to cause a few ripples, but she doubted Axedale had ever seen anything like Penelope Huntingdon-Stewart.

Penny was the ultimate city girl, with her pink floral dress, and her dog in a designer outfit in a handbag, looking as if she went shopping all day and lunched with her friends at the best restaurants.

She looked adorable and sweet, and if there was a scale of femininity from one to ten, Penny would score twenty, but those who dismissed her as a bit of fluff or a bimbo were deceived. Under that fluffy pink exterior was an astute businesswoman.

As she got closer, Bridge could see that Penny was holding a selfie stick as she spoke into the camera. *Starting work already, Penny.*

Penny was much younger than her, and she hadn't seen Penny for years, but she loved to follow her on social media. Penny was bright, funny, and self-deprecating. It was also fun to see glimpses of the society world in which she used to live before she found God and the church.

As Penny approached she put her camera in a side pocket of her bag and collapsed the selfie stick so it would fit in the bag.

"Bridge, hi," Penny said with enthusiasm.

Bridge gave her a kiss on each cheek. "Hi, darling. I love the boots, by the way."

Penny lifted the hem of her dress a little bit. "It's my country look."

"It's so long since I've seen you," Bridget said.

Penny smiled. "It was at Mummy and Daddy's wedding anniversary, at Claridge's."

Bridge snapped her fingers. "That's right. You were telling me about the YouTube channel you had set up, and look how far you've come since then—you successful businesswoman."

Penny blushed and stroked Princess's head. "Oh, you know, it's gone quite well."

"Quite well? Don't be so modest"—Bridge looked down at Princess—"and this must be the famous Princess Baby Bear."

"Yes. Say hi to Bridge, Princess," Penny said.

Bridge ruffled her ears. "I feel like I know her already. I follow your Instagram account. The pictures you post of her are just adorable."

"She is really the star of the show," Penny said.

"Wonderful. Now shall we get going up to Axedale?" Bridge indicated to the church van parked at the side of the road.

"Yes, I can't wait to see Harry again, and the woman who enticed her to settle down. I couldn't believe that she was getting married when I heard about it."

They got into the van, and Bridge started the engine. "You'll realize why when you meet Annie. She and her daughter Riley are just adorable. Harry didn't stand a chance. You'll love her. She's a fantastic cook."

Penny had heard great things about Annie through her own mother, who was friends with Harry's mother. Lady Dorothy, Harry's mother, was full of praise for Annie and what she had done for their family.

Penny turned to smile at Bridge. "And what about you, Vicar? Getting hitched as well, I hear?"

Bridget's face was wreathed in smiles. "Yes, well, civil partnership. The church doesn't allow me to call it marriage, but to Finn and me, it's a marriage."

"Of course it is, bloody outdated church. And where is your dishy magician? I was hoping to meet her," Penny said.

"She's on tour for two weeks, then comes back home for the wedding. You will come, won't you?" Bridge asked.

"I'd love to. You are so lucky—Finn is gorgeous," Penny said.

Bridget laughed softly. "I know. Quite delicious."

Penny chuckled to herself. Bridge said that as if thinking about eating a succulent piece of meat. Bridge had always come across to Penny as someone very much in control of her life, and in touch with her sexual side. Of course, she had heard the rumours about Mistress Black, a persona Bridget had left behind before she entered the church. Or had she? The look on Bridge's face while thinking about her partner Finn belied that.

Penny envied that ability of other people to throw themselves into sexual relationships, explore, have fun, and share that deep connection with a partner. The thought both tantalized and terrified her. Why did other people find it so easy, and she was paralyzed at the thought?

It was something that she had tried to address many times over the last few years, when a yearning for a partner grew and grew inside of her. No one would ever guess that Penny—the dynamic businesswoman, the social media star, who went out with the brightest and beautiful people—had a crippling fear of sexual intimacy.

People thought they knew every little part of her life, they thought every last detail of who Penny was, from sprained ankles to her favourite food, was shared online, but no one really knew the real Penny.

They drove through the gates of Axedale and Penny gasped. "This place is beautiful."

"Wait till you see the house," Bridge said.

As they drove along the road that led up to the house, Bridge slowed when they saw Quade and some of the other estate workers chopping a felled tree at the side of the road.

"Now there's a sight to brighten up your day. Our very own rugged farmer," Bridge said.

Why did she always have to be chopping wood? Penny thought as her stomach fluttered at the sight of Quade in jeans and tight T-shirt, swinging her axe.

Bridge beeped the horn, and Quade looked up. She gave them both the most dazzling smile and waved.

"Gorgeous, isn't she?" Bridge prodded.

Instead of answering Penny said, "I thought she was a farmer?"

"She's assistant estate manager. Harry employed some farm workers for her, so she could do both."

God. Even more Lady Chatterley, Penny thought.

Bridge continued, "She's the sweetest person you could meet, as well as good looking."

"No one could be that perfect," Penny replied.

"I think anyone would struggle to find a flaw in dear old Quade," Bridget said.

Brilliant.

"How's the ankle?" Bridge asked.

Penny's head shot around. "How did you know?"

"Quade told us. We all have dinner here at Axedale once a week. Harry and Annie, Finn and I, and Quade."

It suddenly came clear to Penny why Quade had come back the next morning, and why she had changed her approach to her. All that *Would you allow me?* business.

Penny sighed. "And of course, you all filled her in about me."

Bridget glanced around at her quickly. "Filled her in? I don't—"

"My condition. Hence why she turned up the next day determined to be my knight in shining armour?"

"It wasn't like that, Penny," Bridge said.

"Did you tell her about my epilepsy?" Penny asked.

Bridge said, "Yes, but we didn't elaborate."

Penny didn't reply. Only a day or so here, and people were already feeling sorry for her, but her anxious thoughts were cut short when Axedale house came into view.

"Wow! What a house. Look, Princess."

Princess jumped out of her bag and stuck her nose out the inch or two of open window. She panted excitedly and barked.

Bridget laughed. "Someone's excited. It must be the country air."

Penny had noticed that. Princess had been livelier and more excitable since they arrived in Axedale. Every time she let her out to the garden to do her business, she ran, chased birds, barked, and didn't want to come in most of the time.

"Here we are." Bridge pointed to the steps of Axedale.

She saw Harry, a beautiful blond woman, a little girl, and the largest dog she'd ever seen.

Penny pulled Princess back onto her lap and held her tightly.

Quade watched the church van amble its way up to the front door of Axedale. She hoped Penny had seen the wood and other things she'd left for her.

The other workers had stopped for a drink of water. Quade took a quick drink of her own and noticed the men had gathered around to look at something. She heard Will the under gardener say, "Was that really her?"

"Look for yourself," Andy, one of the manual labourers, said.

"God, she's bloody gorgeous," Will said.

"I think we should put these pictures up in the office," another said.

Quade had to see what they were talking about, so she walked over and pushed into the circle of men. Andy had an open copy of a popular lads' magazine. "What's all the fuss about?"

"It's the woman that just went past with the vicar. Penny Huntingdon-Stewart," Andy said.

Quade grabbed the magazine off him and took a look. There was a double page spread of paparazzi pictures of Penny in a tiny bikini, on a boat somewhere exotic. The spread was titled "Babe of the Week." Quade was hit with conflicting emotions, at once so attracted to Penny, wearing very little, and angry that she was being exploited by photographers and this trashy magazine.

"I don't want this shit anywhere, and if anyone tries to put a picture of Penny up, I'll knock them on their arse. Have you got no respect?"

Will, the youngest of the men, put his head down immediately, and the others stayed quiet, but Andy said, "It's only a bit of fun, Quade."

Quade pointed at the pictures. "These were taken by some sleazy cameraman while Ms. Huntingdon-Stewart thought she was on a private holiday, without her consent. She's being exploited."

But Andy wouldn't let it go. "I think you're taking this a bit too seriously."

"Am I?" Quade had to take a breath to calm her fury. "How would you like it, Andy, if some dick was hiding behind a tree taking pictures of your sister, then selling them? Or you, Will?"

Andy grumbled, "Fine, okay, you're right. I'd knock his teeth down his throat."

Quade let out a breath. "Just have some respect, guys. This is Lady Harry's guest, remember."

Quade looked up towards the house. All she wanted to do was go and check that Penny was okay. Was her ankle healing? Did she need anything done around the house? But she would probably be rebuffed.

The feeling she had gotten when Penny drove past them meant she was going to keep trying no matter how much Penny pushed her away.

Harry saw the tension on Penny's face as she watched her little dog playing on the floor with their giant of a dog, Caesar. Riley was sitting beside the two dogs, rolling a ball around the drawing room floor for them, while Annie, Bridget, Penny, and she enjoyed tea.

"Don't worry, Pen. He might look big, but he's a gentle giant," Harry said.

Penny gave her a tense smile. "She seems happy enough. Princess hasn't been around other dogs very much."

Annie poured out the tea and handed Penny a cup. "How's the ankle? Quade told us you had a bit of a fall."

"Oh, it's fine. No problem at all," Penny said.

Harry sensed it wasn't fine, and she didn't want to push her, but she had promised Hugo that she would watch out for her.

The dogs were barking excitedly. Riley jumped up and said to Harry, "Can I take Princess and Caesar outside, Mum?"

Harry saw Penny tense up. "Maybe just the entrance hall until they get to know each other better. Would that be okay, Pen?"

Penny nodded her head. "Okay."

Once they went out the room, Harry said to Penny, "If you need anything, just let me know. I can have one of my workers bring you down some logs for the fire—"

Penny stopped her. "Honestly. I'm okay. Quade has brought me over lots of wood."

"And showed her how to make a fire eh?" Bridget nudged her. "Sexy Farmer? I saw your post."

"Who is Sexy Farmer?" Annie asked.

Penny felt heat spread up her neck and to her cheeks. She took a sip of her tea and just tried to brush it off. "Quade. I thought my followers on Instagram would find it amusing."

Annie chuckled. "I bet she got lots of likes."

"They are flooding in," Bridget said. "Our rugged farmer will make lesbian hearts flutter across the world."

Penny had to change the subject. So she said to Annie, "You have a beautiful home here."

"Thank you." Annie turned to Harry and smiled adoringly. "Harry's worked so hard on refurbishing it."

Harry returned an even more adoring smile to her wife. "This house would be nothing without you, darling."

Penny could hardly believe this lovesick Harry was the same playgirl she had known when she was younger. It was amazing to watch the power of love right before your eyes. She could see why Harry had fallen for this warm woman. Annie had been welcoming and was obviously gentle and kind, and Riley was adorable.

Harry and Annie continued to gaze at each other lovingly and Bridge said, "They do this all the time."

Harry's head snapped around. "I heard that, Vicar."

"Would you like me to show you around, Penny?" Annie asked.

"I'd love it. Would you mind if I took some video? I promise I won't post it unless you give me permission."

"Of course," Annie said with a smile. "Let's go."

❖

Annie and Penny left Bridge and Harry upstairs to talk while they went downstairs to see the kitchen. Annie saw the grimace of pain on Penny's face. She was obviously hiding how painful her ankle was. Quade had called her stubborn the other night, but after meeting Penny, liking her kind, friendly character, and Harry explaining some of her background, she could see Penny was trying to protect herself in some way.

Penny's grimace disappeared when she walked around the kitchen, which made Annie happy. The kitchen was the heart of their home, and to see it appreciated was nice.

Penny walked around the kitchen holding her camera and smiling. "This is fabulous, Annie. It's a real country kitchen, but a perfect mix of new and old world."

"It wasn't like this when I arrived, I assure you. It was a pile of mess, old teacups, and cobwebs."

"Well, you've done a good job. It's so big too. You can't swing a cat in the kitchen at Northwood Cottage," Penny said as she ran her fingers over the large professional cooker that was Annie's pride and joy.

Annie leaned against the kitchen table and said, "Feel free to film up here anytime you need a bit more room."

"Really?" Penny said.

"Of course. I love your YouTube channel. I watch it all the time," Annie said.

Penny looked surprised. "Do you? I'm sure you're a much better cook than me. I just bumble my way through."

"Hardly. Penny, it takes great skill to come up with clean food that's delicious. I try to encourage Harry and Riley to eat more fruits and vegetables. It's not always easy, but lots of your tips and tricks have helped me to make healthy food more palatable for them."

Penny lowered her camera and was genuinely touched. Annie had been a professional housekeeper, whereas Penny had learned what she knew by trial and error, through her own mistakes. It was wonderful to hear someone like Annie appreciated her show.

"Well, thank you, and I'll take you up on your offer to film here. It'll make an amazing setting for a video."

They were interrupted by a knock at the kitchen door. Quade popped her head around the door.

"Hi, I have something of yours." Quade walked in cradling Princess.

Penny gasped and said, "What happened?"

"She got out the front door and ran to find me. I thought I'd better bring her back," Quade said.

Penny looked at Quade holding Princess gently, just after rescuing her, and felt her heart pitter-patter. She didn't even know that could happen in real life, but it did.

"Thank you." Penny took Princess from Quade's impossibly strong arms. *How am I ever going to find that flaw?*

Chapter Five

That evening Quade saw to her animals and walked back to the house with Dougal. Her thoughts had been filled with Penny since this afternoon. When she returned Princess, and saw Penny in that dress and cute boots, her breath had been stolen by her beauty.

She opened the front door and walked into the empty house. She cursed her bad luck as the universe sent the perfect woman, who just happened to be Penelope Huntingdon-Stewart. Someone completely out of her league and unattainable. Despite their cross words and the stubborn shell Penelope kept for protection, Quade had seen the real Penny once or twice. She saw it today when she handed Princess over to her.

The open love and feeling for Princess dismantled her walls, and she saw a glimpse of the woman underneath. Quade thought of the magazine photos that the men had been looking at, and she seemed like a completely different woman than the one Quade had seen in her unicorn onesie.

Quade wondered if anyone really knew the real Penny. She stopped at the kitchen table and drummed her fingers on the back of chair. She should be getting something to eat, but she felt restless.

She looked down at Dougal and said, "Should we offer to take Princess for a walk?"

Dougal jumped and spun around excitedly.

"I take it that's a yes." Quade let out a breath. She could get to the door and have Penny say she didn't want Princess to walk, again.

Quade looked around her empty house and heard only the ticking of the grandfather clock.

"Well, it's better than sitting here on my own. I need to get washed up first, pal, and then we'll go."

Quade got a quick shower and change of clothes. She sprayed on some cologne and put some wax in her hair and messed it up on top as usual. She wondered if she should do anything different with it.

She was sure the lesbians Penny knew were a lot more interesting than her. Quade shook her head when she realized what she was thinking.

"Don't even think about it. You're not in her league."

Quade quickly finished up, and she and Dougal drove over to Northwood Cottage. When they pulled up, Princess was barking. She'd obviously heard the truck arriving.

They got out and Quade found herself checking her appearance in the mirror.

She closed her eyes and let out a breath. "Stop it."

But she couldn't deny the excitement she felt at seeing Penny again, even though Penny was stubborn and difficult. She was sure there was an extremely sensitive, gentle girl under there.

Quade knocked on the door, and Princess barked wildly. She heard Penny walk to the door and say, "Who is it?"

"It's Quade."

Penny opened the door and Quade's mouth went dry. Penny was wearing a pair of tiny lilac coloured sleep shorts with unicorns on them, and a T-shirt with a picture of a unicorn and the phrase *I believe in Unicorns* emblazoned across her chest. It was tight around her breasts, and Quade couldn't take her eyes off them.

"Can I help you?" Penny said. "Quade?"

Quade heard Penny but had lost the ability to form words, and she'd forgotten why she had come here. Her brain was mush. No one had ever done that to her before, but then no one was Penelope Huntingdon-Stewart. She exuded femininity, and Quade was lost in her beauty. Princess scrambling at her feet finally brought her back.

"What did you want, Quade?" Penny asked again.

"I—I wondered if you had changed your mind about letting me take Princess for a walk."

"Actually, I have. She's got so much energy since we've come here. I'm trying to edit some video and she won't give me a moment. You won't take her far, will you? She's not used to walking," Penny said with concern.

"She'll be safe with me." Quade winked.

Penny looked at her a moment and said, "Okay then. I'll get her jacket on."

"She doesn't need a jacket," Quade said.

But Penny either didn't hear or ignored her as she got Princess ready. A few minutes later she brought Princess, together with her lead and shoes on her paws.

Quade sighed but said nothing.

"Where will you take her?" Penny asked.

It was clearly a wrench for Penny to let Princess go. "There's a forest path that starts over the other side of the road. It leads down to the river, lots of scents and smells for them."

Penny still looked tense.

"I promise she'll be safe with me. Trust me?"

After a few seconds Penny said, "I trust you."

Quade took Princess's lead and said to Dougal, "Okay, pal. Lead the way." She took a step and turned back to Penny. "Penny, you shouldn't really answer the door like that. It could be anyone."

Penny smiled. "I knew it was you, so I knew I was safe."

Quade's chest puffed up with pride. "You'll always be safe with me."

❖

Penny was sitting at her dining room table working, editing the video she had taken of the village and Axedale Hall—or *trying* to work on it.

Ever since Quade left, she had been completely distracted. Every time she tried to concentrate on cutting a particular section of video, her mind wandered to Quade's gorgeous smile, or the smell of her cologne.

It wasn't every day the perfect butch walked up to your door and smiled. Penny let go of her mouse and sat back in her chair. Why did she have to be so perfect, or rugged, as Bridge called her?

She glanced over at her phone, and the likes for Sexy Farmer's picture were still piling up, and she didn't blame them. She wondered why Quade hadn't been snapped up a long time ago.

But it wasn't just her looks—she was kind and gentle, and more. Penny let her head fall back and said with frustration, "Why does she have to be thoughtful?"

Penny switched to the fire-making film on her laptop and watched Quade talk her through everything. Her followers would go wild for this video. Everyone seemed to be wild for Quade, even her dog.

She watched the film and thought, *Just let yourself appreciate her good looks, and her friendship. You won't be here long, and it's not as if you could ever do any more than appreciate—or dream.*

Since her early twenties, Penny had tried hard to work through her intimacy issues. She'd worked with a few different psychologists, and they gave her advice, but she didn't have a partner, someone she trusted to experiment with.

She could never give that trust over to someone she had just met and dated a few times. In any case, it wasn't fair to dump her problems on someone she had just met. That meant she never got to express herself sexually, and she had learned to cope with the frustration of having that part of her life unfulfilled. Finding the flaw, as she thought of it, helped put her off anyone she was attracted to, but Sexy Farmer apparently was flawless.

Penny gave an exasperated sigh. "I never expected this problem when I came to the country."

There was a knock at the door, and Quade shouted, "Penny? It's us."

Penny felt excitement ripple over her body. *It's us.* It was like a momentary glimpse of a normal relationship. She banished the thought quickly and answered the door. Princess jumped up at her excitedly.

"Hi, poppet, did you have fun with Dougal?" Princess panted and licked her face. "I'll take that as a yes."

Penny had never seen Princess so excited before.

"They had great fun together," Quade said. "Lots of scents and smells for them down by the river."

Penny was down on her knees stroking Dougal. "Scents and smells? What does that mean?"

"That's part of why dogs love going out walking. They communicate through scents with other dogs and other animals. It's good for them mentally."

Penny stood. "I never thought of it that way."

After a silence Quade said, "You like unicorns?"

Penny laughed softly. "Yes, I love them. It was a bit too warm tonight for the onesie, especially since I've got the fire going strong. Come in, and I'll get you some more muffins. You said you liked them…in your note."

Quade smiled. "I loved them. How's your ankle?"

"Getting better. It'll be fine." Penny walked to the kitchen but could feel Quade's presence following her.

She picked up a box of muffins and handed them to Quade. "Here you go, they're nice and healthy too. I haven't many boxes left. I'll need to make you some fresh ones, maybe a different flavour?"

"I'd love that. Thanks. Would it be all right to come by each night and take Princess for a walk? Dougal really loves the company. He's been alone for a long time."

The way Quade gazed at her, and the way she said that, made Penny think she wasn't only talking about Dougal. Quade being alone in her farmhouse made her sad. Someone so good-looking and as good-natured deserved someone to love, and she hoped Quade would find it one day.

"Yes, that would be nice. Princess is like a different dog here in the country. She wants to walk, and run, and dig. I suppose you think I treat her like a fashion accessory."

Quade smiled and shook her head. "No, you love her, I can see that. You and Princess have a very different life in London, I suppose."

Penny's heart started to beat hard. That question felt like it had a much deeper meaning.

"Yes, we do, and we won't be here for long," Penny said, mentally putting up a safety barrier between them.

Quade nodded. "Okay, I'll be off then. I'll call for Princess tomorrow."

As Quade walked off, Penny said, "Quade, you know the video I took of you, about making a fire?"

"Yeah?"

"Would you mind if I posted it on my channel?" Penny wasn't sure of the reaction she would get.

Quade raised a questioning eyebrow. "Why would anyone want to watch me teaching you about making a fire?"

You'd be surprised. "It's part of my country experience. This is why I'm down here."

"I'll give you a deal. You can use the video if you keep those daft shoes off Princess." Quade smirked.

"They are not daft," Penny snapped. Then she realized it was silly. "Okay, you have a deal."

When Quade left, Penny set to work on Quade's video, and before too long she had it ready.

She uploaded it and named it *Sexy Farmer makes fire...*

CHAPTER SIX

One week later, Bridge and Annie were in the Axedale ballroom finalizing plans for Bridge's wedding. Staff came and went as they set up tables and chairs around the perimeter of the ballroom. The staff at Axedale were used to preparing for weddings. While Harry, Annie, and Riley lived in the east wing of the house, the west wing had been transformed after refurbishment into a space available for special functions—weddings, special parties, business conferences—and Annie, along with her staff, catered for the events. It was Annie's baby and a good source of revenue for Axedale's upkeep.

Annie held a clipboard and was checking off information with Bridge. "Are you happy with the tables, Bridge? You sure you don't want a top table for the wedding party?"

"No, this wedding is non-traditional. I want everyone just sitting around the dance floor and having fun," Bridge said.

"And the cake before speeches?" Annie asked.

Bridge smiled, thinking about the naughty things she was sure Harry would say in her speech. Bridge and Finn decided they would each have a good friend stand with them as witnesses. Bridge chose Harry of course, and Finn chose Quade.

"Yes, get them over with quickly, I think is best," Bridge said.

Annie wrote on her clipboard and said, "Don't worry, I've warned Harry not to embarrass you too much in her speech."

Bridge laughed. "I'm sure she will, but it's the length I'm concerned with. I want to get to the wedding night as quickly as possible."

Annie play hit Bridge on the arm. "Oh, Bridge. You have plenty of time for that, but you have to celebrate with your friends first. I can't tell you how happy Harry and I are that you're getting married."

They walked into the centre of the ballroom and Bridge let out a happy sigh. "I never in a million years thought I'd get married, Annie. It's more than I ever hoped for. Someone who completes me."

"You must be missing her," Annie said.

Bridge felt a lump come to her throat. She was never given to being gushy and over-emotional, but her love for Finn had changed her in some ways. Being apart from her was so hard. Finn's love made her reconcile her vocation with that part of her that was Mistress Black, and that made her a better person in her day-to-day life.

"I really do. Even though she only goes on tour for a few weeks. I hate sleeping apart from her, and she has offered to retire. It's not as if we need the money, but I think performing is essential to who she is. If Finn gave up performing, I think she would lose part of herself. You know?"

Annie nodded. She couldn't imagine being apart from Harry even for two weeks. Even though Harry retired from her professorship at Cambridge, she still consulted on dig projects, and when she did have to go away on digs, they went as a family. Axedale and the village were Harry's job now.

"We're both lucky, Bridge." Annie thought of Quade. "I wish Quade had the same."

Bridge grinned. "Speaking of Quade—have you seen Sexy Farmer?"

Annie chuckled. "Sexy Farmer?"

"It's Quade. Penny posted a picture of her and a video, and Penny's followers have gone crazy for her."

"Well, no wonder, she is gorgeous. Wait, if Penny called her Sexy Farmer, do you think she likes her?"

Bridge crossed her arms with a conspiratorial smile. "I think it's something we should investigate. Maybe there could be romance on the horizon."

Annie wasn't sure. "Do you think we should? I mean, do you think Penny wants a relationship? I would hate poor Quade to get hurt."

"Let's find out," Bridge said.

Quade stood at the side of the river watching Princess and Dougal play in the water. Since she first took Princess out with them two weeks ago, she had come alive, rediscovering her dog skills, and Dougal loved having another pal, apart from Caesar. Dougal had really taken to Princess, taking care of her and helping her.

If only Princess's owner was as open to help and socialization. Quade had hoped that she would get to know Penny better by dropping by each evening. It was stupid, and she knew that Penny was so out of her league, and only here for a short time, but she couldn't stop thinking about her, and worrying if she was okay, coping on her own in a very new environment.

Quade had been embarrassed when the estate boys had shown her the Sexy Farmer video and picture on Penny's social media and teased her with the name, but the title had at least given her the hope that Penny liked her.

She thought that maybe if she could be a friend to Penny while she was here, it would be enough, but since the first night she had taken Princess out, Penny had been quiet and didn't engage in much conversation with her. It was like a barrier had been put up between them.

Quade whistled, and the dogs came running from the riverbank. Princess was wet and her pretty pink jacket was covered in mud.

"Your mummy is not going to be happy. Let's go and face the music then."

They walked back home to the cottage, and as was her routine, she knocked on the door and walked in. "Penny? We're home."

The room was in darkness, and there were lights on stands, surrounding the kitchen door, pointing inwards. Penny was standing by one big light in a pretty pink skirt and a frilly apron, and was tinkering with one of the lights.

She kicked the base and said, "Bloody stupid things."

"Penny?" Quade said again.

Penny turned around and her eyes went wide when she saw Princess. "What happened?"

"They were playing on the riverbank. It was a bit muddy after the rain last night," Quade said.

Penny hurried over and stripped the muddy coat off Princess. "My poor baby."

"It's only a bit of water and mud," Quade said.

Penny glared at her. "Only a bit of mud? Before I came here, Princess didn't even walk on the pavement without shoes. You convinced me to take them off and look what's happened to her."

Quade was getting annoyed now. "Nothing's happened to her. She had a whale of a time getting mucky, and it'll wash off. She's not a handbag, Penny."

Penny scowled at her, hurried off to get a towel from the cupboard, and wrapped Princess up in it.

"This is the last thing I need," Penny said with frustration. "I was trying to record a video while Princess was out walking, and suddenly all the lights went out. I've got to have this video recorded by tomorrow."

"The fuse has probably just blown because you've plugged in so many lights. Let me check the fuse box," Quade said.

Penny looked panicked and rubbed her temple with her fingers as if she was in pain. "I don't know where the fuse box is. Why did I ever think the country was a good idea?"

"Don't panic. I'll find it. It's probably under the stairs here."

Quade walked over to the cupboard under the stairs and squeezed in. It was full of junk that hadn't been cleared out in a long time. She saw the fuse box and confirmed one was blown.

"Yeah, it's a fuse, all right. The wiring's old in this place—your equipment was probably too much for it."

"Can you fix it?" Penny asked, still with panic in her voice.

Quade got a warm glow inside. It wasn't much, but this was the first time Penny had asked her for anything.

She got out of the cupboard, rubbed the dust off her hands, and then looked Penny in the eyes. "I'll take care of it. I promise you'll be back in business in no time. I need to go and pick up some tools from the farm. Why don't you give Princess a quick dry off, and I'll be back in a flash."

"At my London flat I just pressed a button when the lights went out. My brother showed me that."

"That was a modern fuse box, but this one is a little more complicated," Quade explained.

"I need to get this video done. I have a deadline," Penny repeated.

Quade instinctively reached out and put her hand on Penny's arm. "Don't worry. I'll fix it." Penny looked down at Quade's hand on her bare arm and then back up to Quade's eyes. She couldn't read the strange expression in Penny's eyes. "I'll be back in ten minutes or so. Dougal, stay with Penny and Princess. Look after them, all right?"

Dougal licked her hand. Penny still hadn't said anything since she touched her, so she left.

❖

Penny rubbed a towel over Princess with vigour. "You're not to go paddling with Dougal, Princess. I know you're enjoying this country experience, but there's no need to get dirty, no matter what Quade says."

At the mention of Quade's name, Princess jumped down from the couch and ran to the front door.

"What is this power Quade has over dogs and Instagram followers?" Her picture and video of Quade were fast becoming two of her most popular posts. That annoyed her, not because she was sharing the limelight—anything or anyone that brought extra traffic to her social media was only good for her—but because of the comments that her followers had left. Mainly asking if Quade was her new girlfriend, and if not could they have her? Both questions annoyed her.

Whatever effect Quade had, she'd felt it herself when she'd touched her arm. Her touch sent heat into her body and made her shiver, but that wasn't the most miraculous thing. The most surprising thing was that Penny didn't flinch, or pull away, her usual reaction to another's touch.

It was unnerving.

Dougal walked to her and licked her hand, possibly sensing her uncertainty. He was such a nice dog—reassuring, safe, and steady, just like his owner.

Penny heard Quade's Land Rover pull up outside and couldn't help but feel that unmistakable excitement bubbling in her stomach.

She sighed. Here she was hoping to find that flaw that would give her the excuse to dismiss her intense attraction to Quade, and the opposite was happening. Quade was coming to her rescue like a knight in shining armour.

Penny opened the door and Quade walked in with a large tool bag. Great. Another one of her fantasies. A butch with tools.

"Everything okay?" Quade asked.

"Yes. You do have a lot of tools," Penny said.

Quade walked over to the cupboard under the stairs. "These are just my hand tools. I have a lot more back home. There's a lot of jobs need doing around the farm."

"Tell me you don't have a tool belt in there." Penny held her breath. That would just be too much. A gorgeous hunk of a butch with tools and a tool belt? Her hope of a flaw would die right there and then.

"Not in here, but at home I do. I only need screwdrivers and fuse wire for this job," Quade said as she opened her bag.

Bloody hell. Penny grasped her silver medical warning necklace and tried to remind herself why she didn't let people close.

"Can you point this torch for me?" Quade asked, breaking her from her thoughts.

She pointed it at the box and Quade set to work.

"So, tell me about this intuitive eating thing you do. I've never heard of it," Quade said.

"I'm not surprised," Penny said. "You hadn't even heard of nut milk."

Quade chuckled. "I've not seen any nut milk farms around here, no." Penny let the torch fall a bit. "Keep the light on me, or we'll never get you back in business. Help me understand about what you do."

Normally Penny was happy to discuss her philosophy, but she got the feeling it would sound silly to Quade's ears. "You probably wouldn't be interested."

"Of course I would. I'm always happy to learn, and I'm open-minded. Explain."

Penny watched as Quade cut lengths of wire. She had no idea what Quade was doing. "Well, clean eating, like I told you before, is non-processed, eating as close to nature as you can—"

"I've got that bit. Organic, in other words. And intuitive eating?" Quade said.

"Intuitive eating helps people have a better relationship with food. You make food choices without experiencing guilt, you honour hunger, respect fullness, and enjoy the pleasure of eating." Quade was silent, but Penny could see the corners of her mouth going up. "You're trying not to laugh, aren't you?" Penny could feel her annoyance growing.

Quade cleared her throat and was trying and failing to keep her face neutral. "No, not at all." Quade laughed as she said, "Next time I have a bacon sandwich, I must remember to honour it."

"I knew it was a waste of time to try to explain it to someone like you," Penny said.

Quade laughed some more and said, "Someone like me?"

"A small village cattle farmer who probably doesn't have a care about the animals or the quality of meat you produce."

As soon as Penny said it, she regretted it. Quade's face went stony and Penny knew she had blown it. "Quade, I didn't…"

Quade turned away from her and popped the repaired fuse back in its slot. The lights all came back on, and in the bright artificial light Penny felt even worse. She didn't know what to say to make it right. Quade slammed her tools into her bag and stood up.

"For your information, I raise grass fed organic beef, all the farms on Lady Harry's land are organic, and I won't let anyone say I don't take care of my animals."

"Quade…" Penny tried to talk but Quade just walked out. Penny slammed her hands against her forehead. "What is wrong with me?"

The headache that had been bothering her just made things worse.

CHAPTER SEVEN

The next day Quade was out on her quad bike with Tom, one of her farmhands, driving around fields, checking her cattle, making sure they looked healthy and happy. She was happy with them and pulled up alongside Tom.

"If you can check the top field, I'm going to head on up to Axedale. I have to meet with Lady Harry."

"No problem, boss," Tom said.

As she drove back to the farmhouse, last night ran through her head for the millionth time this morning. What Penny said had hurt. Quade took the welfare of her animals very seriously, but on reflection she realized Penny said what she did in anger.

She should have never laughed at what Penny said. Quade might find it a bit strange, but if it was important to Penny, then she should have respected it.

Quade heard Dougal barking loudly as she neared the field gate. She drove the few hundred yards up to the farmhouse and saw Dougal running for her. He was barking wildly, and then she spotted Princess at her doorstep, barking and shaking.

She knew instinctively that something was badly wrong. Quade parked the quad, and Princess and Dougal ran over. She picked up Princess and felt the tremor that little dogs got when they were stressed.

"What are you doing here? Is your mummy okay?" Quade pulled the Land Rover keys from her pocket and ran to it, carrying Princess. "Dougal, let's go."

Quade's heart pounded, and she felt real fear about what she would find. She drove as fast as she could, but the journey seemed to take so much longer than usual. Especially when she got stuck behind a tractor.

"Come on, come on," she shouted.

Eventually Quade was able to pass and she quickly turned into the driveway of Northwood Cottage. As she got closer to the front of the house, she saw her. Penny was lying in the doorway of the cottage, fitting.

"Shit."

She stopped the car and ran over as fast as she could. Her heart sank when she saw blood coming from the sides of her mouth, meaning she had bitten her tongue, as well as injuries to her arms as they flailed and hit the sides of the door.

Fortunately, her uncle had wanted her to be prepared. He'd taught her how to take care of her aunt in the event of an epileptic fit.

Quade quickly got behind Penny, put her head in her lap, and held her arms so they could not flail any more. "How long have you been like this?" She had to phone the doctor. She managed to get her phone out while holding Penny's arms together with one hand.

"Dr. McTavish? Can you come quickly? Ms. Huntingdon-Stewart is fitting, and she has injuries."

When she hung up the phone she noticed a patch of blood on the side of Penny's head, and her heart sank.

Dougal and Princess sat at Penny's feet looking as worried as Quade felt. Penny's jerky movements calmed, allowing Quade to cradle her head. She wanted to make Penny feel as safe as possible when she came around.

So she stroked her hair and said, "It's okay, Penny. You're not alone. I'm with you, Dougal and Princess are with you. You're safe. I promise I'll keep you safe."

Penny looked so fragile like this, and Quade wanted to protect her from the world. She just prayed that she hadn't hit her head too hard.

❖

Penny became aware of voices, but she couldn't understand the words. Then the fear started to sink in. It had happened again, and the terror made her heart beat wildly. Her eyes sprang open.

The first thing she saw was Quade. Quade was talking to her calmly and stroking her head. The words were garbled, but the tone was calming. Everything about Quade's demeanour was calming. Penny's heart and her breathing started to slow, and she gradually made sense of Quade's words.

"You're safe. I'll keep you safe, I promise," Quade said.

The strange thing was, Penny believed her. The strong certainty in Quade's eyes and voice made her believe.

"The doctor's coming. Just lie still."

This was the part of her condition she hated most. It wasn't even the injuries or the dangers that frightened her so much, it was waking up surrounded by people, often strangers, not understanding what they were saying, feeling impotent, embarrassed, terrified, at the mercy of others, out of control. At her weakest.

"Keep looking at me, Penny, and breathe slowly. You're safe," Quade said.

She felt different. The impotence, the weakness, wasn't as bad when it was Quade who held her. She trusted Quade would take care of her. Penny didn't even feel that when her family helped her after fitting.

That couldn't be right. Could it?

Princess and Dougal ran up to her, and both licked her face. Quade smiled at her and said, "You see? We're all here."

That gave her a warm feeling inside. *We are all here.* She had structured her life as an *I*, an island separated from others, to keep them away from her weakness.

This was a strange, comforting feeling. The comfort was soon replaced by pain when she tried to move.

"Hey, don't move until Dr. McTavish gets here," Quade said.

Penny groaned in pain and was finally able to form words. "Up." She tried to push herself up but her head spun.

Quade eased her down. "Stay still. The doctor's just arrived."

Penny heard a car door shut, and the crunch of gravel underfoot. Her fear and frustration started to gather again. Quade must have felt her tension because she smiled and said, "It'll be all right. I'm here."

She saw the concerned face of Dr. McTavish loom over her. "Ms. Huntington-Stewart? It's Dr. McTavish. I'm just going to look you over."

Quade watched with concern as the doctor checked Penny over. Dougal and Princess sat by her feet, equally concerned. She couldn't describe the panic and fear she had experienced when she found Penny fitting. It had been a long time since she had seen her aunt's epilepsy, but Penny's appeared to be more severe.

It was clearly dangerous for her to live in isolation, and yet she pushed everyone away who tried to help. Quade made a promise to herself, that she wasn't going to let Penny push her away, no matter how hard she tried.

The doctor finally waved her over and said, "I don't think there's a concussion, but I'd be happier if someone stayed with her overnight."

"I'll do that," Quade said immediately.

"No," Penny said firmly, but Quade ignored her.

Dr. McTavish looked between them with concern. "Well, if we could get you upstairs to bed, I'll dress your injuries."

Quade immediately picked Penny up in her arms and walked inside.

"Put down." Penny struggled in her arms.

"You're wobbly, and you're going to bed," Quade said firmly.

A look of panic came over Penny. "No one in my bedroom."

Penny sounded confused, as if she had difficulty forming words. But Quade remembered Penny saying that before. *No one goes in my bedroom.*

She thought it a strange thing to say at the time, and now when she was unwell, even stranger. Quade knew she was private, fiercely independent, but the look of fear on her face was worrying.

"I'll take you in and leave you with the doctor," Quade conceded.

"No…" Penny said.

But Quade just walked through the door and felt Penny tense up like a board. She placed Penny down on the bed and her eyes were drawn to the bedside table, where there were boxes and boxes of medications waiting for Penny. She then looked down at Penny and saw the medical necklace around her neck.

Everything made sense to Quade. These medications, this condition ruled Penny's life. It made her stubborn and led her to push people away. She was terrified of being defined by her condition, and Quade could understand that.

Quade looked into Penny's eyes. "You're not going to push me away. I'll leave you with the doctor."

When Quade went downstairs, she called Tom and asked him to make sure the animals were cared for while she was staying here overnight.

She went to the kitchen and started to make a pot of tea. The kitchen was cluttered with cameras and lighting equipment. She had no idea how Penny coped with all this herself. She saw a notepad on the kitchen counter. There were some notes, ideas for videos, but at the top it said, *Why am I here? To feel better, to get the feel of country life, make some interesting country inspired meals.*

"To get a feel for country life? That's a laugh. She's only been in the village once, and that was to meet Bridge."

She was interrupted by the doctor coming downstairs. "How is she, Doctor?"

"Bloody stubborn, if you'll excuse the language."

Quade chuckled. "That sounds like her."

"Her wounds are superficial, and luckily she didn't bite her tongue too badly, although there was a lot of blood. Her speech is still slow, and she has some of her normal after-seizure problems, but other than that, okay, considering."

"Thanks, Doctor. I'll make sure she's all right."

Dr. McTavish picked up his bag and said, "She insists she's staying alone tonight."

"Don't worry. I'll be here," Quade said. *I can be as stubborn as she is.*

Penny's head was pounding with pain, and fuzzy. She hated the disorientated feeling in her head more than the pain. It was frustrating, but she was determined. So she pushed herself up with one hand, so she could rest her head against the headboard.

"Oh God, my head." She rubbed her temples and cursed how much this was going to hold her back. It usually took three or four days until she was back to normal, so she wouldn't be able to make any vlogs for at least a week.

Penny nearly jumped out of her skin when there was a knock on her bedroom door.

"Penny, it's me."

Quade. She'd assumed she'd left with the doctor. She was backed into a corner. It was bad enough that Quade had carried her into her bedroom, but now she was back.

"I'm okay. Go," she managed to force her brain to say.

But Quade just walked in with the two dogs, carrying a tray with tea. Penny froze, and her chest tightened with panic. *She's in my bedroom, she's in my bedroom.*

Princess jumped up on the bed, and Dougal followed suit. She was surrounded.

"We wondered how you were, and thought we'd bring you tea," Quade said.

Why the *we* thing? Why did she keep saying that? She was never a *we*.

"Don't need tea. Go home," Penny struggled to say.

Quade put the tea tray down on the dressing table and turned to her, arms crossed. "Unless you can get out of that bed and throw me out, I'm staying, so get used to it."

Penny felt fire in her belly, but she didn't have the energy or wherewithal to fight Quade at the moment. She watched Quade pour out tea from the pot and add milk.

"Drink this up and you'll feel a bit better. I even found your weird nut milk in the fridge."

"Not weird," Penny snapped.

Quade smiled and brought the cup over to put on her bedside table. Penny nearly died with embarrassment when she realized her open copy of *Lady Chatterley's Lover* was lying there. Quade stalled while looking at it for a few seconds, cleared her throat, and then moved it to the side to put the tea down.

"Dr. McTavish says you're going to be okay. You just need to rest."

Princess moved on top of her lap, and Dougal licked her hand. She sighed inwardly. Why did everyone have to be so bloody nice?

"I'll call Harry and let her know what happened—"

"No," Penny said firmly.

"But I can't keep it from Harry and Bridge—they're your friends. Besides, I was meant to be meeting Harry. She'll wonder where I am," Quade said.

Penny summoned up all her energy to form the sentence she needed to say. "No, Harry will tell my parents. They'll come and—need space here. Please, Quade?"

Quade was silent for a few seconds and said, "Okay, I'll ask her not to call your parents. She won't if I explain."

It was so frustrating not being in full control of your body. If she had the energy, she would be up getting Quade out of her bedroom. Instead she could hardly lift herself up in bed. She had no control over who Quade told or what she did. Penny hated what this condition did to her.

Quade poured her own tea, and Penny watched with horror as Quade put about five teaspoons of sugar into it. She took a sip and scrunched up her face slightly. "What kind of tea is this you have? It doesn't taste normal."

Penny smiled at Quade's displeasure. "Earl Grey."

"Bloody hell. Don't you eat or drink anything normal?" Quade said, then gave her a wink.

Penny chose to ignore the comment, clearly meant to rile her up.

"Drink your tea then. It'll do you good," Quade said.

Penny didn't want to admit that she couldn't, but she didn't have much of a choice. Her right arm went numb after a fit, and it was pretty debilitating.

"I can't reach. My arm's numb, won't move," Penny said.

Quade's eyes went wide with panic and she put down her tea. "Did you tell the doctor? I can ask him to come back."

"No, you don't need to. I told him. It one of the after-effects I always get. It stays for a couple of days."

Penny waited for the look of pity in Quade's eyes, the look everyone gave. She dreaded it, but it never came. All she saw in Quade's eyes was concern.

Quade walked over, lifted the cup of tea, and put it in her good hand. "Here you go. Anything else you need me to do, just give me a shout."

Penny took a sip of tea and it did make her feel better. After a fit the displaced feeling she got was horrible, but eating and drinking, something so everyday, brought her back to the present.

Quade walked to the door and said, "I'll just go and get some wood, get the fire going in here, okay?"

"Why?" Penny asked.

"Why what? A fire?"

Penny tried hard to articulate her frustration. "Why do you have to be so helpful?"

Quade looked slightly confused. "It's who I am. I'm going to look after you and make sure you're okay, until you can kick me out."

Penny groaned inwardly. Quade wasn't going to leave her alone, was she. Any other woman would give their left leg to be waited on hand and foot by a gorgeous butch like Quade, but the nicer, the kinder she was, just made it more difficult to find that flaw she was looking for.

In the space of a day, Quade had gotten into her bedroom. Her most private space. No one ever got in here, but Quade had just bulldozed in, determined to take care of her. Usually someone as good looking as Quade was full of themselves, and it was easy to find that flaw, that excuse to not let anyone close, but she doubted Quade even knew she was so good looking.

Maybe she should just go back to London when she felt strong enough. Then finding a flaw wouldn't matter. Yes, that was a plan.

CHAPTER EIGHT

Annie was on her knees snipping some chives from the kitchen garden she had planted in their large greenhouse. Her flowers and plants here in the greenhouse were her way of relaxing. The formal gardens outside this space were the territory of the Axedale gardeners, but this was her responsibility. In this temperature regulated greenhouse, she could grow her herbs all year round.

She snipped some more chives and put them in her basket at the side. Annie heard the greenhouse doors open and Harry's voice say, "Annie?"

"I'm over here, sweetheart." Harry walked over and was looking concerned. "I thought you were meeting Quade?"

"She just called. Penny's had an epileptic fit. She found her earlier."

Annie got up immediately and brushed down her jeans. "Is she all right? We better get up there."

"Quade said she didn't want anyone to see. She made Quade promise that she would tell me not to call her mother," Harry said.

Annie put her hands on her hips. "I know you said she's very private, but not letting her mother know?"

Harry shrugged. "She came here from her parents' house. Penny had been staying there since she got out of hospital the last time."

"Hmm. Maybe she feels she's been looked after enough."
Annie walked into Harry's arms.

Harry leaned her head on top of Annie's and sighed. "I
promised her brother I'd look after her."

"Has the doctor been to see her?" Annie asked.

"Yes. Dr. McTavish didn't think she needed to go to hospital.
It was a less severe attack."

"At least that's something. Is Quade still with her?"

Harry kissed the top of her head. "Yes, Penny insisted that she
leave but Quade refused. She's going to stay overnight."

"Really?" Again Annie wondered if Quade had the beginnings
of a crush on Penny. "There must be something we can do."

Harry pulled back and said, "Quade was worried about what
she could give her to eat. I think Penny's clean food philosophy
confuses her. What am I talking about? It confuses me."

Annie chuckled and kissed Harry on the lips. "I know, but it
doesn't confuse me. That's how we can help. I'll make a few meals
up for them, and you can take them up to Quade."

"Perfect idea. Thanks, darling."

Penny fell asleep late afternoon, and so Quade went
downstairs in search of some food for the dogs. As usual, Princess
followed her every move. Quade looked through all the cupboards
and was mostly mystified by the contents. The cupboards had lots
of different herbs and spices, and some bottles labelled *Penny's
Kitchen No Salt Seasoning.*

Quade stared at it. How could you eat food without salt?
There would be no flavour. She shook her head and finally found
what looked like boxes of dry dog food.

She lifted one out and saw *Harrods* printed on the box.
"Bloody hell. You're going to be eating posh food tonight, pal."

Both dogs sat at her feet panting excitedly. Penny had told her
that Princess got the dry dog food with meat on top, and she could

find the meat in the fridge. Quade opened the fridge and found it was more packed with fruit and vegetables than she had ever seen. "She likes her veggies."

The only vegetables Quade tolerated were potatoes, peas, and carrots with her roast dinner on a Sunday. She moved the packets out of the way, expecting to find some fancy pouches of wet dog food, but instead she found a storage container marked *Princess*, and it was full of beautiful pieces of chicken breast.

"Hmm, only the best for you, Princess. Hope you don't mind sharing with Dougal."

Quade made up the meals and put them down for the dogs. Dougal was wolfing his down. It was a treat for him to have fresh chicken breast.

"Take it easy, Dougal," Quade said with a smile.

She loved to see Dougal happy, and he seemed to be happier since he met Princess. Then she realized that she felt happier since she'd met Penny and Princess. In these past few weeks she'd never thought about being lonely once. In fact she'd felt like she had a purpose, a reason to get up every day, and that reason was Penny. Despite the fact that Penny rebuffed her help at every turn, helping Penny was her purpose.

Quade remembered finding Penny convulsing, blood running from her mouth. Her stomach had felt dread like it had never done before. She knew she wasn't in Penny's league, but Quade promised herself that she would convince Penny that she needed a friend, and Quade was the one for the job.

She heard a knock at the door. Quade opened the door to find Harry laden with bags.

"Hi, Harry, come in."

Harry walked in and put the bags on the dining room table. "Annie made some meals for Penny. All you have to do is heat them in the microwave for six minutes, she says."

Quade let out a sigh of relief. "I've been worried about that. I thought I could make her toast, and that was the end of my ideas. There's so many things she doesn't eat."

Harry smiled and crossed her arms. "There's enough for two. You won't go hungry either. How is she?"

"I'm not sure. The after-effects of the attack aren't great. She can't use her right hand, but she says that always happens," Quade said.

Harry's eyes went wide. "That's awful. I'm glad she's got you here. Annie wanted to come, but I told her Penny didn't want any visitors."

"No, she doesn't even want me here, but she hasn't got the strength to throw me out. I'm not going anywhere."

The corners of Harry's mouth lifted into a grin. "You like her, don't you?"

"Of course I like her. I mean, she would rather I didn't, but she can't get rid of me," Quade said.

"No, I mean *like* her." Harry winked at her and she finally caught her meaning.

Quade's throat went dry and she found it difficult to form her words. "Penny? No, no. Don't be daft," Quade said a little too quickly. "Anyway, she's out of my league. She's from your world, not mine."

Harry patted her on the shoulder. "My world is Axedale, just like yours. Don't do yourself down. I'll leave you to it then, and I'll call you tomorrow."

Once she saw Harry out, Quade took the meals through to the kitchen. The dogs were lying together contentedly with full bellies.

She thought about what Harry said and felt her heart pound like it never had. She couldn't court someone like Penny, could she?

Penny woke up slowly and went to stretch. It was only when she felt her arm was numb that she remembered what had happened to her, and the reality of her situation engulfed her. The fear, the frustration, the impotence.

She sighed and shuffled as best she could to sit up. When Penny looked over to the window, she was shocked to see Quade sleeping in the armchair, with her socked feet up on the edge of the bed.

No matter how harsh she was, no matter how much she pushed Quade away, there she was at every turn to save the day. Like some lesbian version of Superman. If it had been anyone else, she would have assumed it was because of who she was, but Quade knew nothing about her other than her famous family name.

Annoyingly, Quade's continued assistance was a kindness, a rare commodity where she came from. Everyone wanted something from her, but not Sam McQuade. The strange thing was, she didn't feel scared or panicked now that Quade had got past her bedroom door. No one had ever done that, and yet here Quade was with the two dogs snuggled together on the bottom of the bed.

No amount of counselling had ever done what Quade had just achieved. Why was that?

Since Quade was asleep, she allowed herself the luxury of openly appraising her. Quade was not only good looking and kind, but she was solidly reassuring. Penny couldn't remember a time anyone had made her feel safe. Perhaps only her beloved father when she was a child, before epilepsy crashed into her life.

Why Quade didn't have a wife, she didn't know. She looked like she should have a wife to come home to, someone to lavish all that love, that kindness, and her gorgeous strong body on.

"I wish it was me," Penny said out loud.

"What? Where? I'm awake." Quade awoke with a start. "Sorry, I fell asleep. Are you all right?"

"Yes. My head feels a bit better. Hopefully tomorrow I'll be on my feet. You didn't have to stay."

Quade rubbed her sleepy eyes. She hadn't had such a relaxing sleep in a while. It had just been too cosy with the fire, the dogs sleeping, and the beautiful Penny lying contentedly asleep.

"I told you. You're going to have to kick me out. I'd only be sitting at home worried about you, anyway."

"I don't need anyone to worry about me. I'm a grown woman," Penny said.

"I didn't say you *needed* anyone to worry—I said I would worry. I fed the dogs while you were asleep. Oh, and Harry came around."

Penny looked worried. "She hasn't told my parents, has she?"

"No. I asked her not to. She and Annie are worried about you, but I put them off from visiting today," Quade said, slipping her feet back into her boots.

"Thank God. It's bad enough having you insist on looking after me."

Penny's remark was sharp and meant as another jibe to push Quade away. So Quade just smiled at her and said, "You're very welcome."

Penny stuck her tongue out at Quade. "You do insist on being so bloody helpful, don't you? I don't know what I ever did to deserve it."

Quade stood up and said quite seriously, "Because you are you, Penny."

That answer totally silenced Penny.

"Are you hungry? Annie sent some meals for you. She said to tell you they were SOS free. What does that mean?"

Penny smiled for the first time. "God bless Annie. Salt-, oil-, and sugar-free food. It's one of the main tenets of my cooking philosophy."

A bit like that nut milk, and Quade couldn't quite wrap her head around that. "No salt? How do you make things taste of anything?"

Penny winked at her this time. "That's one of the things I teach on my channel. How to make things healthy but tasty."

"You must be a bloody magician then," Quade said with disbelief. "But you must know your stuff, because those muffins you gave me were delicious."

"I'll give you some to taste," Penny said.

Quade ran her hand through her hair nervously. "Uh, Annie sent enough for me. I'll bring yours up and eat mine downstairs. Let you have a bit of space."

Penny was silent for a few seconds. "Just eat here, Quade. Princess will follow you wherever you go, and I like her with me."

Was she actually winning Penny over? That sounded like a terrible excuse for sharing her company.

Quade smiled and said, "Thanks, I'd love to have dinner with you, even if it's salt-, oil-, and sugar-free."

❖

Penny watched with amusement as Quade picked her way through Annie's sweet potato and three bean chilli, with brown rice. It was one of Penny's favourite recipes, and it was interesting to taste someone else's version of it. Penny took her last mouthful and was all full up.

She put her cutlery down, and Princess walked up the bed to give her a cuddle. Penny stroked her softly and smiled over to Quade. "How is it, Quade?"

"It's…different. Like nothing I've ever had," Quade said carefully.

"You hate it, in other words," Penny said.

"No, no, I don't, honestly. The flavour is really good. I wasn't expecting it to have so much flavour."

"But?" Penny finished for her.

"I'm not a big vegetable fan, and I've never had beans that weren't in tomato sauce, and as for brown rice—"

"But you're a farmer. You country people are supposed to love vegetables," Penny said.

"I know, I grow them out the back of the farmhouse, but I've only ever liked peas and carrots," Quade admitted.

Penny chuckled. "I'll need to educate you while I'm here, then."

She had said it in all innocence, but Quade's cheeks went red. Quade cleared her throat and put her plate and glass of water on the tray resting on the dressing table.

"So what do you do with them?" Penny asked.

Quade was confused. "Do with what?"

"Your vegetables?"

"Oh, right. Well, I sell them at the local farmers' market. I don't take them myself—we have a collective with the farmers on Lady Harry's land and the next village over, Westwood. They take all our produce over to town."

Penny's face lit up. "A farmer's market? Oh, that's wonderful. Locally grown, locally sourced. That's right up my street. Do you just send your veggies?"

Quade was encouraged. She actually had something positive to talk about with her. "No, my veg, some of my grass fed beef, and my organic home brew, Axedale Ale."

"That's fantastic. I never thought you'd be into the whole organic thing," Penny said with surprise.

"My family has always farmed that way. Long before organic became trendy," Quade said.

"Oh." Penny seemed to take that as a dig, and she hadn't meant it so.

There was a silence. "Are you finished with your plate, Penny?" Quade asked.

"Yes, thanks, but leave the water. I need to take my pills. Can you pass them over?"

Quade put the plate down and picked up the pill bottles and packets. She brought them over and put them down quickly when she saw Penny trying to get up.

"Hey, don't do that yourself." Quade took hold of Penny's good hand and helped her sit on the edge of the bed.

"I'm not an invalid, Quade," Penny snapped, but Quade ignored her.

"Which pills?"

"I can get my own medications." Penny reached out for the first pill bottle, but Quade snatched it up first.

Penny gave a frustrated growl. "I can do it on my own."

Quade sighed. "I know you're independent—"

"Independent?" Penny said angrily. "I'm not independent. I'm at the mercy of a condition that takes over my control. It controls my brain, controls my body, makes me vulnerable to ordinary everyday actions. I can't have a bath, I can't drive my beautiful car, I can't have a normal se—I mean, every time I wake up in the morning, I'm frightened that I'm waking up from an attack, so forgive me if I cherish every little moment of control over my own life I have."

Quade was taken aback by Penny's anger, but she supposed that it was the built up frustration of all she had been through. She handed her the pills.

"I'm sorry. Here you are."

She got up and walked over to look out the bedroom window and give Penny some space. Her heart broke for Penny. To feel all that fear and frustration, and worst of all to face it alone. She wondered if there had ever been anyone special enough to share her load with.

Quade turned around when she heard Penny struggling with one of the pill bottles. She couldn't get it open with one hand. Quade walked over and crouched down. Penny was staring at her feet in resignation.

She didn't take the bottle from Penny. Instead, Quade covered Penny's hand with hers, and Penny looked up, surprised. Quade gripped her hand and took the top off the bottle with her other hand.

"It takes a strong person to ask for help and accept it. My help is freely given," Quade said while looking directly into Penny's eyes.

Penny's lips opened slightly, and her breathing rate increased. Quade felt like she was being drawn to her. She couldn't take her eyes off her.

She and Penny got closer and closer, but then Penny suddenly pulled away, and the moment was gone.

"Thanks, Quade. I'll manage now."

Quade got up quickly. What was she playing at, trying to kiss Penelope Huntingdon-Stewart? She must have lost her mind. *Stop it. She's not even in your hemisphere.*

Annie kissed Riley goodnight. "Have a good sleep, sweetie."

"Night, Mum," Riley said.

Annie then ruffled the large ears of Caesar who was lying at the foot of Riley's bed. He took up more than half of Riley's old bed, and Riley insisted on him sleeping with her, so they got her a bigger bed.

When she first realized how big the Great Dane was going to be, she panicked, but she had fallen in love with the big goofy dog. Watching him run about the estate with Riley was a joy, and she knew Riley would always be safe with that giant by her side.

Harry was waiting by the door. Riley had asked to speak with Harry privately, as she often did. Annie was so pleased that Riley had the joy of another parent to confide in. Harry and Riley were inseparable, and seeing the relationship they had built had warmed Annie's heart.

The question that niggled at the back of Annie's mind was whether Harry would want another child in their life.

"Don't be too long, Harry," she said as she passed her.

"I won't." Harry kissed her softly.

Annie walked to their bedroom and began folding some towels that were on the big four-poster bed.

She sighed when she gazed around the large bedroom. Annie imagined a Moses basket sitting by the window. She had never thought about having another baby before Harry. Riley was her world, and as a single mother she didn't see the need to add to their family, but she felt a need now. One that had been steadily growing since they got married.

Annie had been frightened to broach the subject with Harry for fear of frightening her off. It had been a monumental life change for Harry to have a wife, even more so to have a stepdaughter. Would another child be pushing her too far?

She had to find a way of talking about it, because her body was telling her if she wanted to have another baby, it had to be soon.

Annie jumped when the bedroom door opened. "Did I scare you?" Harry said.

"Sorry, I was lost in my thoughts," Annie said.

Harry wrapped her arms around Annie from the back and said softly into her ear, "Good thoughts, I hope?"

Harry's deep, rich voice always made Annie shiver. "I hope so." Annie tried to change the subject. She turned to face Harry. "What did Riley want to talk about?"

"Oh, she was worried you were going to make her wear a dress to Bridge's wedding. Apparently she saw you looking at dresses online, but she didn't want to hurt your feelings."

Annie laughed. "As if I would even try to put her in a dress. I think the last time she wore a dress was when she was three years old, and that was a struggle."

Harry smiled. "Just like me as a child. I told her that we'll send her measurements to my tailor, and we'll get them to make something similar to my suit."

Annie caressed her fingertips across Harry's cheek. "She's so like you, your ladyship, anyone would think she was your child."

Harry smiled with pride. "She is mine now. I love her with all my heart. She's the future of this estate. I may not be able to pass on my title to her, but the estate and all my lands are hers."

Maybe this was a good moment to broach the subject she had been avoiding.

"It's a big estate, and the village's welfare is a big responsibility for our little girl," Annie said.

Harry smiled. "I'm quite sure she will find someone to share her life with. I think Riley is a romantic. She certainly helped get us together. She loves the story of my ancestor, Lady Hildegard, and her lady, Katherine Aston. Maybe we should play Cupid for Quade like she did for us?"

Annie furrowed her brow. "Quade? What?" They had drifted from the subject that Annie hoped to talk about.

"When I was at Northwood Cottage, I saw a look in her eyes that made me think of what I felt when I was falling for you."

"And what look was that?" Annie said smiling.

"A mixture of terror and complete adoration," Harry joked.

Annie and Bridget had suspected as much, but Annie had some concerns. "She is a lovely girl, Harry, and I'd love to see Quade happy and loved, but is Penny the right one?"

Harry raised an eyebrow. "Why not?"

Annie sighed. "She's Penelope Huntingdon-Stewart, owner of a multi-millon-dollar food brand, and Quade isn't going anywhere. She's a farmer with a farm to run."

Harry gazed lovingly at Annie, took her hand, and kissed her knuckles. "I was Harry Knight, Countess of Axedale, Professor of Archaeology, but none of that mattered when Cupid buried his arrow deep into my heart."

Annie nearly melted on the spot. She placed her hand over Harry's heart. "You are the romantic, Harry. I love it when you talk like that."

"It's true. Every word. You changed my world. I love you, Annie." Harry leaned in and placed the softest of kisses on her lips.

A warm fire was ignited inside Annie, as it always was when Harry touched her.

"Harry," Annie whispered and started to pull Harry's T-shirt off.

"I thought you wanted to talk about something?" Harry said with a sly grin.

"Later." Annie gently pushed her back onto the bed.

CHAPTER NINE

The next morning, Penny felt better. Her head was clearer, and although her arm was still numb-ish, there was feeling coming back. She had managed to persuade Quade to go home and get on with her day, but Quade had promised she would be back later.

It was funny how much had changed in a short time. A few days ago she would have had a panic attack at the thought of someone else being in her bedroom, but after the initial fear and shock, she'd actually had the best night's sleep she ever had.

Penny still awoke with the feeling of terror and fear, but when she saw Quade walk in the room with tea and a big open smile, the fear was banished. The past few days had also taught her that any hope of finding a flaw in the gorgeous farmer was hopeless. She could only console herself with the knowledge that she would be leaving here, once her work was done. No hope for any romance, as much as her body and mind might want it.

The big problem was that Penny felt safe with Quade. To feel safe was something she had hungered for all her life, and now here was some big, strong, hunky, butch farmer, who insisted on running to her rescue at every turn, and who made her feel safe. It was too tantalizing a package. She had to create some distance between them.

Penny heard a knock at the door.

"Hello, it's Bridge."

She smiled. Penny did enjoy the unconventional vicar's company. Princess ran to the door, barking. She got up slowly and opened the door. She was surprised to see Bridge carrying a big wicker basket of fresh produce.

"I come bearing gifts!" Bridge said as she walked in.

"What's all this, Bridge?"

Bridge carried the basket over to the couch and stroked Princess who was jumping excitedly up at her legs. "It's from the villagers. They heard you weren't too well, and there we have it. It's their way of showing they care."

Penny looked through the basket—fresh milk, eggs, bread, jams and marmalades, biscuits and cakes. "But I don't know them." Penny couldn't believe people would be so kind to a stranger.

Bridge smiled. "You're part of the community now. We all look after each other. There's three more baskets out in my car."

"What?" Penny said with surprise. "How did they know?"

Bridge laughed. "You can't sneeze in the village without everyone knowing. Word spreads fast in a place like this."

"It's really so kind," Penny said.

Bridge picked up the box of eggs. "I know a lot of these things you can't eat, like the dairy, but trying to explain that to farming villagers would be like speaking in a foreign language. I can distribute some of the things around the old folk of the village."

"I know. Quade can't understand the concept of nut milk, no matter how I explain it."

Bridge smiled and had a twinkle in her eye. "I hear our rugged farmer has been helping you a great deal. How are you now?"

Penny cradled her numb arm. It was slowly coming back to life, but slow was the operative word. "I'm doing okay. I'll be good as new in a few days." Penny smiled.

"And Quade?" Bridge said.

Penny sighed. "Yes, she's insisted on helping. If I wasn't in such a weakened state, I wouldn't have let her."

Bridge furrowed her brow. "Why?"

"Because I can take care of myself, Bridge. Would you like tea?"

Coming to the country was turning into the worst decision she had ever made. She was going to be suffocated with kindness.

❖

Quade hurried back from Axedale, where she had been helping Mr. Stevens with some new plans for the estate. Lady Annie had the idea of introducing some new animals to the estate—alpacas, goats, pot-bellied pigs—a petting zoo of sorts to give the children who visited Axedale another interesting thing to do.

When alpacas had been mentioned, both Quade and Stevens had thought it was a joke and burst out laughing. They soon understood by the look on Annie's face that alpacas were not a laughing matter.

Then there were the plans for medieval day. Harry and Riley wanted to host a day where families could enjoy the rich history of Axedale and the Knight family, but it took a lot of organizing. She should really be going back to the farm, but she hated the thought of Penny being on her own.

A little voice in the back of her mind was saying she was getting too involved in the life of someone she found attractive. The problem was, Penny was more than attractive. Penny had something inside her that was drawing Quade to her. A need that Penny tried so hard to cover up, something she'd seen in Penny's eyes, when she woke after her fit, and this morning, when Quade walked into the bedroom. The need to feel safe, loved, secure.

Dougal started to bark when he realized where they were going. "Are you excited to see Princess? Good boy."

When they pulled up at the cottage, Quade saw Bridge's car there. Suddenly she felt embarrassed about the bunch of flowers she had in the back seat. Bridge would surely make some jokey remark. Quade had picked them from her own garden before she left for Axedale this morning.

She looked in the mirror. "Who are you trying to kid, mate?"

Bringing flowers was the worst idea ever. Quade let her head fall back against the headrest, feeling sorry for herself.

Dougal's bark brought her out of it. "Okay, okay. We'll go in."

Quade got out of the car, gazed at the flowers in the back, and said, "What the hell. I'm not going to waste them." She ran her fingers through her hair. "Come on, Dougal."

When she got to the door, Quade knocked and popped her head around inside. "Hello, it's only me."

She saw a grinning Bridge and Penny sitting by the fire, drinking tea. Penny gave her a tense smile. Suddenly she felt out of place. Why had she come here?

Princess ran at her and Dougal and covered over the awkward feeling in the room. "Hi, pretty girl." Quade made a fuss over Princess, and then she and Dougal ran to get her toys.

"I see Princess and Dougal are the best of friends," Bridge said.

"Yeah, they took to each other straight away," Quade said.

Quade walked to the couch and Bridge said with a mischievous look, "Are those flowers for me?"

Quade cleared her throat nervously. "Sorry, Vicar. They're for Penny."

Penny took them and said, "Thank you."

"I picked them from my garden this morning," Quade said.

Bridge winked at Quade. "Isn't she the sweetest, as well as gorgeous."

Quade looked down at her boots, feeling the heat burning in her cheeks.

There was another excruciatingly long silence before Bridge said, "Quade, can you help me with some food baskets from the car?"

"Of course." Quade followed Bridge out to the car.

Bridge unlocked the car and started to speak, "So—"

Quade jumped in before she could ask anything about Penny. "How's Finn's tour going? I miss our chats at the pub."

Bridge crossed her arms and leaned against the car. "Ah yes. Your little butch chats. Quite adorable. Yes, she's doing well. Sell-out audiences, but we miss each other terribly."

"At least you have the wedding to look forward to," Quade said.

Bridge sighed. "Hmm. Who would have thought I'd get married?" She leaned into Quade and said, "If a supposed celibate vicar can fall in love with an atheist magician, then there's hope for anyone, especially rugged farmers."

"What do you mean?" Quade said. Surely Bridge couldn't have noticed her attraction, although Harry had clocked it too.

Bridge gave Quade a gentle push. "Oh, come on, Quade. There was electricity in there. It was crackling."

Quade pretended to laugh. "Don't be daft, Bridge. She's a Huntingdon-Stewart. We all studied her family in history class at school. Not to mention she's this internet icon. People like that don't look twice at small-time farmers."

Bridge threw her hands up. "What tosh, Quade. We aren't living in the nineteenth century. Class barriers don't matter any more. Her father won't call you to his study and pay you off or chase you with a shotgun. Don't go looking for obstacles."

"She doesn't want even a friend, Bridge," Quade said, exasperated. "You saw her in there? She's as cold as ice."

Bridge just smiled and leaned in to whisper in her ear, "Then melt her, my dear Sam McQuade. Melt her."

While Bridge and Quade were outside, Penny went back to her dining table and the work she was trying to catch up with. She was so far behind in her scripting and recording of videos, not to mention her cookbook. Her epilepsy tried its best to hold her back in life, but she always came back fighting and more determined.

She was still holding the flowers that Quade had brought.

Penny had been given a lot of flowers in her life. In her circle, flowers were a kind of currency sent by PAs as a matter of course. They were always exquisite, perfectly picked, styled, and beautifully presented by the best florists in London, but they were nothing in comparison to these home-grown flowers, bunched roughly together and wrapped in brown paper, and tied with string.

She threw them down on the table and shouted with frustration, "Why do you have to be so adorable!"

"Sorry?" Quade said behind her.

Penny closed her eyes, realizing she'd been caught. She took a breath and turned around to see Quade holding two baskets of the villagers' presents, looking absolutely gorgeous.

She definitely had to get some space and distance herself from Quade. She knew that a romance with the hunky Quade would force her to address problems that she had never found an answer to.

"Just something I saw on Twitter. You can put the basket on the couch." Penny went back to pretending to look at her laptop, hoping that Quade would take the hint and go.

She could feel Quade's eyes boring into her.

"How are you really? Arm any better?" Quade said.

Again, Penny never looked up and tapped her laptop keys randomly, with her good hand. "Yes, it's getting much better."

She could feel the silence and tension hanging in the air. This woman had seen her at her most vulnerable, when she was not in control of her body. She felt exposed in her presence.

"Don't you think you should be resting?" Quade asked.

"No, I've rested enough," Penny said firmly.

She heard Quade walking towards her, and Penny's stomach tightened with tension.

"What are you doing?" Quade asked.

"Working, I've got a lot to catch up on." Penny looked up and said, "Shouldn't *you* be working?"

"No, I've left the boys in charge," Quade said.

"The boys?" Penny questioned.

"Lady Harry got me some extra help with the farm when she asked me to become assistant estate manager."

Penny looked back at her computer. "Oh yes, well, I mustn't keep you."

Quade sighed in frustration. It was like having a conversation with an icy brick wall. Last night they had talked openly and Penny seemed something approaching normal, but now she was back in her icy shell.

"What exactly is so urgent that you have to work so hard and not rest?" Quade said with a harsher tone than normal.

"I've got to write my blogs and send them to my guy who runs my website, and script videos, so that as soon as I'm able to shoot, I'm ready," Penny replied while still concentrating on her screen.

A thought occurred to Quade. "What are your blogs and videos about?"

Penny sighed. "My new adventure in the country."

Quade was now getting frustrated. "What adventure? You've set foot out of the door once, to meet Bridge and have tea at Axedale Hall. Why did you come to the country, Penny?"

Penny's head snapped around. "Not that it's any of your business, but I came here to de-stress, recover from my last medical problem, and make a country-inspired web series."

"And how can you do all these things stuck in front of your laptop, inside the cottage? You should come out with Princess, Dougal, and me walking, explore the village, meet the people, or is all this just a gimmick for you? You might as well still be back in London."

Penny stood up slowly from her chair, her face full of fury. "Please go."

Quade closed her eyes and gave out an exasperated sigh. So much for melting Penny as Bridget had suggested. It looked like she had iced her up even more.

"Come on, Dougal. See you later, Princess." She walked to the door and said before leaving, "If you need me, just call. I'm always just one call away."

❖

Penny shut up her laptop and looked over to Princess who was sleeping in front of the fire. "Let's go to bed, Princess. This is a waste of time."

She had been staring at her screen for most of the day, her mind filled with Quade's parting words to her this afternoon.

Penny switched everything off downstairs and followed Princess upstairs to her room. Princess jumped onto the bed and got herself comfy. Penny looked over to the chair by the window, and it seemed empty, as did her bedroom. A few days ago her bedroom was her cocoon from the world, and the chair was just a chair, but now it felt empty.

"How can a chair feel empty?" Penny said with exasperation.

She opened up her wardrobe and took out her onesie. It was definitely a unicorn type of night. Once she was changed, which was tricky with one functioning hand and one that was slowly coming back to life, she picked up her iPad and checked her social media accounts.

She had posted comments and replied to questions today, as if she was having a simply wonderful time in the country. None of her followers or fans knew her condition had struck, and she'd actually been laid low in bed, needing someone to take care of her.

Quade had asked her if coming here was a gimmick. Was she right?

This wasn't her idea, but her business partner's. Olivia had pitched to Penny this idea of the city girl in the country, getting mud on her high heels and stumbling through a new environment. The stumbling, kooky, rich city girl had been her image from the first video she'd made, all those years ago.

She'd had no idea how to cook, but taught herself, and put her efforts on camera. Viewers liked it and her following grew. But she was a good cook now. She had grown up and was now a successful businesswoman, a businesswoman who was struggling to cope with epilepsy.

The world had no idea who she was. Her friends had no idea, her business partner, and even her family didn't truly know her. Her fears, her daily struggles, her intimacy problems.

When her mother asked why she never seemed to have anyone in her life, she fudged it and said she had no time for relationships, but last night, when she was alone with Quade, Penny was sure Quade saw through the gimmick, the sham that was her life.

Penny opened her pictures on her phone and looked at the photo of Quade, as she had done many times since she'd taken it. There was something in Quade's open, kind face, something in her eyes that drew her in.

She looked over to the empty chair, then back to the picture. "Princess, shall we text Quade and reach out the hand and paw of friendship?" Princess licked her hand and Penny said, "That's what I thought. Maybe it can be different here. Maybe I can have a real friend."

Penny typed quickly on her phone, *Will you show me your world?*

She didn't normally wait nervously for a reply, but she did this time. Had she pushed Quade too far away?

Her phone finally beeped, and the text only had five words: *You only had to ask.*

CHAPTER TEN

They decided to wait until the end of the week, when Penny would be fully recovered. By the time Saturday came around, Penny was ready for her first excursion. Quade had been getting progressively nervous about their outing as the days went past.

When she'd left Northwood Cottage, Quade had no hope of making a friendship with Penny, but then later on that night came Penny's text.

Will you show me your world?

That text had meant everything to her. She knew, deep down, Penny wanted people to rely on, friends who would support her—she could see it in her eyes—but Penny just didn't know that you could lean on someone without being weak.

Quade had been gazing in her wardrobe for ages. She wanted to look nicer than her usual jeans, boots, and checked shirt, but she had little else. She was a farmer and had little need for fancier clothes.

She turned back to Dougal, who was lying on the bed. "I'm going to look like a country yokel compared to Penny. Mind you, fashion models would look plain next to Penny."

Quade closed her eyes and smacked herself on the head. "Don't say things like that."

As much as she tried to quell her attraction to the difficult Penny, when she was lying in bed at night, she couldn't stop her mind from wandering, and thinking about what-ifs. What if their hands brushed as they walked together, what if Penny stumbled and fell into her arms?

Quade sighed in exasperation. "Why did she have to be so beautiful, and gay?"

If Penny had been straight, she would have kept these thoughts out of her head. On second thought, she'd probably be attracted to her just as much.

The main problem wasn't that Penny was so attractive, although she was utterly beautiful and feminine, but it was the sense that Penny yearned for someone to love her, to care for her, and Quade felt a deep need to be that person for her.

Quade scrubbed her face and then lifted her Sunday shirt and jeans out of the wardrobe.

"This is the best I can do."

She dressed and styled her hair quickly, then both she and Dougal drove over to Northwood Cottage. As usual Dougal was overcome with excitement when he realized where they were going. When they arrived at the front of the house, Quade beeped the horn to let Penny know they were there.

She got out and walked to the door, but before Quade got there, the cottage door opened and she stopped dead and lost all power of thought and speech. Penny was standing in the doorway, wearing vintage high-rise denim shorts with faded pink flowers on them, and on top a little pink T-shirt that showed her midriff, with the words *I believe in Unicorns* printed on it.

On her feet were a pair of pink wellington boots, with flowers matching her shorts, and on her head she wore a straw hat with a pink flower on it.

"Morning, Quade. Will we do for a day in the country?" Penny said.

Quade just couldn't form words to reply. She didn't think she'd ever seen such a beautiful woman in her life. Her legs in those shorts, and the way her tight little T-shirt clung over her breasts, made her mind turn to mush. Penny was femininity wrapped up in a fluffy pink package.

Quade's stomach clenched, and her heart raced. *Say something.*

Penny frowned. "Is there something wrong, Quade?"

Quade averted her gaze to Princess who was sitting in her dog bag with matching pink boots and finally found something to say.

"I—I thought we agreed no dog boots, and no bag. Princess wants to run with Dougal."

Penny sighed and let Princess out of the bag and took her boots off. "You couldn't say something positive, could you?"

If only she knew what Quade really was thinking. Quade led her over to the car and opened the door for her. Once she and the dogs got in, Quade turned to Penny and said, "You look very nice today."

Penny's big smile was back. "Thank you. Where are you taking us?"

"My farm. I thought it would be a good place to start. There's lots of things to see that might interest you."

Penny winked at her. "I'm sure there's lots of things at your farm that I'd be interested in."

Was that flirting? Quade had little experience, but she suddenly felt hot, not to mention entranced by the intoxicating smell of Penny's perfume. She had a flash of pressing lips to the curve of Penny's neck and inhaling her scent.

She shifted uncomfortably in her seat. *Stop this.* When she was alone, it was easier to think logically and rationalize her attraction to Penny. But seeing her this morning just overwhelmed all her rationale.

Something had gone wrong in her brain.

"Quade?" Penny said, trying to get her attention again.

"What? Sorry," Quade said.

Penny narrowed her eyes. "Is everything all right, Quade. You seem a little...distracted."

"No, no, I'm fine." Quade rubbed her hands together over-enthusiastically. "We ready to go?"

Penny lifted her camera from her bag. "I was asking you if minded me filming."

"No, go ahead. I promised to show you the real country for your vlogs. So on you go."

"Great," Penny said.

This was the best idea. She was going to get some great material, and Quade had been more than popular with her followers.

Penny set her camera to record and filmed herself first. "Hi, friends, Penny here. I'm at the start of a new country adventure, and I want to bring you along with me. Today I'm going to visit a friend's farm, and I think you'll all be pleased to see whose farm it is."

Penny turned her camera on Quade and said, "Yes, Sexy Farmer is taking me on my adventure. Say hi."

"Hi," Quade said awkwardly.

"Isn't she adorable, friends? Oh, and no forgetting the other star of the show, Princess, who's made her own new friend." She twisted in her seat, so she could get a shot of the dogs in the back seat. "Meet Princess's new friend, Dougal. Dougal belongs to Sexy Farmer. Isn't he sweet?"

Penny stopped recording and laid the camera in her lap. Quade started the engine and pulled out.

"See, that wasn't so bad, was it?" Penny said.

"No, you're so confident talking to that thing." Quade pointed to the camera.

"It's just what I do. I love it," Penny replied.

"Why Sexy Farmer?" Quade said.

Penny grinned. "Does it annoy you?"

"No, just a bit strange. I'm nothing approaching sexy," Quade said as they drove down the hill to her farm.

"Of course you are. You're a big hunky farmer, and my followers are drooling over you. Besides, I don't want them to know your name. It gives you some privacy."

And some part of you that's just mine.

❖

As soon as they arrived at the farmhouse, Penny jumped out and started taking still pictures of the house and fields surrounding it.

"This place is beautiful. It's so…authentic," Penny said.

Quade let the dogs out the back and walked over to her. "It's what?"

"Authentic." Penny beamed.

Quade raised an eyebrow. "Well, it would be. It's real."

Penny rolled her eyes. "No, it's unchanged, unaffected by modern life."

"Hmm," Quade said.

Penny put her hands on her hips and gave her an indignant look. Unfortunately, in those tight shorts it just made her look all the more sexy. "What does *hmm* mean, exactly?"

"Well, unaffected could mean shabby."

To Quade's surprise, Penny grinned and gave her a playful shove. "You know I didn't meant that. Where to first?"

Penny was really different today. She seemed to have let go of some of the stubbornness and was excited and light-hearted.

"Why don't we take the quad out to see the cattle," Quade suggested.

"A quad bike?" Penny said with concern.

"Don't worry. It's a two-seater, quite safe. Stay here a minute."

Penny watched Quade jog off to a wooden hut by the side of the farmhouse, and a few minutes later, what was more like a red buggy than a quad came driving out.

Dougal jumped about excitedly. He clearly liked going for a ride. Penny opened her bag and said to Princess, "Jump in, Princess. This is dangerous for you."

Quade pulled up beside her and said, "Would you like a ride?"

Penny smiled. Quade did look really sexy behind the wheel of this thing.

"If you promise not to kill me." Penny slid into the bucket seat.

Quade laughed softly and said, "I think I might be hanged, drawn, and quartered if I killed a Huntingdon-Stewart."

Penny gasped when Quade reached over her, and their bodies touched.

Quade must have felt her stiffen, because she lifted the seat belt and said, with panic in her voice, "I was just buckling you in. I'm sorry."

"No, no. I'm sorry. I'm just not used to being so cl—Can we just forget about it, start again?" Penny said.

"Yes. Hold onto Princess tightly." Quade whistled, and Dougal jumped into the back.

Penny held Princess with one hand, grasped her hat with the other, and squealed as the quad sprang to life and started to move.

"Don't panic. It's perfectly safe," Quade said.

"How far away are they?" Penny couldn't see anything but an expanse of grass, and Axedale Hall in the distance.

"Not far. Just around this bend. They usually congregate around the old oak tree. Gives them a nice bit of shade."

Penny had to raise her voice to be heard over the noise of the quad. "They aren't dangerous, are they?"

"Not at all. Aberdeen Angus are known for their tame temperament," Quade said.

Penny noticed the way Quade talked with pride when she spoke about her animals. She obviously cared about them.

"Aberdeen Angus? I think I've cooked with that beef."

They drove over a bump, and Penny got a fright.

"They're a well-respected Scottish breed. Fantastic animals," Quade said.

Penny spotted a group of men over by the side of the field. They turned around and Quade raised her hand to them.

"Who are they?" Penny asked.

"My farmhands."

"Oh."

They turned a bend and she saw the tree Quade had been talking about. "There's hundreds of them."

Quade smiled and shook her head. "No, just the one hundred. I have a bull too, but he's in a separate field with a few steers to keep him company."

Penny was lost. "Stop, you're talking farmer-speak. What's a steer?"

"A castrated male. It makes them less aggressive. For a small farm like this, one bull is enough, and Boris is definitely more than enough for us." Quade smiled proudly when she said that.

Penny did a double take. "Boris?"

"Yeah, he's quite the personality, and very good at what he does, so we keep him in another field when his services are not needed."

"His services?" Penny laughed. "How romantic. I hope you don't talk like that to the ladies you entertain."

Quade smiled tensely and red rose to her cheeks. She was *embarrassed*. How sweet.

Could she really be that sweet?

Quade slowed the quad as they got nearer to the herd and finally stopped. The cattle mooed loudly when they saw her.

"Stay there and I'll help you out." Quade jumped off, then walked around. Dougal followed suit. "Let Princess out of that bag. She'll be fine now."

Penny opened the bag and Quade lifted Princess down to Dougal. They immediately ran around together. Quade then offered her hand to Penny. Penny stared at her hand.

Why did Penny seem so tense? Quade had noticed that before, especially in the quad when she helped with her seat belt.

Didn't Penny trust her? She thought about taking her hand away but somehow knew she had to try to get Penny to take her hand. She kept her hand out and held Penny's gaze.

Penny's hand had a slight tremble as it moved to hers, and then when she clasped it, Penny held it tight and let out a breath, as if she'd overcome something. What that was, Quade didn't know.

When she first met Penny, her friends had advised her to offer help, not just bulldoze in and give it. Maybe this was the same. She just had to keep offering kindness, and her touch.

"Let me introduce you," Quade said.

Penny kept gripping her hand. "Are you sure it's safe?"

Quade gave her a reassuring smile. "Yes, trust me. They love nothing more than a back rub and ear scratch. They won't hurt you."

"Back rub?" Penny said with surprise.

"Yeah, come on." Quade led them over to the tree. The dogs entertained themselves chasing each other.

One of the cows walked forward a few steps, and Penny jumped behind Quade. "It's really big. The don't look that big in pictures."

"They're perfectly docile. Look." Quade stroked the animal's neck. "You see? Come and talk to him."

Penny edged forward and patted him gingerly. "What kind is he?"

"This is a young steer," Quade said while she scratched its ear.

Penny started to relax and smile. "They are quite gentle, aren't they?"

"Told you. Look around this whole space." Quade indicated with her arm. Penny turned and followed Quade's direction. "They graze here, free range, and over at the other side of the field is one of my barns where they can take shelter, with lots of straw and everything they need."

"This certainly is organic farming. You really are doing it right. Can I film here?" Penny asked.

"Yeah, go ahead." Quade's chest puffed out with that compliment. "We are inspected every year to keep up standards, or we don't get a license renewed."

When Penny got her camera set, she turned to Quade and said, "Quade, I'm sorry I made assumptions about your farm when I first met you."

"That's all right. You didn't know me," Quade said generously.

Penny looked her straight in the eye and said, "No, really. All this, everything you do, is what I believe in." Penny looked down. She hesitated for a second and then touched Quade's hand. "Thank you for showing me this."

❖

Penny swept the video camera around so she could get a panoramic shot of Quade's garden. After a hair-raising run in the quad back up to the farmhouse, Quade led her through the side gate to her garden.

"It's wonderful," Penny said.

The garden was split into large beds with flowers, plants, and vegetables. Quade clearly put a lot of work into this.

Quade's face beamed with pride as it had done with her animals. "Thanks, let me show you the vegetable patch."

Quade was so different from anyone she had met or socialized with. Many of her acquaintances used the buzzwords clean eating and insisted on organic produce, but like her purchased them at their local expensive supermarket or deli. None of them knew the hard work, sweat, and pride that went into its production. But Quade knew.

Quade crouched down by the side of the vegetable patch, and Penny laughed as Princess sat by her feet.

"She really likes you," Penny said.

"I could say the same thing about you and Dougal, Penny." Quade indicated to her side, where she was surprised to see Dougal trotting along beside her.

"You're a sweet boy." Penny ruffled his head and joined Quade by the vegetable patch. "You know, I just realized something."

"What?" Quade asked.

"Everyone else I know insists on calling me Pen, but you call me Penny. Why?"

"You told me your name was Penny, so that's who you are to me," Quade said.

There was a tenderness in Quade's words, a tenderness that made her breathing more rapid and, unusually for her, made her open up. Just like when they were in the cattle fields, she took Quade's hand, and she didn't feel threatened or scared. Then she sought out the touch of her hand again.

"My family calls me Little Pen."

Quade nodded sympathetically. "And you don't like that?"

"No," Penny said. "They don't mean to, but it makes me feel like the little girl who can't take care of herself."

Why was she telling Quade this? No one knew that. Something about this big, strong, unpolished, down-to-earth farmer made her feel safe. Every night when she went to bed, she never felt as safe as she did the night Quade stayed with her.

"I'll never think of you that way. You're Penny, a strong, successful businesswoman."

It meant so much for Quade to say that to her. She saw her as a woman, not a girl with a condition.

"Everyone calls you by your last name. Can I call you something that no one else does?" Penny asked.

"Sam?" Quade replied.

Penny smiled and shook her head. "Sammy."

Quade widened her eyes. "You're right. No one calls me that, but I'd be happy if you did."

Something passed between them then. Penny didn't know what it was and couldn't explain it, but it felt like she had stepped over a barrier, probably of her own creation.

"Show me your veggies then."

Quade gazed back at her with a more than friendly smile. "Okay. In this bed I have cabbage, Brussels sprouts, carrots"— Quade pointed to the next bed along—"then potatoes, onions, greens, kale, and runner beans along the wall."

Penny's eyes widened. "Kale? You've just said a clean eating vlogger's magic word."

"Really? I never thought about growing it until the farmers' collective suggested it. They always sell out at the farmers' market. Come and I'll show you."

They walked over to the next bed and Quade pulled out some kale from the ground. "We'll make up a basket of veg for you to take home."

Penny reverently touched the kale with dirt clinging to the bottom. "Vegetables fresh out of the ground and straight into the cooking pot? You're giving me shivers of pleasure."

As they had done earlier in the day, Quade's cheeks went adorably pink.

"I know what I could do. A video making a recipe only from ingredients from your garden. It's perfect! Everyone would love it," Penny said.

"I told you I would give you inspiration, didn't I?" Quade said.

Penny smiled and her eyes sparkled. "You do, Sammy. You do."

Quade stood up quickly and brushed down her jeans. "We better get you inside for a cup of tea before my purple carrots tip you over the edge."

Penny gasped. "Purple carrots?"

Quade poured the tea and carried it over to the table.

"It's a perfect country kitchen. Much bigger than mine at the cottage," Penny said.

Quade gave her the tea and said with a hint of amusement in her voice, "Authentic?"

Penny laughed. "Exactly."

"It needs decorating, but white is all I've ever gone for. I wouldn't know what other colours to choose."

Quade looked over at Dougal's bed and saw that Dougal and Princess were curled up together. She indicated for Penny to look over.

"Aww, they're sharing a bed. Isn't that the cutest? I don't think I've ever seen Princess as happy since she's come to the country. I think she was a sheepdog in a previous life."

"Dougal is glad to have her too," Quade said.

"How long have you lived here alone?" Penny asked.

"Five years. I was brought up by my aunt and uncle. My aunt died twelve years ago, a heart attack, and my uncle went five years ago to a stroke."

"I'm sorry." Penny surprised her by covering her hand with hers. "Have you never met anyone you wanted to make a home with here?"

Quade looked down into her mug of tea and tapped her fingers on the side. "There aren't many lesbians to choose from in a small village."

Penny furrowed her brow. "But what about the nearest town? There must be a gay bar, or go to London."

"Finn is always trying to convince me to go to a club in London," Quade said.

"Why don't you go? Don't you want to meet someone?"

Quade looked up and gazed directly into Penny's eyes. "Yes, I want to meet someone to love more than anything in the world, but me in a club? I mean, am I likely to meet someone who would want to be a farmer's wife in a London club?"

Penny felt like that question was pointed at her, and she panicked. Quade was looking for a wife. She couldn't be that to anyone, although she had gone further with Quade that she ever had with any date.

"Who knows. What about a dating app?" Penny suggested.

Quade picked up her phone and then dropped it back down. "Are you kidding? I can make a call on this thing, and that's it."

Penny picked up Quade's phone. "An iPhone? You don't look the type for an iPhone."

"I'm not. Harry got them for the estate management team. I'm not good with computers."

"Wait," Penny said, "you've got *my* app. It's the only one you have."

Quade looked a little embarrassed. "Uh, yeah. Riley put it on for me. I wanted to understand what you did."

That touched Penny. Even when she was being cold and pushing Sammy away, she was interested in what she did. She looked up at her and said, "You've never asked about my family."

Quade took a sip of tea. "I supposed everyone asked you that, and it probably annoyed you."

"Why?" Penny asked.

"Because you want to be your own woman. Not your surname."

Penny felt another chip of ice crack and melt from her heart. How did she know that? How could she know her so well after such a short time? Connecting like this with someone was not only strange for her, it was unheard of.

"You're very perceptive, Sammy."

"Not really, you just have to listen. So many people talk and don't listen these days."

Penny had an idea. "Would you mind if I put some of the social media apps on your phone? Just so you can see what I do?"

Quade smiled. "I'd like that."

Penny's fingers started to fly across the screen, and as she set up some of the apps, she started to talk. "I don't want you to get the wrong idea. My family are the best. I love them so much. There's my mum and dad, my brother, my sister, then I come last. The baby in more ways than one. They've always babied me, for the best of intentions. They're always frightened I'll get hurt because of my condition."

Quade nodded in understanding. "Epilepsy can be almost as frightening for your loved ones—I know."

Penny looked up from the phone quickly. "It didn't seem to frighten you, when you were helping me."

"My aunt had it. My uncle taught me how to take care of her when it struck," Quade said.

It couldn't be. Quade understood her condition as well? Could she be any more perfect? Penny was beginning to think the universe was playing one big cosmic trick on her, dangling the perfect partner in front of her, knowing she couldn't take her.

"I see. Well, I've just spent six months at home being babied, and I need to be myself again," Penny said while still installing the apps.

"I suppose it was hard growing up as a Huntingdon-Stewart. A lot of expectations?" Quade asked.

"You could say that. Not from my parents, but everyone in my family is so accomplished. My brother is the youngest ever professor of mathematics at Cambridge, my sister is Under-Secretary-General for Humanitarian Affairs at the UN, and you know who my mother and father are. Really difficult for a young girl with epilepsy and dyslexia."

"Dyslexia?" Quade said. "That must have made school really difficult."

"It did. I was terrible at school. I became so frustrated that I gave up trying. It was only when I got older that I worked through it and found ways to help myself."

There was a silence, and then Penny put Quade's phone down on the table. "I've never told anyone that before."

Quade smiled at her. "I'm glad you trusted me, and I'm really proud of you for overcoming all those obstacles and becoming a successful businesswoman."

Penny sighed. "Not all the obstacles. I can't do live TV. I was always frightened my epilepsy would strike while I was under pressure. I suppose you know what happened to me six months ago?"

Quade shook her head. "Not really. Harry mentioned something but not the full story."

Penny couldn't believe there was anyone in the country who didn't know and hadn't laughed at the viral video.

"Don't you ever go on the internet? I was all over it," Penny asked.

"No, I only ever go online to order farm supplies, and my computer went completely kaput last week. I've had it about ten years."

"Good God, well, my business partner, Olivia, convinced me to break my rule about live TV. If I could do it, then there might have been an offer from the production company for my own series, so against my better judgement, I did it, and I paid for it."

"You had a fit?" Quade took her hand and squeezed it in support.

"Yes. It was one of the most terrifying experiences I've ever had. I woke up in terror, with strangers around me, and a studio audience watching as I was given first aid. The fit was much worse than the one I just had. It lasted too long. I couldn't even begin to move or talk. Everything was a blur, like I was out of time with everyone else. I lost consciousness again, then woke up in hospital. Only to find the video of it had gone viral, was being watched all over the world. I wanted to crawl into a hole and die."

Quade looked angry. "Don't ever say that. The people that shared that video are sick."

Penny felt tears come to her eyes and fought hard to keep them back. "I shouldn't be telling you this. I never talk like this."

"Maybe you need to. You can trust me." Quade squeezed her hand tightly.

Penny started to panic. She was exposing too much of herself. She had to get away. She slid Quade's phone across the kitchen table and stood up abruptly.

"Can you take me home now?" Penny said.

Quade appeared confused. "What? Why? What's wrong?"

"Just take me home now, please, or I'll walk. Princess? Come now."

Once she got hold of Princess, she marched out of the farmhouse and waited by the Land Rover.

Quade came out, followed by Dougal and clutching the basket of vegetables they had picked for Penny. "What have I done wrong, Penny?"

"Nothing, just take me home. I need to be home." Penny's whole mind and body were in panic. It was too easy to talk to Quade, too easy to touch her, and she was going to expose herself too much. Quade scared her.

Quade sighed and got in. The drive back to Northwood Cottage was excruciatingly tense. Penny's mind just kept telling her, *You need to be alone. You need to be alone.*

When they arrived, she thanked Quade and ran into the house. She slammed the door shut and burst into tears.

"Why can't I be normal?"

CHAPTER ELEVEN

A few days later, Harry was in her study, reviewing some edits for her new book on the Roman occupation of Britain, when she heard children screaming and shouting, running down the hall. There was a time when that would have sent her into a rage, but not now. Now that she had Annie and Riley, it made her smile and gave her a warm glow.

Riley had her best friend over after school. The alpacas were being delivered today, and it had caused great excitement. It was wonderful to be able to give Riley wonderful new experiences, and a much better childhood than she ever had.

Apart from when Bridge came to stay during the school holidays, Harry had always been alone. Since she didn't go to the local school, the other children were distant, and her father's reputation hadn't helped. Axedale was a huge estate and house for a child to be alone in. At least Riley had a good friend. She remembered what Annie had said the other day, about Axedale being a big house for Riley to take care of on her own.

There was something they could do to give Riley support. A sibling. Harry couldn't quite believe she was thinking about this, but the more she did, the more she liked the idea.

Her grandfather had once told her that houses like these were meant to be filled up with children. Maybe he was right. Her heart melted at the thought of seeing Annie pregnant and looking after her, but would Annie want another child?

She'd had Riley a long time ago and had never mentioned wanting more children to her. Maybe she thought one was enough. Harry looked up at the portrait of her favourite ancestors, Lady Hildegard and Lady Katherine, that hung above her fireplace.

"I bet you would have loved to have a baby with Katherine, Hildegard, if you'd had the technology."

Her mind was made up. Harry would talk to Annie about having another baby, but she just had to find the right time to bring it up.

Annie had invited Penny for a cup of tea, and to make firm plans for filming in the Axedale kitchen. Penny was taking notes on her iPad, and Princess was ingratiating herself with Annie by sitting on her knee and getting lots of strokes.

"I know things are going to be busy leading up to Bridge's wedding," Penny said. "Why don't we make it the next week?"

Annie looked at her own calendar, where she kept all the Axedale bookings, and said, "Any day but Friday of that week. We have an anniversary party in the east wing then."

Penny was impressed by how good Axedale looked, and by the improvements the couple had made. She had heard it was in a state of disrepair a few years ago.

"Do you enjoy that side of things? The hospitality business part?"

Annie took a sip of tea. "Yes, I do. It's not as if we have to do it for the money, but everything we do with the house—weddings, parties, business conferences—all bring money into the village. More people to buy things in the shops, and more jobs here on the estate, while the visitors keep coming. It's too big a house not to do something constructive with it, I think."

"What does Harry think?" Penny asked.

Annie chuckled. "Oh, she just lets me get on with it, really. As long as they don't get in her way, she doesn't mind. When we refurbished the public end of the house, I had a professional kitchen added, so we can keep our own kitchen to ourselves. And anyway, I've worked all my life. I can't just look after Harry all day, although she does take some looking after."

Penny laughed along with Annie at that description. "It really is so nice to see Harry settled down and happy. She's so different, if you know what I mean."

"Don't worry. I know what she was like, but she had some issues to overcome and needed the right woman to help her."

Annie's description reminded her of her own fears, the intimacy issues that had held her personal life back all these years.

Penny stared down at the table and made imaginary circles with her fingertip. "Do you think there's someone for everyone like that?"

"To help them understand love?" Annie asked.

Penny cleared her throat, feeling a little uncomfortable. "Yes."

"Of course, but then I'm a romantic. Before I met Harry, I vowed to hold out for my one true love. The one my heart yearned for. Then I met the womanizing Harry Knight, who didn't believe in love."

"And what happened when you met?" Penny asked.

Annie had the biggest smile and she whispered, "I made her believe."

Could Quade be the one to make her believe she was capable of a relationship?

After a silence, Annie said, "To change the subject completely, how are you getting on with Quade? I understand she was showing you around."

It had been three days since she had seen Quade, and they'd felt like the loneliest days. She hadn't come to take Princess out for her evening walk, and Penny couldn't blame her. Penny had panicked. She'd told Quade things she had never told anyone, and she just wasn't used to it.

The feeling of missing someone was also new. Everything seemed to remind her of Quade. The fresh vegetables in the kitchen, her book at bedtime, *Lady Chatterley's Lover*, which gave her some hot thoughts about Quade, and then there was Princess who was pining for her.

"Yes, I had a lovely day with her at her farm, and then I— Well, I left on bad terms."

Annie lifted both their teacups and took them to the sink. "Oh, don't worry about that. Quade's not the type to hold a grudge. Just talk to her. She's one of the nicest people you could meet."

No. She just couldn't find one flaw in her character, that was why she was so frightening.

They heard children's footsteps running down the stairs. Riley stopped halfway down with her friend and leaned over the banister. "They're here, Mum. The alpacas!" And then they ran away again.

"Can you tell she's excited?" Annie joked. "Would you like to come up and see our new friends? It would make a good video clip for you."

Penny's mind lit up with the prospect. Alpacas were hilarious and cute in any video, but when added to her country experience, could be fantastic for internet hits.

"Thanks. Come on, Princess."

As they walked out of the large Axedale entrance hall, Annie asked, "Are you sure you're feeling better now?"

"Much better, and thank you for the meals you made. They were perfect," Penny said.

She saw Annie's eyes were drawn to Harry, who was well ahead of them, holding Riley's and her friend Sophie's hands, the large Great Dane walking by their side. She sighed in contentment.

It must have been wonderful to look and feel that way about someone. Harry was gorgeous, in a different way from Quade. Harry was polished and oozed sex appeal, while Quade was ruggedly sexy and didn't know how attractive she was. Going by the response to the picture she'd posted of Quade, everyone seemed to agree. She should have been snapped up years ago.

As they rounded the corner of Axedale Hall, they saw a group of estate workers standing by a large fenced-off area occupied by a horsebox-style trailer.

"Why the alpacas, Annie?" Penny asked.

"I thought it would be a nice to have something to interest the children who visit here with their parents. Everyone loves alpacas, and I thought they'd be a good place to start. We're eventually going to have goats, hens, the whole petting zoo experience."

"That's a great idea." Penny smiled.

"Riley thought it was, but you should have seen the faces of Harry, Quade, and Stevens the estate manager when I suggested them."

Penny laughed. "I can just imagine. Was Harry easy to talk around?"

"Harry's always easy to talk around." Annie winked at her.

When she turned back to face the field, she saw Quade was one of the people helping with the alpacas.

"Quade's there." Penny stopped dead. "It'll be awkward. I'll just go home."

Annie grasped her arm, "Don't be silly. It'll give you a chance to talk. She's a good friend to have while you're here, Penny."

While I'm here. She was reminded again that she had the perfect excuse to escape her burgeoning attraction. She was going home to London in a month or so.

"Okay."

Quade walked up the ramp of the truck to help with the last alpacas out. After a lot of research, they had decided on four females to start with, and they'd see how they settled. Annie hoped they might breed with them at some point. Baby alpacas would be a good attraction.

Jack, one of the estate workers, was struggling with the last alpaca.

"Quade, this one doesn't want to move," Jack said.

"Stand back from her," Quade told him. She approached the more dominant female from the side and slowly and gently took hold of her harness.

She stroked its nose while she said in a soft calming voice, "Hello there. You don't like to be handled, eh? I know another girl like you who is independent and doesn't like to be pushed into things."

Quade's gaze drifted over to the fence where Penny, Harry, Annie, and the children were watching.

"I know you're scared, but we've got a lovely pasture for you and your girls to live in, and a wading pool to cool off in, if you'll take that first step."

Quade could tell her soothing voice was calming the animal, even though it couldn't understand her words.

She knew as well that Penny's eyes never left hers, and she was sorry now for not going over to Northwood Cottage and trying to mend what had happened in her kitchen. Quade had been confused and angry at the start but soon came to realize that Penny was simply scared. A scared young woman frightened of showing anything but the ditzy city girl.

She should have gone back to see her. Quade patted the alpaca a few more times, then took a step forward, and the animal followed suit. She then took two and three steps, and soon the alpaca was walking down the ramp to join its pack mates.

Everyone clapped as it bounced off towards its friends. Quade turned back around and saw Penny struggling to keep Princess in her arms, while holding her video camera.

I'm not giving up on you.

Quade strode over to the fence and took Princess from Penny's arms. "Hi, I'm sorry I haven't been around to take Princess for a walk. I was trying to give you some space."

"You're apologizing to me? I was wrong. I—why do you have to be so nice and understanding, Sammy?"

Quade smiled at her warmly. "It's who I am, and who I always will be."

"Yes, you will, won't you?" Penny said.

Quade couldn't quite tell if that sentence was good or bad. She decided to change the subject. "Do you like the alpacas?"

A big smile erupted on Penny's face. "I love them. I got some great video, and going by Riley and her little friend, they are going to be a big hit."

Quade looked down to where Harry, Annie, and the girls were. They had a bucket of food and had enticed a few of the alpacas over to the fence.

"Yeah they will. I was sceptical at the start, but they'll have a good life here. That's for sure."

"What did you say to that one that didn't want to get out of the truck?" Penny asked.

Quade tickled Princess behind the ears and looked at Penny's beautiful green eyes.

"I told her that I understood she was frightened to take these new steps, but if she was brave enough and took them, that there was something wonderful waiting for her."

Penny clearly got her meaning. In fact, it felt like there was no one else here but them gazing into each other's eyes.

"Sammy? Would you come to my cottage tonight? I could show you how I make an episode of my show, and then we could eat dinner."

"I would love to." This was Quade's chance to melt Penny as Bridge suggested, because as much as Penny was out of her league, and she probably wouldn't be here for long, Quade was falling for her. She wanted to be the person who taught her love wasn't scary.

❖

Penny felt nervous. Not nervous like going in for a business meeting kind of nervous, but more of a giddy excitement. Giddiness was not something she was associated with. Ditzy, yes, but not giddy.

That was the only way she could describe the feeling she had in her stomach at the thought of Quade coming to watch her record and make dinner. She scrutinized her cream dress with pink flowers in the mirror above the fireplace and checked her hair. Luckily her ankle was feeling good enough for her to wear heels again.

"Do I look fabulous, Princess?" Princess didn't respond. "No, I didn't think so. How can she make me feel so nervous?"

Penny picked up her signature 1950s frilly apron and walked to the kitchen to check on dinner. She thought since Quade was watching, she would do a simple video but cook something extra special for her.

She figured Quade would like simple but tasty food, and she was trying to apologize, so there would be no making her eat extra healthy tonight. Penny looked in the oven and saw that the beef casserole she was cooking was doing okay.

There was a knock on the door, Penny jumped out of her skin, and Princess ran for the door, barking and going crazy.

Penny clutched her chest in an effort to calm a rapidly hammering heart. "Dear God, she's here."

She hurried back over to the mirror to have one last check of her hair, then pointed at her own reflection.

"No matter how nice, how kind, how sexy, or how adorable she is—don't fall for her charms any more than we already have. We won't be here forever. Got it?" she asked herself.

Penny nodded back and walked to the door, repeating in her head, *She's just a friend, just a friend, just a fr—*

She opened the door and saw Quade with a bigger and more beautiful bouquet of flowers, wearing a suit jacket with her jeans, and a shirt and tie. If that wasn't gorgeous and adorable enough, she looked down to Dougal, and he had a doggy bow tie around his collar.

"Aww! Look at you, sweet boy." Penny crouched down and ruffled his fur.

"Dougal thought that we should make an effort tonight," Quade said.

"He looks so handsome." Penny stood up again and said to Quade, "You both look handsome."

"You look beautiful, Penny," Quade said.

Penny's stomach was turning cartwheels. Not only did Quade look good, but she could smell her gorgeous cologne. "Come in then."

Quade walked in and handed over her flowers. Penny inhaled the scent and hummed. "These smell beautiful. Flowers don't usually have this strong a scent."

"They do when they've come straight from the ground," Quade said.

Penny giggled. "Don't go getting me all excited with your organic goods."

Quade brought out another box from behind her back and handed it over nervously. "Eh…I got you these too. I hope they're okay."

Penny put down her flowers on the coffee table, unwrapped the roughly wrapped paper, and found something that just screamed Quade's adorability: a box of dairy-free organic chocolates. Even though dairy-free was alien to a farmer like her, she went out of her way to get something she knew Penny would like.

Penny's heart was certainly getting a good workout tonight as it resounded with appreciation for Sam McQuade.

"Where did you get something like this around here?"

Quade looked as if she was nervously waiting on her approval. "I didn't. I drove to Waldenworth. It's our nearest town."

"How far away is that?" Penny asked.

"About forty-five minutes?" Quade replied.

Penny groaned internally. How could she ever hope to keep her emotions under control with Quade? When she was impossibly kind and gorgeous?

I could so fall in love with her.

"Are they the right kind of thing?"

"Yes, perfect. Thank you so much, Sammy." Penny took a breath and moved to kiss Quade on the cheek. It was meant to be a quick peck, but Quade's scent made her lips linger on her soft skin.

Get away before you go somewhere you can't ever go.

"Excuse me. I'll just put these flowers in water."

❖

Watching her Penny be Penny Huntingdon-Stewart was a strange experience. Quade was sitting on a stool by the kitchen door, while Penny recorded at the kitchen counter. There were three cameras, all placed at different angles, and lights all over.

Penny was so confident talking to the camera, almost as if the viewers were in the same room as her. This taught her that she got to see the real Penny, because she didn't show any insecurities, worries, or stubbornness in front of the camera.

That gave Quade some satisfaction. Even if Penny was being difficult, bad tempered, cold, or closed off, at least she was seeing the real Penny. None of Penny's audience had ever seen her open and vulnerable like she had been when she lay in Quade's lap after her epileptic fit.

Penny lifted up one of the cameras and pointed it at Quade. "I have a surprise for you, friends. Sexy Farmer is with me tonight. "Say hi, Sexy Farmer."

"Hi," Quade said nervously.

Penny laughed. "As you can see friends, she's very talkative. Now today we're going to show Sexy Farmer how you can milk a nut. Which was exactly what she said to me the first time I met her."

Quade watched in awe as Penny's features shone and came to life in front of the camera. She could see why this was important to Penny. This was hers, something she had built with no help from her family, or family name.

Quade just couldn't get over how beautiful Penny was. She loved everything about Penny. She loved the way Penny ran her pink painted fingernails through her wavy blond hair and tucked it behind her ear. The way she ran the tip of her tongue over her deep pink lips when she was thinking, and the way her laugh set Quade's heart on fire.

She'd never seen anyone as beautifully feminine as Penny. If someone had asked her to dream up the perfect woman, Quade's imagination couldn't even come close to the reality of Penny.

Quade had imagined kissing Penny many times, but the dreams didn't feel half as exciting as when Penny had leaned in and kissed her cheek. It took everything in her to not take Penny into her arms and make her imagination come true. Being so close to her, feeling her lips on her skin, and being surrounded by her perfume made Quade want her so very badly.

But Penny didn't go for lesbians like her. Quade had looked with interest at the social media apps Penny had put on her phone. She flicked through the pictures of Penny in her London world, going to events and parties, and felt even further away from her. They were so different, and Quade had seen with her own eyes what type of woman Penny went out with.

She was always at events with a young good-looking tomboy or dapper butch, some well known and some not, but all extremely handsome and well dressed.

She could never compete in jeans and boots. The one thing she did notice in the pictures was Penny was never close to, or even holding hands with, the women she was with, and she was reminded of their day at her farm. It took effort, almost courage, for Penny to take her hand, but she had taken her hand.

There must be many hidden depths to that icy wall she kept around herself, and as Bridge had said, it was her task to melt her. But was she up to the task?

She turned her attention back to Penny and heard her say, "That's all for today, friends. More from the country soon."

Penny turned the camera on her again. "Say goodbye, Sexy Farmer."

Despite her embarrassment, Quade gave a brief wave. "Bye."

Penny stopped filming and let out a breath. "That was great, having you here. It's going to be a popular video."

"It was interesting. I never knew you could do things like that with nuts," Quade said.

Penny walked to her stool with a wicked smile on her face, and the glass of nut milk she had made.

"Taste it, then, Sexy Farmer."

Quade loosened her tie. She was starting to feel really hot. She had the urge to pull Penny into her arms but resisted.

She took the glass and sniffed it in suspicion.

"It won't bite you—it's just made from nuts," Penny said.

"That's what I'm afraid of." Quade screwed up her face.

Penny put her hands on her hips. "Do you eat kidneys? Liver?"

"Of course. Steak and kidney pie is one of my favourites."

Penny leaned over, and whether it was intentional or not, Quade got an up-close view down into her cleavage. Her breasts looked so round, so full. A heavy beat started to pound inside her. She wasn't used to constant sexual arousal, but since Penny had come to the village, it was frustratingly real.

Penny whispered in the sexiest voice, "You can eat offal from an animal, but you're afraid of nut milk? Are you a butch or a mouse, Sammy?"

Quade could either pull Penny to her, rush whatever was growing between them, and risk upsetting Penny, or drink the dreaded nut milk. So she brought it to her lips and drank back the whole glass.

"Well?" Penny said.

Quade mulled it over. "It's not as bad as I thought, but I'd rather stick to the moo variety."

Penny burst out laughing and reached out and wiped a dribble of milk from her mouth.

The laughter died and there was something quite different hanging in the air. Wiping the drop of milk from her mouth turned into a caress. Quade slowly put her hand on top on Penny's, and after a few seconds, she felt the tension in Penny's hand.

Penny pulled it away. "I'd better check on dinner."

"That was delicious. You're a great cook," Quade said as she finished her last bite of dinner.

Penny couldn't stop smiling. It was such fun having dinner with someone who she got on well with. Someone she trusted, and who she knew wouldn't push her into something she wasn't ready for.

Penny had enjoyed watching Quade eat. She seemed to really enjoy her food, and it made Penny feel warm inside to feed Quade.

"I didn't used to be. When I left my parents' house, I couldn't boil an egg." Penny pointed to Quade's plate. "And don't expect so unhealthy a dinner the next time. I just wanted to make something I knew you'd enjoy to say sorry for the other day. Next time there'll be more colour on your plate."

"What do you mean?" Quade said.

"Eat the rainbow. Purple, oranges, yellows, and lots of green. That's what makes you healthy."

Quade rumpled up her nose cutely. "That sounds like vegetables to me."

"Exactly." Penny winked.

That was another new thing for Penny. Flirting. She never indulged in it as it might land her in a situation that panicked her, that she'd have to talk her way out of, but with Quade, it was fun, and she felt comfortable indulging in it.

Quade laughed. "As long as you cook them, I'll give anything a try."

"Are you ready for dessert, or do you want a break?"

Quade patted her stomach. "A break, I think. I'm stuffed."

Penny stood up and picked up her phone. "Why don't we sit in front of the fire for a while. I can show you our picture."

Before they'd started dinner, Penny had taken a picture of them together and posted it online. Her followers appeared to love Quade, so she gave them what they wanted.

Penny led them over to the couch and pointed to the two dogs, sprawled out in front of the fire. "They're quite contented."

Quade took a seat on the couch. "No wonder, after that beef dinner you gave them."

Penny picked up her iPad and flopped down beside Quade. She kicked off her heels and put her feet up.

"Okay, you ready to see what the world thinks about you?"

When Penny got no immediate response, she looked at Quade and saw her eyes almost caressing her legs and feet, and surprisingly she didn't panic.

This is fine. It's Quade. It's safe.

"Quade?"

"Oh, sorry. Yes." Quade turned her attention to Penny and fidgeted with her tie.

Penny was excited when she saw the likes and hits their picture had received. "Wow, this is amazing, look at all the likes and comments."

Quade leaned in to look closely, and Penny felt warmth spread up the right side of her body. Usually close proximity to people turned her cold, but Quade was warming her up.

"You really are popular," Quade said.

Penny smiled. "Read the comments, Sexy Farmer."

She had to stop herself from giggling too much as Quade's eyes went wide at some of the appreciative comments and improper suggestions.

"How does it feel to be popular? There's some proposals in there too," Penny said.

"They don't even know me." Quade again fiddled with her tie.

"They don't need to know you. They're appreciating your other attributes. I should put videos and pictures of you online every day—my internet traffic would go up by fifty per cent." Penny thought it was adorable how embarrassed Quade was.

Quade couldn't get more adorable if she tried, or could she?

When she pulled at her tie again, Penny said, "What's wrong with your tie? You seem uncomfortable."

"I never wear ties. I just wanted to look a little smarter for you," Quade said.

Penny reached for her tie without thinking and started to take it off slowly. "You don't need to change for me, Sammy. You're perfect as you are."

Penny pulled the tie from Quade's neck a bit at a time, all the while getting caught up in Quade's gorgeous eyes. She was drawn in closer, and closer, and her fingers grazed Quade's neck as she unbuttoned her shirt button. *I want to kiss her.*

She was a few inches away from Quade when Quade lifted a hand to touch the side of her face.

It's Quade, it's just Quade.

Then, as always happened, the memory of regaining consciousness after a fit at school ran through her mind. She was looking up at a crowd of kids laughing at her. Caught at her most vulnerable. It couldn't happen again.

Penny felt the ice she was used to coursing through her veins.

She pulled back quickly and just stared at the iPad screen, gripping the sides tightly.

She hated herself for being like this with Quade. She was so kind, so nice. She deserved someone who could love her like a normal woman.

Quade stared at Penny, trying to work out what was going through her mind. They had almost kissed, and then Penny looked terrified. She had to say something, something to ease her tension.

Quade held out her hand. She didn't take Penny's hand or get too close to her. She simply invited Penny to hold her hand. It was her choice whether to take it.

A short time passed, and then Penny looked at her hand, lots of thoughts seeming to pass through her head. Quade wished she could chase Penny's fears away.

Penny grasped her hand and held it softly. She put down her iPad and used two hands to hold Quade's.

Quade was so happy to even have Penny holding her hand. Any little touch from Penny meant she trusted Quade that little bit more.

Penny ran her fingertips over her calloused hands and said, "Our hands are so different."

Penny's soft skin and painted nails felt wonderful against her rough skin. "Mine are a bit of a mess," Quade said. "Working outside—"

Penny cut her off. "No, they're perfect. They are who you are. You have strong hard-working hands, but you use them with tenderness looking after your animals, and your garden."

There was a silence for a minute or so. Quade was simply enjoying Penny's touch and didn't want anything to make her feel pushed or wary. She wondered what it was that made her so frightened of touch.

Quade thought back to what they were talking about before, and how excited Penny had been about the picture she'd posted.

"Why are likes, internet traffic, whatever you call it important to you?" Quade asked.

Even as they spoke, notification after notification pinged on the iPad lying on the couch. "It's the core of my business. I'm a brand, so the more people interested in me, or my life as a brand, the more money I make in advertising, through sponsorships from big companies wanting me to use their products in my videos. The higher my profile, the better business offers I get. There's an American food channel interested in making my show over there. My business partner is talking to them just now, and if this time in the country goes well, it could be on the cards."

"You want to go to America?" Quade's happy feeling fell away. She felt disappointed. Which was silly. Quade always knew that Penny would be leaving Axedale sometime, so what did it matter if it was London or America, or Timbuktu. She would leave, and the thought hurt her.

"I want to launch my brand overseas, in every country. I've made my name here, so it's the next step."

"Why?"

"Why?" Penny let go of her hand and turned around to face her. "What do you mean, why?"

Quade felt some annoyance building inside her. "Why is it the next step? You've a successful business. I assume you have enough money, going by the Ferrari sitting in your driveway, so why the need to go abroad?"

"Because you've got to keep going, keep changing, keep moving, or you'll be left behind. The business world I'm operating in is getting bigger and bigger. There are more and more competitors in the field of food vloggers. I have to keep pushing."

"What's wrong with standing still to enjoy life?" Quade said with anger in her voice.

Penny pulled back from her. "Why do you sound so annoyed all of a sudden?"

"I'm not annoyed. I just think you're missing out on life, because your head is constantly in your phone or your tablet. If you looked up, you would see a life waiting for you."

"I have a life, thank you, Sammy. A very active social life in London."

Quade snorted and sat forward in her seat. "So I saw on the apps you put on my phone."

"What's that supposed to mean? And why has this conversation suddenly turned into an argument?" Penny snapped.

"It hasn't. I just think you should slow down and enjoy life."

"Oh, you do, do you? People have told me that my whole life, but look where I got to? Millions of followers and a thriving business."

"Followers, not friends," Quade said.

Penny looked hurt.

I've blown it. Idiot. "I'm sorry. I didn't mean that. I just wonder when it will ever be enough." Quade stood up and said, "Dougal, come on. Thanks for dinner. I'll call around for Princess tomorrow." Penny was quiet. So she patted Princess and walked to the door. "I'm sorry if I ruined tonight. I just want—"

Quade wanted to say, she wanted more, she wanted to know Penny was going to stay, but Penny was never going to be a farmer's wife.

"It doesn't matter." Quade walked out the door.

Chapter Twelve

Penny was lying in bed feeling utterly depressed, with Princess curled up at her side. Why had her perfect evening turned into an argument? Their time together always seemed to.

Quade was so kind and understanding, and even when she had freaked out about the nearly kiss, Quade had taken it in her stride and offered her hand, without pressure to take it.

Penny grabbed the pillow on the other side of the bed and put it over her face. She screamed her frustration into it. "Why does she have to be so bloody perfect!"

She threw the pillow away and found Princess looking at her strangely. "Well, she is perfect."

Penny had never found the perfectly coiffed women she met at parties and events attractive. No, since she was a teenager, if she fantasized about her perfect woman, it was always a manual worker, always with tools, lots of tools, and usually a tool belt. Her hunky farmer definitely fit the bill—*infuriatingly* fit her bill.

No one had ever forced her to question if she really could get over her intimacy problems, but Quade was making her wish she was different. The thought of Quade's calloused, hardworking hands touching her made her hot. She closed her eyes and thought about those hands running down the side of her neck, her chest, and gently grasping her breast.

Penny's eyes sprang open. She was wet and aching with just the thought of Quade. What would it be like to be actually touched by her?

"Don't go there, Penny. Don't."

She turned over on her side and tried to cool down. The chair that had felt strangely empty since Quade slept in it was looking at her. No one had ever gotten closer to her than Quade, and she had never felt as comfortable with someone. Maybe Quade could be the one to help her explore her sexual side. Could it be? Penny trusted her, even though they always seemed to argue, but did Quade like her that way?

Quade had been helpful and kind, even when she didn't deserve it, but was she just like that with everyone? Tonight their conversation went downhill when Penny said she wanted to expand her business to different countries. Maybe Quade was disappointed that Penny had plans to leave, but then that was always the plan.

"Princess, I'm so confused."

Harry's eyes fluttered open and she looked at the time. Six o'clock. Annie was lying on her side, so Harry scooted up closer, spooned her, and wrapped her arm around her middle. She loved early morning, when there was no one but her and Annie.

She pressed her face into Annie's neck and inhaled her scent. It was beautiful, but everything about Annie was beautiful. A few years ago she would never have believed that she would want one woman in her life, and would even share her bed every night with one woman, but Annie was the answer to the question she never knew had been asked of her.

Now Harry couldn't do without her. Annie had cast her love spell over her heart and Axedale and brought them all back to life.

Annie's neck was too tempting. Harry brushed her blond hair from her neck and gave her feather-light kisses. Annie shivered and moaned as she woke up. Harry was more than delighted that as much as Annie came across to the world as the perfect housewife, she also craved sex and was happy to keep up with Harry's high sex drive.

Annie enjoyed what she called sleepy sex, and Harry was more than happy to oblige. She ran her hand under her silky nightdress, and her sex started to burn. Harry had the overwhelming urge to thrust into her wife. She grasped her hip and pulled her close, just to tease herself.

Annie reached back, grasped Harry's hair, and pulled her closer. "Morning, sweetheart. Someone's woken up frisky. What time is it?"

Harry smiled and kissed her shoulder. "Just after six."

Annie took Harry's hand from her hip and pushed it up onto her breast. "You know, when I worked for you, I was already up and starting my day of work."

Harry squeezed her breast gently and laughed softly. "Now you're Lady Annie, so you don't have to, although I used to have fantasies when I heard you up and about back then."

"What kind of fantasies?" Annie moaned as Harry trailed her fingers from her breasts down her stomach.

"Oh, I had all kinds of fantasies. You drove me wild because you were never interested in just sex. You drove me wild, frustrated me, and courted me until I fell in love."

Annie was so wet. Harry barely had to look at her to turn her on, but to wake up to Harry touching and kissing her was enough to make her melt.

"Tell me some of them, and let me feel you," Annie said.

Harry pulled off her T-shirt and boxers and was skin to skin with her wife. Annie took Harry's hand and pushed it into her underwear.

Harry cupped her sex. "You're wet." Harry groaned.

"I'm always wet when you touch me. Tell me," Annie said.

Harry slipped her fingers into Annie's sex and felt how wet she really was. "Oh God, I love you."

"Tell me," Annie repeated.

Harry could hardly think. All she wanted to do was make her wife come, and thrust till she came herself.

"Well, there was the one where you brought me breakfast in bed and gave me a lot more than breakfast, but my favourite was coming down to the kitchen, where you were baking, rolling dough at the kitchen table, with your apron on—"

Annie laughed. "I knew you had a fetish for my apron."

Harry split her fingers around Annie's hard clit and rubbed in soft almost barely touching strokes, just the way Annie liked.

Annie's hips started to thrust, and Harry couldn't help but join in. "Yes, you know I do. There's something that turns me on about that kind of domestic scene. I'd kiss your neck, and you'd pull my hands on your breasts and ask me to make you come. I'd lift up your skirt and make love to you on the table."

"You have a thing about the kitchen table too." Annie groaned as her orgasm started to build.

"I have a fetish with anything and you. You are everything to me." Harry hastened her touches, as she could tell Annie was close. Annie reached back and grasped Harry's hair.

"I love you, my darling Annie," Harry whispered.

It was enough to tip Annie's orgasm over the edge. She went rigid and grasped Harry's hair tightly.

"Oh God. You're so good at that," Annie said, trying to get her breath back.

"I'm glad you think so, my lady." Harry's hands went back to squeezing Annie's breasts. She was so turned on and wet and was desperate to come.

Annie reached back to Harry's hip and pushed her bottom into her groin. "Come, sweetheart."

Harry didn't need to be asked twice. She positioned herself against Annie's buttock and started to thrust, all the while keeping her hand on Annie's breast. Before she was ready, Harry was thrusting erratically and pressing her face into the curve of Annie's neck.

"Fuck." Harry groaned, then fell back onto the bed.

Annie rolled into Harry's arms, while Harry caught her breath. "I love sleepy sex with you, your ladyship."

Harry laughed. "I know you do, and so do I, my darling."

"I bet Bridge doesn't have sleepy sex," Annie joked.

Harry laughed. "No, I think one has to be very awake for what she has in mind."

Annie squeezed Harry tighter. She thought about how happy she was, but what was going round and around in her mind was consuming her every thought. Did she really want to spoil this moment by bringing up the thoughts that just wouldn't leave her head? What if Harry's attitude changed? What if she pushed her too far?

But she had to say it or she would go insane. She took a breath to speak but Harry cut her off.

"Can I ask you something, Annie?" Harry tensed up as she asked the question. Harry was never tense.

"Of course, anything." Annie had no idea what this was about.

"I know you had Riley a long time ago, and maybe one is enough for you, but I wondered if you ever thought about having another baby—with me, I mean."

Annie was stunned. The subject that she had been frightened to bring up had just come from Harry's mouth. She rolled on top of Harry and looked down at her in shock. "You want to have a baby with me?"

"Yes, it was what you said about this estate being really big for Riley on her own. I grew up alone in this place, and I hated it. My grandfather always said these big houses were meant to be filled with children. I thought it would be nice to give Riley a little brother or sister."

Annie was so astonished and filled with joy that she started laughing.

Harry looked at her with confusion. "What did I say? You don't like the idea?"

Annie calmed her laughter and caressed Harry's handsome face. "Like the idea? I've been trying to find a way to bring it up. I've wanted another baby with you since we got married, but I was frightened I'd be pushing you too far."

Harry shook her head. "Don't ever keep things like that to yourself. There is nothing you could want that would push me too far. I'm not the old Harry with a foot out the door. I have two feet under your kitchen table, and all of me is invested in our family. Promise me you'll never keep anything you want to yourself again?"

"There is one more thing," Annie said.

Harry smiled and ran her hands through her hair. "What?"

"I'd like your baby." Annie waited for the penny to drop.

"You mean—you don't want me to—"

Annie laughed. "No, sweetheart. I'd like to use your eggs, and we could have a little baby Harry."

It was Harry's turn to laugh. "I thought you wanted me to—Of course we can do that. I'd love you to carry my baby."

Annie hovered inches from Harry's lips and whispered, "Don't worry. I'm the mummy in this family."

Just as they were about to kiss, they heard Caesar's low bark coming from Riley's room.

"Riley's awake. Get your clothes on, Harry," Annie said in panic.

Harry grabbed her boxers and pulled them on quickly, as the sound of paws and feet thumped down the hall.

They both sat up in bed against the headboard, just in time for the door to burst open and the Great Dane and Riley to come bouncing into the room and jump on the bed.

"Harry, Harry, we need to go and check on the alpacas before school!"

"Okay, we will. Just hang on a second," Harry said.

Harry disappeared into the en suite bathroom to clean up, and Riley cuddled in beside her mum, while Caesar lay across Annie's lap, enjoying her attention.

Annie put her hand around Riley. "Did you have a good sleep, sweetie?"

"Yeah, but I'm so excited to see how the alpacas are," Riley said.

It gave Annie such satisfaction to see how happy Riley was here at Axedale. She loved Harry so much, and Harry gave her such a rich and varied life. They were living the dream.

Harry came back into the room and smiled. "Where's my space gone?"

Annie grinned back at her and said, "And you're sure about what we talked about earlier?"

Harry plonked herself down on the bed and pulled Riley onto her lap. "I couldn't be surer."

Riley looked at her strangely. "Surer about what?"

"Nothing for you to worry about, sweetie. Go and take Caesar out to do his business, and Harry will get dressed," Annie said.

"Okay, Mum," Riley said. She and Caesar ran away down the hall leaving Annie and Harry alone.

Just then Annie's phone beeped with a text message.

"Who is it?" Harry asked.

"Bridge. She says she hears that Penny and Quade may be getting closer and thinks we need to give them a little push."

"I don't think you should interfere. If it happens, it happens," Harry said.

"Harry," Annie raised an eyebrow. "Remember hot choco surprise?"

"Yes. The magic elixir that finally melted my heart?"

Annie leaned her head on Harry's shoulder. "That along with fudgie-wudgies. Sometimes love just needs a little push—a little sprinkling of magic dust."

"I forgot you were the witch who made all the love potions in this village. Well, it certainly worked on me." Harry kissed the top of her head. "Speaking of fudgie-wudgies, is it baking day soon?"

"For you, yes." Annie kissed her cheek.

Chapter Thirteen

Penny woke up the next morning ready to try to break some boundaries. Quade was the first person in her life who'd threatened to melt the ice that froze her body when anyone got close. She had to explore it and push herself.

Quade had texted her earlier and said she would drop by for Princess earlier than usual, so Penny got ready to go with her.

Her mobile rang. It was her business partner, Olivia. "Hello?"

"Pen, darling, how are you?"

Penny walked to the fireplace and checked her hair in the mirror. "Fabulous as ever."

"Wonderful. I love the new videos. Who's this new hunk you've found?"

"A local farmer who's been really kind to me, that's all," Penny said.

She didn't like the idea of giving too much information about Quade. She felt protective of her friendship with her.

"Your social media people say everyone is going mad for Sexy Farmer. Like an are-they-or-aren't-they sort of thing. Your last book has shot back into the top ten in the book charts. Try to get her in more of your videos and posts, Pen."

Penny felt angry. They never normally argued, because Olivia was driven by business, as she was, but now Penny's priorities were changing.

"I'm not using her for business, Olivia. She's—" Penny struggled to describe what Quade was to her.

"She's what? Pen, you don't have relationships, but this friendship is good for business, so it would be in your interest to give the impression of romance."

Olivia was so cold about it. Was that what *she* had been like? Until she came to Axedale, her life had been this picture-perfect image, about being seen with the right people, and her every thought was whether something was good for business. Her thoughts were changing.

There was a knock at the door and Princess ran to it, barking and spinning. "I have to go, Olivia. There's someone at the door."

"Okay, darling. I've got you a book signing, since your last cookbook is hot again. I'll email you the details. Keep up the good work."

"Bye," Penny said.

The whole conversation had annoyed her, maybe because it reminded her of who she was, and how she behaved.

She walked to the door and tried to calm Princess, so she could open the door. Princess had never been so happy as she was since she'd been here, Penny thought. She was like a different dog.

Quade was right. She had been looking at life through a lens for so long, she had forgotten to live it.

Penny opened the door, and her heart thudded. Quade looked adorably unsure of herself.

"Hi."

Dougal jumped up to give her a hug. Penny ruffled his ears and kissed his snout. "Hi, Dougal."

"I need to take the dogs out earlier than usual. It's the pub quiz night—we have a team."

"I know. Bridge invited me. She says you're one down with Finn being away," Penny said.

Quade sighed. "I'm sorry. I should have asked you. I just didn't know if, after last night, it—"

"It's all right. Let's just forget about that. I was hoping I could come walking with you today."

Quade appeared surprised. "Yeah, of course. If you'd like."

"Give me a second and I'll get my things."

Penny came back to the door wearing a pink poncho with ladybirds on it, over her little denim miniskirt, and matching ladybird wellington boots. Quade had the urge to hug Penny for being so sweet, and at the same time make love to her for being so sexy. How could someone be so sweet and sexy at the same time?

"Ready?" Penny said.

"Yes, okay." Quade had never expected this when she arrived at Penny's, after last night.

She thought she would get an icy reception from a closed-off Penny, but it was the complete opposite. As they started to walk, Quade realized that Penny didn't have her camera equipment with her.

"Where's your camera? Don't you want to take some video and pictures of the walk?" Quade said.

Penny smiled and said, "No, I just want to enjoy the walk with you and me."

Wow. Penny was really different today. What had happened?

When they came to the end of Penny's driveway, Penny tried to put on Princess's lead.

"It's okay, Penny, they walk without the lead," Quade said.

"But there's a road. I know Dougal is well trained but—"

Quade brought her fingers to her mouth and whistled. Both dogs stopped dead and sat by the edge of the road. Then when Quade checked the road was clear, she made a clicking sound in her mouth. "Go." The dogs darted across the road and onto the forest path.

"You see? I've trained her while I've been walking her. She's a good dog."

Penny looked at her dreamily. "That's amazing."

Quade felt a surge of excitement run through her body. Penny was looking at her the way she had dreamed of.

❖

Penny could feel the ice in her veins slowly melting away, drip by drip, as she walked with Quade. The way she handled the dogs, the way she took care of her as they made their way over some difficult paths, everything. Quade was her dream.

They reached the river and walked down to a little sandy area. Dougal and Princess ran to the edge of the water and barked excitedly.

"What do they want?" Penny asked.

Quade took a ball from her pocket and threw it into the water. Both dogs ran in to catch it. Penny hurried down to the shore after Princess.

"That's too dangerous for her, Sammy. She's only small."

Quade smiled at her. "Don't panic. She'll be fine. I'm here."

I'm here. Those few words made Penny's heart soar. Princess was safe when Quade was around, and Penny felt safe. Penny remembered waking from her fit in Quade's arms and feeling safe because Quade was there, and all the nights since Quade had stayed with her, she hadn't felt so safe.

Quade was strong, and solidly reassuring. The safety that she had been craving her whole life. What would it feel like to be held and loved in those strong reassuring arms? For the first time in her life, she wanted to find out.

Penny turned back to the water and laughed as Dougal and Princess splashed around. She took a deep breath of fresh country air and felt a kind of peace.

"This place is beautiful, Sammy."

Quade took a step closer to her. "I'm glad you think so. It's a special place to live."

"You were right last night," Penny said while still looking out at the water.

"Right about what?" Quade said.

Penny turned to Quade. "About life passing me by while I look at my screens, and through lenses. It's nice to stop and live. I've never done it before."

Quade held out her hand, as she had a few times. Never forcing or taking but offering. "There's a life waiting for you, if you want it."

Did Quade mean with her? Or was she reading too much into it? Could she live a rural life with Quade? She didn't know if she was capable, but maybe, just maybe, she could try.

She took Quade's hand and smiled. "Thank you for showing me."

Penny felt the urge to open up. She wanted Quade to understand her, what made her the damaged, stubborn woman she was.

"I know you think I'm stubborn and slightly crazy," Penny said out of the blue.

Quade turned and looked at her with surprise. "I don't think that."

"No, you do. Everyone does, but I can't help it. It's ingrained in me and difficult to change."

"Do you want to change?" Quade asked.

Penny nodded and squeezed Quade's hand even harder. It felt like she gained some of Quade's strength when she did it.

"I want a life that's more than through a lens," Penny said.

Quade smiled. "There's lots more life for you to see, come on." Quade never let go of her hand but shouted to the dogs, and they set off again on their walk.

After walking for another five minutes, they stopped at a run-down walled area, with big iron gates on the front.

Penny walked up to the gates and peered through. There were lots of mini gravestones covered in vines, some broken in half or crumbled away.

"What is this place? It looks so creepy," Penny asked.

Quade walked to her side and whispered in her ear, "It's the old pet cemetery."

Penny squealed and hid behind Quade's back. Quade laughed at her reaction. "What's wrong? There's nothing to be scared about. It's just where the Knight family buried their pets, favourite hunting dogs, things like that."

Quade loved the feeling of Penny wrapped around her back.

"That's so creepy. It's like something from a horror film."

Quade put her arm around Penny and ushered her to her side. "No, it's not. The family loved their pets. That's a nice thing, like we do for Dougal and Princess. Let's go in. It's really interesting."

"No way am I going in there, Sammy." Penny took a few steps back.

Quade took her hand and opened the gate. "Anyone who's brave enough to drink nut milk can walk into a graveyard. Come on."

Penny followed Quade reluctantly. She walked carefully around the little graves, frightened to walk over them.

"Look," said Quade. "Read the inscriptions."

Penny looked down at the nearest stone and read, "*Here lies Winston. Born 1918, died 1925. Faithful friend of Lord James Knight, Earl of Axedale. He was only a dog but was human enough to give comfort in hours of loneliness and pain.*" Penny grasped Quade's arm. "That's so touching. He sounds like he really loved Winston."

"Yeah, there's quite a few like that. Harry told me the story. James was Harry's grandfather's older brother. He came back from serving in World War I, with shell shock. They'd call it post-traumatic stress these days. He was gay and had watched his lover killed. When he came home, he tried to kill himself, but the family rallied around, and his sister got him the dog as a puppy, to try to help him cope, and he did. They went everywhere together, and Winston was a kind of service dog, before anyone had ever coined that term."

Penny reached down and touched the stone with reverence. "That's such an amazing story. What happened to James, do you know?"

"He lived until his fifties I think but never married or had children, so the title and lands passed to his younger brother, Harry's grandfather."

"You're right. This isn't creepy. I'm glad you brought me here." Penny smiled at Quade.

As Penny started to walk around the other stones, Quade said, "I've always found this graveyard a really nice place to come. Despite how horrible human beings can be to each other, animals always find a way to make things better."

"I wish I had brought my camera now. I'd love to take some pictures," Penny said.

"Can you not use your phone?" Quade asked.

Penny sighed. "I didn't bring it."

"Wait, are you really Penelope Huntingdon-Stewart? You never have that thing out of your hand."

Penny strolled back up to Quade and stuffed her hands in the pockets of her poncho. "I was trying to live life, like you said, and spend time with you, without the internet being with us."

Quade shook her head and laughed, then took her own phone out of her pocket and handed it over to Penny. "I only meant look up now and again, to see life, but I appreciate the sentiment. Take some pictures and I'll send them to you."

Penny went around all of the stones taking pictures, her head full of possibilities for vlogs. Axedale was just full of material, and someone who was changing her outlook on life.

"Are you sure she'll be all right?" Penny said to Quade.

Bridge watched the interaction between Quade and Penny with interest across the pub table.

They had arrived for the pub quiz that evening, and there was a new closeness to them. Bridge and Annie both thought they would be perfect for each other. She could see a vulnerability in Penny, and Quade was the sort of person who was looking for someone to take care of. Quade was kind, generous, and selfless. She had so much to give a woman, and Annie and Bridge weren't going to let Quade's chance at a happy ever after pass her by.

Quade replied to Penny, "Yeah. They'll be fine. The dogs would just have been bored sitting under the pub table. At your house they'll be warm, have toys to play with and food, and you know Dougal will take care of Princess."

"Yes, I know," Penny replied with a dreamy look upon her face.

Bridge nudged Annie to check out the way the pair were looking at each other adoringly, and Annie winked. Time to put operation magic potion into effect.

At the break during the pub quiz, Harry arrived back at the table with a tray of drinks. "Here we are. Campari for you, Vicar, orange juice for Pen, vodka and tonic for you, darling, and two pints, for Quade and me."

"Thanks, mate," Quade said.

When Harry sat down, Annie turned to Bridge and said, "When's Finn home, Bridge?"

Bridge smiled inwardly. This was how they planned to start casting the magic potion. She took a sip of her drink and said, "Saturday. Her last show is on Friday in Glasgow."

She couldn't wait to get Finn to herself again. It was too long since she'd touched her, and run her hands though her gorgeous hair.

"Isn't that sweet?" Annie leaned into Harry. "And then we look forward to your wedding. Quade, are you bringing anyone to the wedding?"

Quade looked at Annie in panic. The woman she wanted to ask was sitting right beside her, but she couldn't just ask her on the spot. It would be too awkward.

"Um…no." Quade stumbled.

Penny stared down at the table, clearly feeling as awkward as she did.

"You know, Quade, I think it's time you started looking for Ms. Right, unless you think she's just going to fall into your lap," Bridge said.

Please don't do this to me, Bridge. She gazed at Penny, but she looked away quickly.

"Give me your phone." Bridge held out her hand.

Quade pulled it out of her pocket and gave it to Bridge warily. "What are you doing?"

"Annie and I are going to make you a profile on a dating app. Those little lesbian hearts will be all of a flutter when they see you," Bridge said.

"Yes." Annie added, "You have to get yourself out there, Quade. Now, what are you looking for, blond, brunette, redhead?"

Quade closed her eyes and wished the ground would open up and swallow her.

❖

Quade and Penny shared an uncomfortable silence as they walked back to Penny's cottage. Bridge and Annie asked her all these questions about her perfect woman, to set her up on the dating app, and the perfect woman had been sitting beside her the whole time.

What Bridge and Annie had meant as a bit of fun had caused embarrassment for Quade and made Penny go extremely quiet, with what Quade thought was annoyance. Could Penny be jealous? How could Penny be jealous? She could have anyone she wanted. But if it was the other way around, Quade would be jealous. She was jealous when the estate workers were drooling over Penny's magazine photos, or when she looked at Penny's social media pages and saw her attending parties with women who could never love and take care of her the way she should.

Did she actually just say love? She sighed inwardly. She was falling for the unattainable Penelope Huntingdon-Stewart. Brilliant.

As they walked along, Quade's phone started to beep, and with each beep, Penny started to walk faster, her heels clattering across the cobbles.

"Why is my phone beeping like mad?" Quade pulled it out of her pocket and looked at the screen.

"Your dating profile," Penny said sharply. "Just like Bridge and Annie said, all those little lesbian hearts will be fluttering."

Penny tried to cover her annoyance, as she had done in the pub, but her patience was wearing thin. The thought of Quade taking someone else to Bridge's wedding was just awful. Jealousy was a new emotion for Penny. She'd been so used to trying to keep potential suitors away, that there was never a reason to feel jealous over anyone.

But Quade was different. Everything was different with Quade. Just after convincing herself to open up to Quade and see if she could explore something more, Bridge and Annie had to come up with this. Now these bloody women were going to beat her to it, because any other woman wouldn't be screwed up like her and frightened of intimacy. No, one look at Quade and they'd be jumping in her bed.

They arrived at the cottage and Quade said, "Is there something wrong?"

"Wrong? Of course not. Why would there be?" Penny said a little forcefully. They stopped at the front door while Penny fumbled, trying to get her keys out.

"Because we spent a nice day together, and since the pub, you've seemed annoyed about something. I don't know what I've done wrong."

Penny gave her a false smile. "You've done nothing wrong. Now go home and reply to all your lovelies waiting for a message back. Then you can pick one for the wedding."

Penny put her key in the front door lock and struggled to get it to turn. She was so angry.

Quade stepped in, put her hand on Penny's, and calmly helped her turn it. "I don't want to take any stranger to the wedding. I would have asked you if I thought you'd come," Quade said.

Penny was caught by surprise. She turned around into the circle of Quade's arms. "You would?"

"Of course I would. You're the most beautiful woman I've ever met. You're kind and gentle, but at the same time so strong. I don't know if I could have been as strong and determined if I had been through what you had. But I'm just a farmer. I'm not anywhere good enough for you."

Quade's words penetrated her heart. No one had ever said anything like that to her in her life, and meant it. She was overcome with an urge from her heart, and this time she couldn't stop herself.

Penny planted a very clumsy kiss on Quade's lips. Their noses clashed, and Quade let out a moan in pain. Then as soon as the urge surged through her, the fear kicked in. She hastily pulled away from the kiss, hurried though her front door, and slammed it shut. Penny pressed herself against the inside of the door, eyes closed and breathing hard.

She kept repeating, "What have I done? What have I done?"

Her first amorous advance to anyone, and she'd nearly broken Quade's nose. She'd totally embarrassed herself, and how could she ever get over her fear of intimacy if a kiss was too much for her? Everything was a mess.

The dogs came running through the cottage, delighted to see her, seeking love and attention. She heard Quade say, "Penny, open the door. We need to talk."

She couldn't face Quade. Penny just wanted to run upstairs to her bedroom, put on her unicorn onesie, and hide from the world.

"I don't want to talk. Just go, Sammy," Penny said.

Please go, please go.

Princess, hearing Quade's voice, started to bark at the door, making the situation worse.

"Penny…" Quade said.

The barking, the embarrassment, and the fear all twisted into anger, and Penny shouted, "Just go, Sammy. Now!"

There was silence from the other side of the door for a minute, and then Quade said, "I need Dougal."

Penny was starting to feel overcome with emotion, and the tears started to tumble unrestrained from her eyes as she handed Dougal out the door. She shut and locked the door and ran upstairs to the safety of her bedroom and threw herself on her bed.

CHAPTER FOURTEEN

The next morning Penny got up and dressed early and walked down to the vicarage. She just had to talk to someone, or she could risk losing the one person who made her want more.

She got a few looks from the locals, as she usually did. There weren't many country women who wore frilly short dresses, high heels, and—today—a flower pinned in her hair, not to mention carrying a dog in a handbag.

Penny arrived at the vicarage and hesitated before she knocked. This was a bad idea. The whole thing was a bad idea.

She should just go back to London and get away from temptation. Penny turned around to walk back the way she came, but the image of Quade holding her so tenderly in her arms stopped her.

If she didn't try, she knew she would regret it for the rest of her life. Penny let out a breath and marched back to the door.

"Here goes, Princess." Penny knocked on the door and had to wait ages before the vicar answered.

Bridge was wearing a scarlet red silk dressing gown. No one would ever suspect she was a vicar.

"Penny? You're out early." Bridget yawned.

She'd clearly just woken up. "I'm sorry, I shouldn't have come so early. I just needed to talk."

Bridget opened the door wide. "Don't be silly. My door is always open. Come in and have a cup of coffee."

As Penny walked in the door she saw a very rumpled Finnian Kane walk down the stairs in her boxers and T-shirt. Her trademark haircut was all over the place and looked as if she'd had a busy night.

"Finn, come and met Penelope Huntingdon-Stewart. I was telling you about her," Bridge said.

What a strange way to meet the famous magician. She'd clearly interrupted their first night back together.

"Pleased to meet you, Penelope," Finn said, shaking her hand. "I've heard all about you from Bridge."

"I'm sorry, I didn't think Finn was back yet." Penny was regretting ever having the idea to talk to someone.

"I surprised her," Finn said with a smile that erupted into a big yawn.

They'd definitely had a busy night. "I shouldn't have come."

"Nonsense. Don't worry about that." Bridge put her arm around Penny. "Come into the kitchen."

Bridge turned back to Finn and said, "Finn, be a dear and put some clothes on before you give Mrs. Long a fright when she arrives to start cleaning."

Finn said, "Your wish is my command."

Bridge chuckled and said under her breath, "Oh, I know."

Finn ran back upstairs, and they made their way to the kitchen. Penny sat, and Bridge switched on her coffee machine and got a bowl of water for Princess.

"Here you are." Bridge put the bowl on the floor, and Penny let Princess down. "Now, what can I do for you on this fine morning, Pen." Bridge started making the coffee.

Now was the part she was dreading. Could she say it? She had struggled even talking about it to therapists.

"I suppose I'm in need of a kind of confessional," Penny said.

Bridge brought over coffee and sat down. "Well, I'm certainly not a Catholic priest, but I'll give it a bash."

Bridge crossed her legs and Penny saw she was wearing the most exquisite heeled slippers. Even in nightwear, Bridge was beautifully dressed. They were very much alike, although Bridge was older, and she was so confident in herself. Penny couldn't imagine Bridge running in fear from a kiss, if the rumours about Mistress Black were true, and now seeing the satisfied, happy smile on Finnian Kane's face, she knew they were true.

Penny only wished she could have the courage to make Quade feel that way. She wrapped her hands around the coffee mug, tapped her nails against the surface, and tried to think of how to start.

"I have—I mean, I need advice because I have feelings for Quade."

Bridge put her coffee down and clapped her hands together. "How wonderful. Have you told her? I'd be so overjoyed to see Quade happy. She's been alone for such a long time."

"No, I haven't told her. That's the problem, or in other words, I have a problem."

Bridge leaned closer. "What kind of problem? The only problem I can foresee is you might frighten poor Quade to death when you get hold of her. You've been out with a few people—"

"I haven't. That's the problem," Penny said.

"But I've seen you at your parents' parties and glitzy events with a partner in tow. Usually gorgeous, I might add," Bridge said with a wink.

"They were escorts—well, not escorts in the sense that they were paid, just people that my business partner put me in contact with. Someone who thought it would be mutually beneficial to be seen together. Actors, singers, things like that."

Bridge shook her head in disbelief. "I don't understand, Pen. You're young, beautiful, why would you need to do that?"

Just as she was about to speak, Finn came into the kitchen, dressed and fresh from the shower.

"Sorry for interrupting you. I thought I'd have a walk down to the village shop. Would you like anything?"

Bridge grasped Finn's T-shirt and pulled her down to a teasing kiss. "Just you, when you come back. Don't be long."

"I won't," Finn said with the goofiest smile on her face.

Bridge smacked her softly on the backside. "Be good and run along then."

Penny could only imagine the happiness of having that kind of closeness with another human being.

"You were saying, Pen?"

Penny sighed. "I'm not good at that."

"What, darling?" Bridge said with a look of confusion on her face.

Penny pointed to where Finn had been standing. "That. What you just shared with Finn. I haven't had much experience. I could never fully trust anyone—because of who I am, I never knew if I'd be in the tabloids the next day—and then there's my condition. It can make me really vulnerable. It became easier to push people away."

Just saying it out loud brought tears to Penny's eyes.

Bridge immediately covered Penny's hand with hers. "Oh, my dear girl."

"There hasn't been anyone who's made me want to learn how to be different."

"Until Quade?" Bridge finished for her.

Penny got a hanky from her bag and wiped her eyes. "Yes. Sammy is like someone I created in a dream. She's kind, strong but gentle, and Princess just adores her."

"Not to mention scrummy?" Bridge added, smiling.

"Yes. She's exactly my type. I've never met anyone quite like her. Everyone I've ever known in my social circle has been so polished, but Sammy is—"

"Ruggedly butch?" Bridge said.

Penny nodded. "But can I ever have what you and Annie have? I've never tried to let someone in, and I'm not sure how to. I kissed her last night, made a mess of it, and ran inside the house. I was so embarrassed. I think I confuse her, and quite frankly I don't know why she is still my friend, or if she's interested in me."

"Oh, Quade's interested. You just have to watch the way she looks at you. She adores you, Pen."

As much as that news made Penny happy, it also made her even more stressed. She wrung her hands and looked down at the table like an embarrassed teenager. "I've heard that you would be a good person to talk to…about things like this."

Bridge laughed. "You mean Mistress Black? Tongues do wag in society circles, don't they?"

"How can I learn to let someone in, Bridge? If I don't take this chance, she could be snapped up by any woman from that stupid app you put on her phone last night."

"Oh, that? Darling, it was just to give the pair of you a push in the right direction. Annie and I could see how you felt about each other."

"Really?" Penny felt a sigh of relief.

"I'm not a professional relationship counsellor," Bridge said.

"If you were, what would you say?"

"I would tell you not to worry about the destination, about where a relationship could lead. What do you think Quade would like with you at the moment? Does she want to get you into bed?"

"No, she's not like that. Besides, at the moment, I think she would like one day together without us arguing," Penny said jokingly.

"You see, you have a place to start. Sex isn't the be all and end all of a relationship. Jolly nice, but the most special times are when Finn and I are alone, lying together quietly, and I know she loves me. That's the special time. You need to learn to lower those barriers one step at a time."

"I don't think many women would have the patience to be with me," Penny said.

Bridge leaned in and said, "Quade is not just any woman. She's traditional, old-fashioned in the nicest possible way."

Penny smiled, and her heart fluttered thinking of how sweet Quade was. "Yes, she is. She brings me flowers from her garden, no matter if I've been bad tempered or tried to push her away. She still comes calling to my house with flowers."

"She's dreamy, isn't she?" Bridge said.

"She even drove to the next town to get me dairy-free chocolates. Can you believe that? Even though she doesn't understand the whole dairy-free thing. If my followers knew just how adorable she was, they'd be beating down her door."

As Penny explained it to Bridge, she was even more convinced of what her heart felt for Quade.

Bridge took a sip of her coffee. "I can believe it of Quade. It sounds like she's courting you, in Quade's adorably old-fashioned way."

"Courting me?" Penny said with squeak. "Do people even do that any more?"

"Yes, people who want more than to get you in to bed. People like Quade," Bridge said.

"I've given her so many mixed signals, Bridge. She probably doesn't want to talk to me." Penny sighed.

"Stuff and nonsense, Pen. She may be a little wary, but you just have to bat those beautiful eyes at her, and she'll come around. Woo her."

Penny said with surprise, "Woo her?"

"Yes, and be honest with her about your anxieties. I don't think you'll find a more understanding person in the world, but one thing—"

"What?" Penny's heart and head were swirling with exciting possibilities but also fear.

"Be sure of what you're doing if you want to do this. Quade means a lot to us, and you have a life away from here. Quade's livelihood is here."

Penny tapped her fingers on the table. She couldn't think beyond telling Quade how she felt or think about a long-term relationship. That was too scary, but she knew she had to explore what she felt, and that she could never hurt Quade.

"It's hard for me to think about what comes next, but I won't ever intentionally hurt her. You and Finn make it work. She's a famous magician and tours, and you're a country vicar."

"Very true. I just needed to say it, because we love Quade," Bridge said seriously.

Penny nodded. "So how do I woo her?"

Bridget grinned. "Use your feminine wiles, and your talents."

Penny laughed. "What talents?"

"Cooking and baking. I happen to know a woman who has the recipe for Quade's favourite cake."

Penny grinned. "Really?"

❖

Quade was driving her Land Rover through the village when she spotted Finn walking out of the post office. She pulled in at the side of the road and put her passenger window down.

"Finn? You're back early."

Finn smiled when she saw who it was and walked over to the window. "Hi, Quade. Yeah, I wanted to surprise Bridge."

"Are you headed back home?" Quade asked.

"Yeah, I just went to get a newspaper."

"Hop in," Quade said. "I'm on my way to see the vicar anyway."

"Great." Finn jumped in.

"So how was the tour?" Quade asked.

"The shows went really well, and it got great reviews. I think going back to basics with my magic was the best idea I've ever had. To interact with an audience again felt good, although I really missed Bridge."

Quade smiled. "She missed you." She envied the close bond Finn had with Bridge. It was all she'd ever wanted, but she was falling for a woman who blew so hot and cold, she didn't know whether she was coming or going. One minute she was being pushed away, the next being friends, then arguing, and to top it all Penny kissed her, then ran. It had been clumsy, but all she'd ever wanted. Why was Penny running from a kiss that she initiated? Her dream of kissing Penny did not end like this.

"I can't wait for my next adventure," Finn said.

She had the biggest smile on her face and Quade couldn't help but smile along with her. "Your wedding?"

Finn ran her hand through her hair. "Yeah. Imagine me getting married?"

"You're a very lucky person, Finn. Bridge is a beautiful woman," Quade said.

She turned into the vicarage driveway.

"I know. The luckiest—oh, Harry's tailor is bringing the suits for a final fitting at Axedale on Sunday."

That was the only thing that was worrying Quade about standing as a witness with Finn. She had to wear a suit. Quade hated being dressed up in a suit. It just wasn't her.

"Okay," Quade replied.

As they pulled up at the vicarage, Finn said, "What was it you wanted to see Bridge about?"

"I—" Quade drummed her fingers on the steering wheel. "I wanted some advice, but since you're here too, I'd like to talk to you too."

"Sure. Let's go in and get the kettle on," Finn said.

Finn got out of the car and Quade sat alone for a few more seconds. Could she talk about this? She had to.

She let out a breath and got out. As they walked in the door, she heard Finn say to Bridge, "Quade's here. She wants to talk."

CHAPTER FIFTEEN

Penny had a busy day trying to get through her work by lunchtime. She'd finished a blog on her country walk and discoveries in the graveyard and sent it to Dario, who headed a small team that managed her social media output, and then was free to start work on her wooing mission.

Bridget had sent her to visit a Mrs. Castle, who had been head cook at Axedale. She was a delightful old woman who welcomed her in for tea.

Bridge had phoned ahead, and Mrs. Castle had her file of recipes waiting for her. There were so many wonderful recipes, and Mrs. Castle said she could come back to copy more if she'd like, but there was one that was Quade's favourite. A deliciously rich, chocolatey Black Forest gateaux.

Of course she didn't have the dairy ingredients, so she stopped off at the shop. Luckily, they had the few essentials. She didn't take any video or pictures of herself baking this. This was private, just for her and Quade—just for them, if there was a them.

Penny spent all afternoon making sure it looked perfect, and it did. The white whipped cream was thick and sumptuous, and the cherries on top looked ruby red, sitting in their own delicious juices.

She closed the cake box that was sitting on the dining room table and said, "I hope you appreciate this, Sammy. It'll do my clean eating, dairy-free image no good."

Penny took a shower and changed. Bridge had said to use her feminine wiles, and so she chose a dress she hoped Quade would like. A designer minidress with a floaty tulle overlay of birds of paradise and beautiful flowers. She got the impression Sammy liked her hair down, so she gave her blond hair a slight wave and let it cascade over her shoulders.

She looked at Princess and said, "Just you to make even prettier, poppet."

Penny took one of Princess's doggy outfits from the wardrobe and got her ready quickly. By five o'clock, they were ready. Penny picked up the cake box and said to Princess, "Are you ready to go a-wooing?"

Princess panted, excited that they were going out.

"Let's go."

When they reached the entrance to Quade's farm, Penny's arms were struggling with the weight of the cake. She stopped at the bottom of the drive to catch her breath.

"This thing weighs a tonne, Princess." After catching her breath, she walked up the trackway, taking care not to end up falling on her backside like the first time she came here.

When the farmhouse came into view, she saw Quade crouched down by the wooden fence that bordered her fields.

She's gorgeous. She's my perfect dream, but can I be hers?

Princess pulled at her lead when she saw Quade, and Penny let her go. Dougal and Princess met up at the farmhouse, jumped around excitedly, and ran over to Quade.

Penny walked closer as Quade stood up from her task. Her heart started to thud wildly when she saw Quade was wearing a tool belt.

"Oh my God, oh my God." Penny gripped the cake box tightly and gulped. It was her fantasy. Part of her wanted to run, and the other wanted to run to Quade. She ended up standing stock-still in the driveway. Quade greeted the dogs and strode towards her.

Quade made her toes and everything else curl. Quade was real, with rough edges, not polish, with working hands that could touch her soft body and feel rough, but tender. In her quiet moments, she had imagined those hands grasping and cupping her soft breasts, and that image had stuck in her mind, heating up her nights, and fuelling further fantasies.

But in those fantasies, she could respond. In her mind she could leap into Quade's arms and be pushed up against the barn wall. For some reason barns and straw bales played a vital part in her fantasies. This wasn't a fantasy though. This was real life, where she was nervous about taking that next step.

Her breathing grew shorter as Quade strode purposefully towards her. That sexy tool belt, those jeans, those boots—

"Penny? Is everything all right?"

Penny panicked and forgot why she was here. "Um...I was—"

Wooing. You're wooing.

"I brought you a cake," Penny spluttered and handed the box straight to Quade.

Quade looked at the box and then Penny. There was something else going on here that Quade wasn't quite picking up. She never expected to see Penny today, after last night. When she had asked Bridget advice about how to handle their situation, she'd advised her to listen, to follow Penny's lead, so she would do just that.

"A cake? Thank you. Do you want to come in?"

Quade offered her arm as she had done before, letting Penny make the decision. Penny took her arm.

"You look beautiful today, Penny," Quade said.

"Thank you."

Penny was beautiful every day but especially today. Her dress was lovely, and her hair perfect. Quade had the urge to follow her fantasy and lift Penny into her arms, as she had the first time they met, and kiss her. She imagined Penny's perfectly painted nails digging into her neck as they made love.

But as it was, she had a cake box in her arms and no nerve to tell Penny what she wanted.

When they arrived at Quade's cottage, they went straight to the kitchen. Quade put the cake box down on the kitchen table and began to unclip her tool belt. She noticed Penny's eyes glued to her belt area. She glanced down quickly, afraid her fly was open, but it wasn't.

When she looked back up, Penny's eyes had travelled to the tool belt in her hand. Interesting.

"What did I do to deserve a cake?" Quade asked.

"It's not just any cake. I made it specially from one of Mrs. Castle's recipes. Take a look," Penny said.

Quade lifted the lid on the box and was astonished to find the best looking Black Forest gateaux she'd ever seen.

"Bridge said it was your favourite, and I could get the recipe from Mrs. Castle," Penny said nervously.

Quade was so touched and surprised. "It was, I mean, it is. My aunt gave Mrs. Castle the recipe. I always got it on my birthday instead of a birthday cake."

"It not dairy-free or anything. No nuts were harmed in the making of this cake, so don't worry. Does it look okay?"

"It's the best looking one I've ever seen. Thank you. I haven't had one in so long."

Quade wanted to touch Penny, to hug her, thank her for her sweetness, but she didn't want to push her.

She held out her hand, and when Penny grasped it, she took a chance and kissed the back of her hand.

"Thank you. This was really kind," Quade said.

Penny gave a little gasp at the touch of her lips, but then smiled. "I'm glad to have made you happy. I wanted to apologize for last night, and maybe talk about it. I seem to be always apologizing to you."

"Of course we can talk. Let me put the kettle on," Quade said.

Penny had done the easy part. The wooing with the cake had gone down really well. She gave herself a gold star for that, but now the difficult part—talking.

How could she explain her situation? She'd never considered it before. No one who had ever shown an interest in her had made her want to take this chance before.

They had taken their tea and gone to sit on the couch in the living room. The fire was crackling, and the dogs were sprawled in front enjoying the heat.

As if reading her mind, Quade took her hand and said, "You can tell me anything, Penny."

She looked down at their clasped hands. It would be nothing much for most people, but for Penny it was proof that she could get used to closeness with Quade. Holding hands was no longer scary—it was nice.

She gazed at Quade's handsome, open face and knew she was safe. She was always safe with Quade. Penny decided to start with her growing feelings.

"I know we didn't start off as the best of friends. No, that's not true. You tried to be my friend and I pushed you away," Penny said.

"I think everyone needs someone to rely on," Quade said. "You were new to the country, and I knew you would need help with things, if you let me."

"I know I was difficult, but yes, I really did need help. You see, I'd just spent six months being mollycoddled by my family after my very public epileptic fit, and I was trying to break free. Be my own person again."

"I can understand that," Quade said, then started to chuckle. "I definitely knew you were your own person when you opened the door looking like a unicorn."

"You like my unicorn look?" Penny smiled.

Quade winked. "Oh yeah. Really cute."

Penny was silent, trying to work out the words to say and build up the courage. "I—since then I've enjoyed your company, despite appearances sometimes, and I've developed feelings for you."

Quade had been sure there was something between them, but to actually hear Penny say it was something else.

"What does someone like you see in me, Penny? I'm just a farmer. You're a smart, beautiful, successful businesswoman, and a Huntingdon-Stewart."

"Are you kidding?" Penny said. "You're kind, strong, gentle with your animals, and tender, just like my dream—"

Penny stopped abruptly as if she realized she'd said too much, and her cheeks went pink.

How could she be someone's dream? Quade was astonished.

"When you took care of me after my last fit, and you stayed with me, it was the safest I've ever felt, and every night since I've missed you, like you should be there. It's all because of you."

Tears came to Penny's eyes and Quade turned around to face Penny, holding her hand tightly. "Hey, don't be upset. You have to know I feel the same. The first time I saw you walk up my driveway, you took my breath away, and I've tried to take care of you since. I never in a million years thought I was in your league."

"Of course you are, Sammy, but I'm not upset because of how I feel. It's because what I feel for you has made me face some things I've never had to before."

"What is that, sweetheart?"

Quade felt Penny's hand tremble, and she remembered all the little clues she had picked up along the way. The way she flinched when touched, the stubborn attitude to do everything herself.

She tried to help Penny say it. Quade held up their joined hands. "Is it to do with this? Being close with someone?"

Penny nodded, and she dried her tears. "Yes. I've never had a relationship. I've never even slept with someone."

Quade squeezed her hand. "You find it difficult to trust, let people in?"

Penny wiped her eyes. "Yes. I never could, not until I totally trusted them anyway. The women I met wanted into my bed, and I wanted just to hold their hand and test whether I could trust. I hate to show the real me, because that's always been what people have laughed at."

"Why would you say that?" Quade asked. "Why would anyone laugh at you, Penny?"

"When I was at boarding school, I was about twelve when my epilepsy developed. I was at the top of the stone stairs in the entrance hall when I had my first attack. I fell down the stairs, broke my leg quite badly, but to me that wasn't the worst. When I came out of it, there were teachers pinning me down. I couldn't talk, I couldn't move. I was confused and helpless."

"I'm so sorry. That must have been so scary for you." Quade stroked the back of Penny's hand with her thumb.

"What made it worse was all the other girls crowded around the teachers, looking down at me, whispering, laughing, I felt so vulnerable."

"Kids can be so cruel." Quade's heart broke for Penny. It was no wonder she had so many fears.

"Ever since, I've always kept that vulnerable part hidden. I don't want to be laughed at again, and I've always been frightened I'll have a fit while I'm being close with someone, and I'm completely vulnerable."

Everything about Penny fell into place. Quade considered carefully how to respond. She didn't want to say the wrong thing. Rather than talk about the intimate side of her worries, she asked, "What did you feel when you woke in my arms from your fit."

Penny thought carefully. "I felt safe. I always feel safe with you, Sammy. Do you know you're the only one, outside my family, that's gotten past my bedroom door?"

Quade shook her head. "I didn't, but I understand why."

"You do?"

"Yeah, the first time I saw all your medications by the side of your bed, I knew that it was your most private space. The side of you that you didn't trust anyone else to see."

Penny gave her a small smile. "You understand me like no one else has, but you deserve someone who won't try to kiss you and break your nose."

Quade chuckled. "I don't deserve anything. Never in my wildest dreams did I ever think a beautiful sophisticated woman like you would have feelings for me. I'm the luckiest person in the world that you even look my way."

"Don't say that, Sammy. You're gorgeous, you're Sexy Farmer."

Quade smiled. "Well I'm glad you think so, but I have to ask you something, Ms. Huntingdon-Stewart."

"What?"

"Would you allow me to court you?" Quade asked.

"But I'm supposed to be wooing you," Penny said.

Quade furrowed her brow. "Who told you that?"

"Bridge. She said I was to woo you."

Quade smiled and shook her head. "Don't listen to Bridge. She always has to be in charge. I do the courting—that's the way it is."

"Okay, okay." Penny laughed. "I'd be delighted to be courted by you, Sam McQuade, but—"

A look of worry was back on Penny's face.

"No buts," Quade said. "Do you know what old-fashioned courting means?"

"Flowers, walks, that kind of thing?" Penny said.

"Yes, it can include all those things, but mainly what it means is *slow*," Quade said.

"Slow?"

"Slow, and getting to know each other slowly, building our relationship slowly, and getting comfortable with each other, so that whatever happens, happens naturally, and never until you are absolutely ready. That's the way I was brought up to behave when I had romantic feelings for someone."

Penny pulled Quade's hand to her lips and kissed it. "I think that's the nicest thing anyone's ever said to me, Sammy. Thank you for understanding."

"I always understand you. You never have to feel scared or pressured with me, okay?"

Penny nodded. "I've never wanted to explore this with anyone before. I just hope I can be everything you want."

Quade ran the back of her hand along Penny's arm. "Penny, I don't have huge experience with women. Compared to Harry or

Bridge, I'm a novice at best, so I have no expectations other than what you want to share with me."

"Okay, I suppose at least one of us should know what they're doing," Penny joked.

Quade reached out and cupped Penny's cheek. "The slow scenic route seems good to me. Now, can I get some of that delicious looking cake?"

The tension broke and Penny laughed.

❖

Penny decided that gateaux should be for dessert since she heard Quade's stomach rumbling. Quade sat at the kitchen table with Princess enjoying her attention, while Penny looked in Quade's fridge.

"Eggs, bacon, milk, cheese? Don't you have anything else to eat?"

"There's some potatoes in the pantry," Quade said.

Penny sighed and turned back to find Quade's eyes locked on her bottom. It made her smile. Since their talk, Penny felt like she'd crossed another boundary, and a weight lifted off her shoulders. She felt like she could relax and enjoy what was growing between them without worry about where it might lead. Penny trusted Quade, and no matter how Quade insisted she would court her, Penny was going to do a fair bit of wooing and enjoy the experience.

She stood up and put her hands on her hips. "I thought you farmers needed to eat big meals all day? You must do, to give that strong body of yours the energy." Penny winked at Quade.

Was she actually flirting? And enjoying it? Penny's heart was more free than it ever had been. Because of Quade she could now try to enjoy those little sweet beginnings of a relationship that she never could before, and she decided she was going to revel in it.

"We do, but if you only know how to make egg and bacon, bacon and egg, and egg, bacon, and chips, it's hard."

Penny was horrified at Quade's diet. "You can't eat that three times a day. How do you cope?"

Quade ruffled Princess's head and set her down on the floor. "Well, if I'm working at Axedale, Annie makes us lunch, and I usually go to the pub for dinner, or there's the fish and chip shop. Then on Sundays I go to Axedale for Sunday lunch."

Penny shook her head and tutted. "That needs to change, but for right now how does an omelette sound?"

Quade beamed. "Sounds brilliant."

Penny went back to the fridge, then said, "Do you have any spinach in your vegetable garden?"

"Yes," Quade said slowly and reluctantly.

"Excellent."

Forty-five minutes later, Penny brought over two plates to the table. She put Quade's down in front of her, and Quade rubbed her hands together.

"This looks so good."

The cheese omelette with toast on the side looked like something you'd get at a restaurant, and she couldn't wait to dive in.

Penny put her own plate down and went back to the cooker to get a frying pan.

"There's one more thing," Penny said.

Quade looked in horror as Penny spooned some wilted green leaves onto her plate.

"What is that?" Quade prodded it with her fork as if it might be dangerous.

Penny grinned. "It's sautéed spinach. Spinach grown by you, so it's even better."

Penny put the pan down and took her seat. Quade looked at Penny's plate and saw no green at all, only toast. Why was she being singled out for this torture?

"You don't have any?" Quade pointed with her fork to Penny's plate.

Penny began to spread jam on her toast. "That's because I've got nothing to have it with. I could have had a stir fry with your beautiful vegetables, but you've no garlic, chillis, soy sauce—I really need to take you shopping." Penny crunched into her thick cut toast.

Quade couldn't think of anything worse than eating that green splodge, so she started on her omelette, hoping that Penny would forget about it.

"This tastes so good," Quade said.

Penny took a drink of water and said, "Would you like to come for dinner at my cottage? When you haven't got any other offers, of course."

"Really?" Quade said excitedly. "Wait? What other offers have I got?"

"All the ladies from your dating app. Oh, and my fans would love to cook for Sexy Farmer." Penny waggled her eyebrows.

"As if. That would be great, to come to yours. Dougal would love it too."

Dougal barked and jumped up on one of the kitchen chairs.

Penny laughed. "What's he doing?"

Quade cut off a piece of cheesy omelette and held it out for him. "He always sits up here begging for scraps and keeps me company. It's not much fun eating on your own."

Penny gazed dreamily at her, and then pulled out the other chair. "Princess? Up."

Princess jumped up and Quade immediately gave her a share of the food.

"You're not alone now," Penny said.

Quade looked around the table and for the first time since her aunt and uncle died, the farmhouse felt alive again.

"Don't think I've forgotten about that spinach, Sam McQuade."

Dammit.

❖

Quade drove Penny and Princess back to Northwood Cottage after spending a lovely evening together. After they ate, Penny and Quade talked and talked until they realized it was midnight.

It was such a revelation to be able to talk to Quade about her insecurities and have Quade chase them away.

They stopped outside and Penny said, "Thank you, Sammy. I never thought I'd be able to talk like this to anyone."

Quade turned around in her seat. "Don't worry about any silly fears in your head. You're safe with me, Penny. I'd never expose any of your secret fears or personal life. You're beautiful, kind, and a good mum to Princess. You deserve someone to take their time to show you how good a partner they could be."

Quade would be the perfect partner, she knew. Quade was a once in a lifetime chance at happiness. Once someone won her love, Penny was sure that she would love them for the rest of her life.

"Thank you for understanding, anyway, and sorry about hurting your nose last night. I suppose I was trying to show you how I felt, but I messed it up and felt foolish."

Quade smiled. "Everything will come right in its own time. Like the seasons in the countryside. You wait until conditions are right. You don't force them."

Penny could have melted in her seat. Quade was a girl's dream. "You know, I was attracted to you from the first time I saw you. I tried for the longest time to find a flaw in you—that's what I usually do, you see. When I find someone attractive, I find a reason, a flaw in their character, to put me off, and I always have, but not with you. I couldn't find one flaw. All I found were things that I dreamed of in a partner."

Quade blushed sweetly. "I have lots of flaws, believe me."

"Not to me," Penny said.

They gazed at each other silently for a few minutes. Penny's heart was thumping wildly, and she wasn't scared.

She felt herself being drawn closer to Quade, and then Quade broke the silence by saying, "Let me walk you to your door."

Quade got out, and Penny tried to calm her racing heart. Quade helped Penny out and took the bags they had filled with vegetables from Quade's garden, then whistled for the dogs.

The dogs jumped out and ran to the door.

"Here, let me take some bags, Sammy," Penny said.

"Oh no. Taking you home and carrying your bags is part of the courting process," Quade said.

Penny followed her to the door. "So when do I get to woo? I think it's only fair."

"Penny, you woo me every time you smile at me, every time you frown at me, even, every pretty dress you wear, every unicorn onesie you wear, and everything you cook for me. You're wooing me all the time."

Penny sighed with happiness. "Thank you. That was a lovely thing to say."

She unlocked the door and Quade carried the bags into the living room.

"So tomorrow at six for dinner?"

"I can't wait," Quade said.

There was a moment when Penny actually hoped Quade would kiss her, but she just reached for her hand and kissed it.

"Goodnight, Penny."

"Night, Sammy. Sweet dreams." *I know mine will be.*

As Quade walked to the door, she turned her head back to say, "I will—oh, and enjoy your book."

Penny was confused. "What book?"

"The one on your bedside table." Quade winked and walked out the front door with Dougal.

Penny felt her cheeks grow extremely hot. She had seen it.

CHAPTER SIXTEEN

The following week was one of the happiest Quade had ever had. After a hard day's work, she and Dougal went to Penny's for dinner. They enjoyed a great meal, and Penny even went to the trouble of making two different meals, one health-conscious for Penny, and what Quade would call a normal dinner for her. Although with every meal, Penny added more vegetables to her plate.

Penny was determined to improve Quade's palate and crowd out the more unhealthy choices, and if Penny wanted her to try them, Quade would. She was fast becoming completely enamoured with Penny. Every day they spent together, the more Penny relaxed, and the funny, sweet, woman she was came through.

Today Penny was filming in the kitchen at Axedale Hall, and Quade was having a suit fitting for the wedding which was a week away. Quade was helping Penny set up her equipment—putting lights up, setting them, and positioning microphones. Riley had taken Dougal and Princess to play outside with her and Caesar, to give Penny some quiet to record. Princess was used to being on camera, Penny said, but since she'd met Dougal, her inner dog had come to the surface and was a bit loud and playful.

Quade had hardly been able to take her eyes off Penny. For her recording she was wearing a fifties-style pink skirt with a large white poodle on it and a tight white blouse, with a pink neckerchief. She reminded Quade of her childhood crush on Olivia Newton-John in *Grease*. Quade always wanted to be Danny, driving one of those cool cars, with Sandy in the car beside her.

Now she had her own version in front of her and she wanted to kiss her so badly.

"Is this light okay, Penny?"

Penny was standing behind the large kitchen table setting out her ingredients, bowls, and kitchen equipment. She looked up and was dazzled by the light.

"A bit more to the right, Sammy."

Quade moved it and Penny said with a sexy smile, "Perfect. I should use you as my assistant for every video."

Quade's heart fluttered as it did with every compliment Penny gave her. "Anytime. I'll do anything for you, you know that."

Penny gazed at her silently for a few seconds, then put down what she was holding and walked over to her.

She took Quade's hands and stepped closer. "I do know that. You know, all my life I thought being strong meant doing everything myself, but I was wrong."

"Why?" Quade asked.

Penny felt like she was falling deeper and deeper for Quade with every moment she spent with her. Quade was so easy to fall in love with, and that was frightening but made her feel elated at the same time.

"I was wrong because since I've had you in my life, I feel stronger than I ever have. Knowing you are behind me has given me such confidence."

Quade slipped her hands around Penny's waist and inched closer. "I'm glad to hear it. You are the strongest person I know, sweetheart."

Penny smiled, her heart thudded, and their lips inched closer. "I like it when you call me that."

It was going to happen. They were actually going to kiss and Penny wanted nothing more in the world than to feel Quade's lips on hers. Just as they were about to touch, the kitchen door burst open and they moved apart quickly.

Penny cursed her bad luck. She was so ready to kiss Quade, but she smiled when a grinning Annie and Bridget walked down the stone steps.

"Sorry, did we interrupt something?" Bridget teased.

Quade's cheeks were adorably pink as she was sure hers were as well. "No, just getting set up."

Annie said, "Sorry, we've been banished from the drawing room, so Bridge doesn't see Finn's wedding suit. They're waiting for you, Quade."

Quade sighed. "Okay, I'll go."

Penny reached for her hand. "You'll look very handsome. It'll be fine."

Quade had confessed to Penny over the last week how she was dreading getting trussed up in a suit. It wasn't her style at all. Harry and Finn wore suits with ease, but Quade found even ties strangled her. Penny had calmed her by reminding her she was doing this for her friend, and it was good to put yourself out for friends.

Quade kissed her on the cheek and whispered, "I want to finish this sometime later."

"So would I," Penny whispered back.

Penny couldn't help but gaze at Quade as she ascended the stairs out of the kitchen.

"There is the look of a love-struck woman," Bridge said.

"How are things going with you and Quade?" Annie asked.

Bridge nudged her and said, "Most of the internet thinks they're a loved-up couple."

Penny was a little embarrassed, but it was a new feeling to share things like this with friends. Olivia knew some things about her life, but not all.

She was coming to realize that this little community's fondness for Quade was whipping her up in a romantic haze. They all wanted Quade to be happy, and she only hoped that she never let Quade or them down.

"All my followers are swept up in their romantic notions for me, and those that aren't would like to have Quade for themselves."

Penny walked over to the kitchen table and continued to set up her knives and utensils.

Bridge sat on the edge of the table. "Well, it might be because you're posting pictures of you two together all the time."

Bridge turned to Annie. "You know, I heard our Quade has spent every evening over at Northwood Cottage."

Annie smiled. "Oh, really. That's a good sign."

Penny shook her head. These women were determined for a happy ending to their love story. Was that what she and Quade were having? A smile crept on her face. Yes, yes, they were.

"She comes over for dinner," Penny said. "I'm wooing her, and she's courting me, we've decided."

Bridget winked at her. "Good girl. You'll be fine. Take it slow and you'll wind up where you want to be."

"So," Annie said. "Can we watch you record?"

"Absolutely, but if you're here, we need to get a selfie to post." Penny picked up her phone, gathered Annie and Bridge around her, and held up the camera. "Say cheese."

"Cheese," they both replied.

Afterwards Penny edited the picture quickly and got ready to post it on Instagram.

"I'll say, fun and games with Lady Annie and…" She looked over at Bridge and said,

"I think since we've got Sexy Farmer, we'll call you Sexy Vicar."

Bridget laughed. "Oh, do please."

Quade and Harry were sitting on the couch watching Finn getting fitted by Harry's tailor, and waiting for their own turns. Quade had to admit that Finn looked great in her wedding suit. It was what Finn called steampunk, a kind of exaggerated Victorian suit, Quade would have said. It was black with a deep red waistcoat, and of course Finn's signature top hat.

"She really pulls off the top hat thing, doesn't she?" Quade said to Harry.

Harry chuckled. "Yes, she certainly cuts a dash. So, how are you and Pen coming along? Any movement on that front?"

"Yeah, well, I have dinner with her every night. She loves to cook for me, and I'm courting her, taking it slow, you know?"

"I do," Harry said. "Annie courted me and I never even realized until I nearly lost her. If it's Pen you want, don't hesitate like I did."

"You did?" Quade said.

Harry nodded. "I ran away in fear, and Annie was packing to leave for another posting. If I hadn't convinced her that I wanted to change my life, I would have been heartbroken."

"I didn't know that." Quade had only seen Annie and Harry's romance from the outside and had assumed that after Annie melted her heart, their love story was a smooth journey, not a rocky road.

Quade wouldn't let that happen to her. She wanted Penny and would go as slow as it took to win her heart.

"I'm going to do anything to keep her in my life. She wanted to make a video of my workday. A day-in-the-life sort of thing. Do you mind if we film my job up here?"

Harry smiled and patted her leg. "Of course not. Have fun and win her heart, Quade."

Finn jumped down from the box she was standing on and gave a bow. "I'm ready for my greatest show ever. Who's next?"

Quade nudged Harry. "You go, mate."

She wanted to put off wearing the suit as long as possible.

Penny made her way to the drawing room. Annie said this was one of the many drawing rooms, music rooms, writing rooms, and every other room under the sun in Axedale Hall. Penny's family home was a mansion in Mayfair, but nothing to the sheer scale of Axedale Hall. She wondered how Harry, Annie, and Riley didn't get lost here.

She opened the large doors to the drawing room and peeked her head around. The normally good-natured Quade was standing on a raised platform and had a frown on her face. The poor tailor was trying to adjust the jacket with great difficulty. Quade shifted and fidgeted the whole time.

"Ms. McQuade. If you could please stay still."

Quade pulled at her collar and tie and said with frustration, "It's Quade, and how can I keep still when you keep poking me?"

Before the situation got any worse, Penny said, "Mr. Havers? Lady Annie has tea ready for you in the kitchen. Why don't you take a break?"

Mr. Havers sighed and nodded. "Thank you, miss."

When he left, Quade jumped down from the box, opened her collar, and pulled her tie loose. "Bloody man."

Penny walked over to her. "What's wrong, Sammy?"

"Have you been sent to make me behave?"

She said that more sharply than Penny had heard Quade speak before. "Now, now. I came because I wanted to see your lovely suit."

"It's not lovely. I hate being trussed up like this. I feel like I can't breathe." Quade put her hands over her face and rubbed it vigorously.

Penny followed her instincts and slipped her hands inside Quade's jacket and round her waist. "Now look at me. What's really bothering you?"

Quade hands fell and went to Penny's waist quite naturally. "It's just not me. You should have seen Finn and Harry—they look like they were born to wear these stupid things."

Penny remembered Bridget's advice to use her feminine wiles to woo her. Maybe they could also be used to calm her down or distract. She was a novice at this, but she'd give it a try.

Penny placed the flat of her hand on Quade's chest. "Sammy, I know it's not you, and you don't like it, but this is something you are doing for your best friend. We talked about it."

Quade let out a long breath. "I know. I really tried, but look at me."

She started to trace her fingernails over the crisp white shirt. "I think you look rather dashing, actually."

"You do?" Quade's tone of voice changed.

Penny grasped Quade's loose tie lightly. "Yes. I know it's not you, but I for one will be so happy to dance with you at the wedding looking so sexy."

"You will?"

She pulled on the tie and pulled Quade closer. Quade's eyes became alive and her breathing deepened. Penny could hear Quade's breath shorten, and see the rapid rise and fall of her chest. She felt powerful having this sort of effect on Quade. The anxiety she once had now gave way to excitement, want, and aching for Quade's lips.

Penny realized Quade was allowing her to come to her, always wanting Penny to make that choice. Why had she taken so long to do this?

Nothing made more sense than falling into Quade's deep blue eyes and feeling the warmth of her lips. Her eyes closed, and their lips met without the fanfare or trepidation she had always worried about, but just quite naturally.

Quade's lips were gentle, soft, and heart-meltingly sweet. She felt Quade's hands slowly and softly cup her cheeks, and the tip of her tongue trace her upper lip. That one small touch made Penny's knees weaken, and a small moan escaped her throat.

Just when she thought Quade might deepen the kiss, she pulled back and smiled at her.

"Thank you, sweetheart," Quade said.

Penny, still a little dazed, said, "What for?"

Quade caressed her cheek. "For trusting me, for believing in me, and for making me feel better."

"Can I bring back Mr. Havers then?" Penny asked.

"In a few minutes." Quade grinned and moved back in to kiss her.

Chapter Seventeen

Quade stood outside Northwood Cottage waiting on Penny coming out. Today Penny was shadowing her for a day-in-the-life vlog.

They decided it would hold Quade's work back too much to follow her from half past five in the morning at the farm. So they started by following Quade's midmorning work up at Axedale and would finish on the farm.

Since their first kiss the other day, they had spent every moment they could together, exploring their new-found closeness, and strengthening their bond and trust. Bridget had been right about patience and time. Penny had relaxed more and more, and their intimacy deepened, as well as their kisses, every day.

As much as their kissing and touching made Quade ache for more, ache to touch and kiss Penny's body, she was in no rush to get there. She was enjoying this old-fashioned courtship. Penny was not a woman you wanted to rush. You wanted to savour every look, touch, and kiss you were fortunate enough to have bestowed on you.

Her gaze was drawn to the Ferrari that had sat in its slumber since Penny arrived. It had puzzled her why Penny owned something she couldn't use. Her thoughts were interrupted by the cottage door opening and Princess's barking. Then of course Dougal's loud barks started. Quade got out of the car and lifted Princess up into her arms.

"Good morning, beautiful girl."

Penny walked over and said, "Are you talking to me or my dog?"

Quade looked up and her heart thudded as it always did when she saw Penny. She put Princess down next to Dougal and leaned in to kiss Penny. "Both."

"That's all right then. How do I look for a mucky day in the country?" Penny spun around and Quade's eyes went to Penny's gorgeous looking bottom in tight jeans.

She had warned Penny to wear something sensible, and Penny's version of sensible was jeans with sparkles and diamanté, and Quade started to laugh when she looked down at Penny's feet and saw her wellington boots of choice were white and pink with a large unicorn print.

"You look beautiful, and as near country as you could ever get, Penny. Especially those boots."

Penny beamed a smile and waggled her hips. "I was saving them for a special occasion."

Quade put her arms around Penny's waist and pulled her in close. "I'm honoured then."

Penny put her bag down on the ground, wrapped her arms around Quade's neck, and kissed her. "Good morning, Sammy."

Quade couldn't resist slipping her hands from Penny's waist to her pert bottom. "I love you in these jeans."

Penny gave her a quick kiss. "Thank you, Sexy Farmer. You know, I'm getting bombarded with questions from my followers about us. And my subscriber numbers have gone through the roof."

"Really?" Quade said.

"They're fascinated by us—are they or aren't they?"

"And what have you told them?" Quade asked.

Penny gave her the sweetest smile. "Nothing. I've told them nothing. This is just ours."

In their little bubble of Axedale, Penny was safe to explore her new-found love life, her special relationship with Quade. She was frightened that if the real world crept in, things would change.

Quade kissed her nose. "That's a nice thing to say. Are you ready to go?"

"Yes." Penny picked up her bag and pulled out her camera. "Would you mind doing one more little thing for me, Sammy?"

"Anything."

Penny rummaged around in her bag and brought out two clip-on microphone packs. "I promise I won't post anything before you approve it, but it will really help with the recording."

"I trust you. Of course I will."

"Great." Penny wired Quade up and put the pack in her back pocket. "Let's go."

❖

The Land Rover pulled in to the stable block behind Axedale, and Quade brought it to a halt.

"So who works here?" Penny held the camera in front of Quade.

"There's about one hundred staff who work at Axedale. The majority are outdoor staff, and then the house and hospitality staff who work for Lady Annie. The outdoor staff are based in this office and are sent out to do their particular jobs."

They got out and Quade led Penny with her camera into the office. The guys were sitting around have a morning cuppa.

"Morning, boys. I've got Ms. Penny with me today. She wants to see how we do things."

"Hi, boys. Nice to meet you," Penny said.

All the men's eyes went wide, not quite believing this beautiful woman from the magazine was right before their eyes.

Young Will said shyly, "Hello, miss."

Then the rest found the courage to greet her.

Quade laughed to herself. They had plenty to say when Penny was just a picture in a magazine, but now they were like frightened rabbits.

"Everyone got their assignments for today?" Quade asked.

They all nodded.

"Andy, take some people and check on the deer herd later. Make sure they're all in good health."

"Will do," Andy replied.

"Great," Quade said. "We're going to feed the alpacas. See you later."

They got back into the Land Rover and drove up to the alpaca enclosure, and Quade got out the feed bucket. Leaving the dogs in the truck for the moment, Penny followed Quade over to the pen. She whistled the same way she did for her cattle.

"Do they understand commands?" Penny asked.

"I'm not sure, since I'm not an expert on them, but I try to treat them as I do my cattle. It's all I know."

Penny laid her head on Quade's shoulder. "You're so sweet."

"I'm not," Quade said, showing her embarrassment.

Penny giggled. "Of course you are. Right, I'm going to film you feeding them. On you go."

Quade took the bucket over to the feeding station, and the alpacas all followed her.

"They're so goofy!" Penny shouted.

Quade spread out the feed and scratched one of the friendliest ones behind the ears. "I know. Just wait till the pot-bellied pigs arrive. It'll be even sillier around here."

The ringing of Quade's phone silenced her. She saw it was Tom ringing her from the farm. "Hello? Tom?"

Tom explained that one of the cows had gone into labour, and it was taking too long. Quade hung up quickly and hurried over to Penny. "We have to go now."

"What's wrong, Sammy?"

She explained about the cow. "Tom thinks she may be in trouble."

"Well, let's go," Penny said.

❖

Penny had never seen Quade so worried, so concerned. She truly did care for her animals. They drove at breakneck speed back to the farm and hurried out of the truck. "Penny, will you put the dogs in the house?"

"Yes, on you go," Penny said.

Quade ran up to the barn and disappeared through the door.

"Dougal, Princess? Come on and we'll get you inside."

Once Penny settled the dogs, she made her way up to the barn. She was unsure if she should just walk in. Deciding to take a chance, she pushed open the barn door and saw the cow pacing around with a heavy looking udder area, making the cow equivalent of moaning noises. Quade had her arm around the suffering animal, stroking her neck and trying to calm her.

Tom, Quade's farmhand, was standing a few paces back.

"Come on, girl. You'll be all right. We'll look after you."

Penny didn't want to spook the animal, so she walked to the hay bales that were stacked from low to high and sat down, trying to get out of the way.

Quade said a few words to Tom and walked back to talk to her.

"How is she?" Penny asked.

Quade rubbed the back of her head. "Her confinement's taking too long, but the vet's on his way. I can get Tom to take you home. We could be here a while."

"No," Penny said quickly. "I mean, unless you want me to go?"

Quade gave her a tense smile. "I'd like you to stay, but it might be difficult for you to watch."

"I'm tougher than I look." Penny smiled.

Quade leaned down and kissed her cheek. "I know you are."

Penny had never watched anything more scary or beautiful. For the longest time, Quade and Tom were worried and tense, and

Penny was caught up in those feelings too. She sensed that Quade would be devastated if she lost one of her animals this way.

The tension was so palpable that Penny had to stop herself from biting her precious nails. She gradually moved from the hay bales at the back up to where Quade was standing. She stood with her arm around Quade, trying to give her comfort, while the vet tried his best to help the cow and the unborn calf.

As the birth progressed, Penny found herself gripping Quade more tightly. "Will she be all right? She sounds like she's in a lot of pain."

"I hope so. She's in the best hands." Quade put both arms around Penny and kissed her head.

Five minutes later, Penny watched in awe as a big calf was born onto the straw. "It's here, it's here."

"We need to make sure it's healthy first. We're not out of the woods yet." Quade let go of her and hurried over to where the vet was.

Penny watched as all three of them, Quade, the vet, and Tom, held the calf and cleared its airways.

Please be okay, please be okay, Penny prayed.

"Sammy? Sammy? Is it okay?"

Finally, Quade turned around and smiled. "He's made it."

Chapter Eighteen

Quade sighed with contentment, watching the new calf being licked and taken care of by its mother. Something that could have turned out so very differently.

She turned her head and smiled. She had her arm around Penny and Penny was leaning on her chest, sleeping. Penny had done so well for a townie and had been a great support for her. Quade didn't feel alone any more. Working hard during the day and going for dinner with Penny in the evening was her idea of a dream. If only it could be like that every day.

I'm falling in love with you.

She had started to have little niggles in her mind about what would happen next as she sat there keeping an eye on the calf. Quade imagined this was what it would be like to have Penny as her wife, having her support no matter what came up. But Penny was only meant to be here a short time. They hadn't talked about it, and Quade was frightened to bring it up in case she got an answer she didn't like.

Quade kissed Penny's brow and thought she better get her back to the farmhouse. It was a bit late to take her home. The mother and calf were safe enough now, so she stood up and lifted Penny into her arms.

"Come on, sweetheart. Let's get you home."

Quade stopped in her tracks. The farmhouse wasn't Penny's home, but could it be?

Penny put her arms around Quade and nuzzled further into Quade's neck.

She carried Penny back and greeted the excited dogs as she entered the front door.

The barking of the dogs woke Penny from her snooze. She jumped when she became aware she was being carried.

"What's happening?"

Then Penny realized she was in Quade's arms. *It's Sammy, you're safe.*

Quade stopped at the bottom of the stairs. "I thought it was too late to take you home. I was going to put you in my bedroom—I mean, I'll sleep in the spare bedroom."

If it was anyone else in the world, Penny would be certain this was a ploy to get her into bed, but not Quade. She looked into Quade's deep blue eyes and saw that her intentions were completely honourable, and she could trust her with everything, every little secret that she hid deep down in her soul.

"That sounds like a good idea."

Penny didn't insist on walking the rest of the way, like she did the last time. She was quite happy to stay in Quade's arms for as long as possible.

Quade carried her upstairs and placed her on a brass bed with a patchwork quilt on top. The dogs arrived seconds later.

"Excuse the room. It could do with decorating, but I never seem to find the time," Quade said.

"It's warm and cosy, Sammy. That's all you need," Penny reassured her. "Oh, do you have a T-shirt or something I can sleep in?"

"Yeah, give me a sec," Quade said.

When Quade left the room, Penny checked her phone quickly. She had hundreds of notifications, but she didn't want to check them now. Her online life didn't seem as important any more, not now that she had looked up from the screen as Quade had told her to and found a life.

She did check her emails and saw that one was from Olivia. She had set up the public appearance and book signing for a few days after Bridge and Finn's wedding. Penny frowned when Olivia suggested bringing Quade.

Penny could see right through Olivia's intentions. Olivia wanted to cash in on the excitement and gossip over her relationship with Sexy Farmer. The thing was, Penny had intended to ask Quade to come with her, to show Quade her world in London.

The last thing she wanted to do was give Olivia what she wanted, but why should she let it spoil her plans?

Quade came back in with a white T-shirt for her. "It's a bit big, but it'll work, I think."

Penny smiled and took it from her. "It'll be perfect."

Quade stuffed her hands in her pockets and rocked on her heels nervously. Penny supposed it was strange for Quade to have another woman in her bedroom.

"Sorry I don't have anything with unicorns on it," Quade said.

Penny laughed. "I'll need to leave one of my unicorn nighties here for when I stay over."

Penny realized what she had said. It was clear her trust was growing and growing, and wherever Quade was, Penny wanted to be. She remembered the night that Quade had slept in the chair at her house, one of the most peaceful nights of sleep she'd had. She wanted that again.

Penny's heart began to pound. Could she ask?

"I better say goodnight then," Quade said.

"No," Penny spluttered.

"No?" Quade said with confusion.

Penny touched her fingers to her forehead and tried to form her words. "Would you stay here with me?"

Quade's eyes went wide with shock. "You want me to—"

"Sleep here," Penny said quickly. "Just to sleep. I'd like to be close to you, in a way, without…"

Quade nodded and smiled, catching her meaning. Penny wanted to take the next step and enjoy being close to Quade without any expectations. "I'll just go and get changed."

Quade left and Penny started to panic. Why had she said that? It was easier to handle in her mind than in reality. She quickly got changed into Quade's T-shirt, took off Princess's little outfit, jumped under the covers, and pulled them right up to her neck.

The anxieties that she had started to forget of late were swirling around her stomach like a snake. She'd never slept in the same bed with anyone, apart from her sister.

What would happen if she had an attack again? *I can't handle this.*

Quade was nervous as she got changed into fresh boxers and a T-shirt. She had gone for a super fast shower after she'd left Penny. There was no way she was going to spend her first night sleeping beside Penny smelling like a barn.

She quickly sprayed on some cologne Bridge had given her for her birthday, then took a moment to calm her nerves. Penny was the one who had worries about letting someone in. She had to be strong for them both.

Quade walked through her bedroom door and found Penny lying as stiff as a board, with the covers pulled right up.

She's worried.

"Penny, you don't have to do this. I'll sleep in the spare room."

"No, please," Penny said, "I really want to."

Quade told Dougal to get down off the bed, and Princess followed him to his basket.

She got under the covers and tried to stay as far on her side of the bed as possible. The atmosphere was tense, and they both lay silently for the longest time before Quade felt she had to say something.

"So, here we are."

"Here we are," Penny replied.

Quade had to find some way of making Penny relax. "So what recipe are you doing in your next video this week?"

She heard Penny let out a breath she'd been holding. "Well, I thought I'd do lentil curry with cauliflower rice."

Quade turned her head to look at Penny. "What, rice with cauliflower mixed through it?"

Penny laughed all of a sudden and reached across the divide between them to take her hand. That was a huge step. "No, silly. Rice made from cauliflower."

Quade screwed up her face. "Rice made from cauliflower, rice made from cauliflower," she repeated trying to make sense of it.

Penny scooted over the bed and leaned up on her elbow. "You say that like you did with nut milk."

Quade's heart was happy to see Penny so much more relaxed. She wanted Penny to trust her more than anything. "Yours is a strange world where you can milk nuts and magically turn cauliflower into rice," Quade joked.

"You make it sound as if I come from some magical kingdom." Penny laughed. "I'll soon have you familiar with all the strange food from my world."

"I don't have to try cauliflower rice, do I? I have to draw the line somewhere," Quade said.

Penny leaned to within a few inches of Quade's lips and whispered, "If you want any of my kisses you will."

"Ah, you've found my weakness, Ms. Huntingdon-Stewart."

Penny giggled and gave her a peck on the lips. "Speaking of my world—can I ask you something?"

Quade turned over on her side so they were facing each other. "Yeah, anything."

"A few days after Bridge's wedding, I have to go to London. I have a public appearance to do at a bookshop—signing books, things like that."

This was what Quade was dreading. Penny was going home.

"I hope you have a good time," Quade said a little sharply.

Penny took Quade's hand and lifted it onto her hip. "I was hoping you might come with me."

"With you?" Quade couldn't have been more surprised.

Penny stroked the side of Quade's face with her fingertips. "Yes. If you can get someone to look after the farm for you. I thought we could go down the day before and stay at my parents' house. I'd like you to meet them."

"You would?" Quade was gobsmacked. Penny wasn't trying to find a way out.

"So do you want to? I'd like you to come to the signing with me. If you can't get anyone to look after the farm, or you don't want to—"

Quade grasped Penny's chin lightly. "I would be honoured to meet your family and to visit your world in London."

She took a chance and kissed Penny, taking care to be as gentle as she could. It was Penny who responded by making the kiss deeper and running her fingers through her hair.

Quade couldn't help but run her hand under Penny's T-shirt and onto her bare thigh.

Penny moaned, but everything was getting too hot too fast. Quade was so turned on and Penny wanted slow. She wasn't going to ruin this first step and this trust that Penny had given her.

She pulled out of the kiss and said, "Penny, I care for you so much…" She didn't want to admit she was falling in love in case it spooked her. "I don't want to move too fast. Courting is slow, remember?"

"You're right, but you make me feel so hot, Sammy. I want you to know that," Penny said.

Quade laughed. "Me too. Believe me."

Penny laid her head on Quade's chest and put her arm around her waist. "Can I sleep like this?"

"I'd love it." Quade had never felt so happy in her life. Penny, her Penny, was wrapped around her and feeling safe and trusting her. It was perfect.

They lay in silence, and then Penny said out of the blue, "Now I know how Lady Chatterley felt being with Mellors the gamekeeper."

"How did she feel?" Quade asked.

"Horny," Penny replied.

Chapter Nineteen

The day of Bridge and Finn's wedding finally came around and the whole village was mobilized for the wedding of the year. Penny had stayed with Quade the night before, as they had every night since the evening the calf was born. Penny was loving the close, safe feeling she got from being with Quade.

Every night spent together created another layer of intimacy between them, with some pretty hot kissing sessions. She was praying that she would have the courage to share more of herself with Quade soon.

Quade was so patient with her, despite the fact she must have been really frustrated. But each time Penny felt she had to apologize, Quade told her that anything worthwhile was worth waiting on.

She was just perfect, Penny thought.

Penny was setting out Quade's wedding suit that had been delivered the day before. She knew Quade would need some reassurance because she still wasn't comfortable in a suit. Quade had gone out with the dogs to pass some instructions to Tom, who was looking after the farm and the dogs today.

Penny heard the front door slam shut and the sound of paws running up the stairs. When the dogs came tumbling into the room, Penny held out her hand. "No dirty paws on the bed, you two. Stay down."

Penny stroked both dogs and they ran off happily. It was so wonderful to see Princess so happy. When she first arrived in Axedale, mud on her little dog's paws might have brought on one of her fits, but now it was a sign that Princess was having fun.

She heard Quade stomping up the stairs, but when she didn't come to the bedroom, Penny went in search of her. She found Quade in her office smacking the side of her computer.

"What's wrong, Sammy?" Penny asked.

"I need to order some supplies and this stupid piece of s—rubbish won't come on."

Penny looked closely at the ancient looking thing. "I think you need to buy a new computer, Sammy, and join the modern world. A laptop would be good for you. Then you could use it anywhere in the house."

Quade rubbed her forehead. "I wouldn't know what to ask for or what to choose."

Penny sensed that some of Quade's tension was really about the wedding and wearing the suit. She took Quade's hand and said, "Why don't we go computer shopping when we go to London? I'll help you."

Quade let out a breath. "That would be great. I really need a decent computer."

"Now that's one worry dealt with, come and get ready. You have to pick up Finn soon."

Quade took a shower, and when she walked into the bedroom she found that Penny had put on her dress and was applying her make-up. The sight stopped Quade in her tracks and she was hit with a bolt of lust and want.

She stood silently and watched Penny carefully apply her lipstick. There was something so female, so erotic about the act. Quade was hungry, hungry to touch, to kiss Penny, and to have Penny kiss her with those sexy lips. She seemed to be in a perpetual state of horniness these days. Just having Penny sleep beside her was enough to turn her on, but all the kissing and touching they were doing was making her ache.

Quade couldn't stop herself for walking over. Penny jumped when she realized Quade was behind her. "Sammy, you scared me to death."

She bent over and kissed the curve of Penny's neck, and she moaned. "You're so beautiful."

Penny stood up and wrapped her hands around Quade's waist, then dipped her fingers under the band of Quade's Jockey shorts. "You make me want to forget we have a wedding to go to."

Quade grinned. "You make me want to forget I'm an old-fashioned lover, and to be honest, I'm nervous because you mean so much to me. I wish I was a confident lover like I bet Harry and Finn are. I bet they weren't nervous about their first times with Annie and Bridge."

"Harry had a lot of practice before Annie," Penny said, "and Finn just does what she's told, I think."

Quade narrowed her eyes. "Does she?"

Penny put her arms around Quade's neck and chuckled. "Don't look so shocked. Have you never seen the leather strap on Finn's wrist?"

"Yeah, I thought it was a fashion thing. You know she has this gothic style."

Penny smiled and shook her head. "Bridge has the chain that attaches to it."

"You mean…I knew Bridge was bossy, oh, and she has that scary whip." Quade's eyes went wide.

"What whip?" Penny asked.

"It used to be a joke between us. I didn't think she was serious." Quade felt a momentary sense of panic. "Wait, you don't—"

Penny threw her head back and laughed. "Don't worry, Sammy. I like my butches on top. I mean, I've never experienced it before, but my fantasies never include whips, or making you kiss my shoes."

Quade pulled her closer. "You have fantasies?"

"When you're scared to let people behind your walls, your fantasy world becomes quite important, and it never consisted of whips."

Quade grinned and kissed Penny's neck. "What do your fantasies consist of?"

A touch of pink came to Penny's cheeks. "Oh, you, tool belts, you fixing things, barns, and bales of hay are a favourite."

Quade laughed. "Why barns?"

"People always get up to no good in barns in films, TV, and books. They have an earthy erotic feeling."

"Funny," Quade said, "I've never thought of anything erotic as I've stacked hay bales, but I will now."

"Kiss me," Penny said.

Quade was just about to when an alarm on Penny's phone went off. She grabbed it and shrieked, "You're supposed to be leaving in twenty minutes, Sammy. Put thoughts of barns and hay on hold, and let's get you ready, handsome."

The gold music room of Axedale Hall was full of noise, laughter, and chatter as they waited for Bridge and Harry to arrive at the altar.

Although called the music room, the space was huge, and there was plenty of room for the two hundred guests that were invited. The chairs in the room were divided by an aisle down the centre, but guests were encouraged to sit anywhere, no matter which of the wedding party they knew.

Quade and Finn were sitting next to the altar, which was an antique oak table. The local registrar would perform the legal part of the civil partnership, and then Bridge's friend Kate, a vicar from Manchester, was conducting the blessing afterwards.

Quade's attention was drawn to Finn's fingers drumming nervously on her top hat which was resting on her lap.

"Are you okay, mate?" Quade asked.

"I'm more nervous than I've been in my life, but at the same time I can't wait to get married. You know what I mean?"

Quade glanced over to the front row of seats and gazed lovingly at Penny, who was chatting to Annie and Bridge's mother, Cordelia Claremont. Next to them, Harry's mother was in deep conversation with Riley, another example of love healing all those emotional wounds held inside, and Riley was sweetly holding Mrs. Castle's hand.

"There's nothing I want more than to be married, Finn."

At the moment she said those words, Penny turned to look at her and smiled sweetly. Quade felt all the empty spaces in her heart expand with love. *I love her.*

"Penny's beautiful, Quade. Don't let any fear you have get in the way of what you want," Finn said.

"I want Penny with all my heart, Finn, but one day I'm afraid she's going to leave here."

"Then tell her you love her. Give her a reason to stay. I stayed," Finn said.

The music room doors opened and the housekeeper gave Finn and Quade a nod.

"It's time, Finn."

"Have you got the rings?" Finn said in sudden panic.

Quade tapped her pocket and smiled. "Yes. Don't worry. I'm really good at the boring stuff."

They took their places at the altar, the guests stood, and Quade reminded Finn to put on her top hat. The music started, and Quade heard Finn gasp a huge intake of breath. When she turned in the direction Finn was looking, she saw Bridget Claremont, not as the vicar, but as the utterly gorgeous, sexy woman she was, holding the arm of her best friend Harry.

Bridge's wedding dress consisted of a tight red corset on top, and a full black dress, overlaid with red lace. In her hands she held deep red roses, simply bunched and beautiful. The colours matched

Finn's black steampunk suit and red waistcoat. They matched each other both outside and in, and Quade prayed that she and Penny could match together as well.

❖

After the meal and speeches, the staff cleared the tables in the ballroom, and the dancing started. Harry and Annie were dancing together slowly on the dance floor, content to be in each other's arms.

Harry was happy. The day was a success, and now all the guests were either talking happily or dancing. Her mother, Lady Dorothy, was engaged in deep conversation with Bridge's mother, Cordelia, Annie was in her arms, and her friends were happily married.

"Did you make sure Martha was settled when you took her home? Did you remember the cake for her?"

Mrs. Martha Castle, Harry's childhood cook, was like another grandmother to Riley and so important to them. She didn't have the best of health and struggled to stay after the dinner, so Harry drove her home and settled her in.

"Yes, I got her tea, put her favourite TV show on, and the nurse was coming to help her to bed in an hour. She's fine."

"Good. What a beautiful day it's been," Annie said.

Harry kissed the side of her wife's head. "You planned it perfectly. You're so good at organizing events. Did I ever tell you that Axedale wouldn't be half of what it is without you?"

Annie smiled with satisfaction. "Once or twice."

"You're like the general of the Axedale army and I just need to stand well back and let you get on with it."

"Is that why you escape to your office then?" Annie asked.

"Sometimes, but then my heart misses you so much I have to come and find you."

Annie leaned in and whispered in her ear. "Like the airing cupboard incident?"

"Exactly." Harry waggled her eyebrows.

Last week Harry was feeling a little deprived of Annie's attention, as Annie was knee-deep in wedding preparations. So Harry whisked her off for a private word, and they ended up making love in the airing cupboard upstairs. It had been thrilling.

Annie turned her head to the side and gasped. "Oh my God, Harry. They look so adorable."

Harry turned to where Annie was looking and saw Riley, who was wearing a replica of Harry's suit, trying to dance a waltz with her best friend Sophie.

Harry grinned. "I think our little centurion has an eye for a pretty girl."

"I think so," Annie agreed.

"How sweet," Bridge said, as she and Finn danced up beside them. "Another little heartbreaker."

"If Harry has any influence on her, I'm sure she will be," Annie joked.

"Very funny," Harry said. "So, what time are you two leaving?"

Finn looked at her watch. "About half an hour, I think. Our flight is at twenty past seven tomorrow, so we'll need to be up at the crack of dawn."

Bridge softly smacked Finn's backside. "Not that she'll be getting any sleep. Will you, darling?"

"I can sleep on the plane." Finn grinned goofily.

"Before you two start early," Harry said, "let me dance with my friend."

Harry gave Annie's hand to Finn, and she took Bridge's.

"Do you see our lovebirds over there?" Annie pointed to Quade and Penny dancing closely on the other side of the room.

Bridge smiled. "I have a good feeling about those two. Imagine our Quade with Little Pen?"

"Bridge, you will remember to aim your flowers at Penny, won't you?" Annie said.

"Of course, but as Harry will tell you, I wasn't very good at sport at school, so my aim may not be the best."

"Try your best," Annie said. "We need one more happy ending in Axedale, and if Quade doesn't get it with Pen, I don't know if she ever will. She's head over heels in love."

❖

Penny and Quade walked back to the farmhouse hand in hand, Penny carrying her heels. Penny's phone was going crazy with beeps of notifications.

"What are your people all excited about now?"

"My people?" Penny laughed.

"You know what I mean."

Penny took her phone from her clutch bag and opened up her Instagram account. "It's the picture I took of us together at the reception." Penny began to laugh as she read through the comments.

"What is it?" Quade asked.

"They seem to be particularly excited about Sexy Farmer wearing a suit. I think you could have your own successful social media account. They fancy you so much."

"Don't be daft. They don't know how boring I am in real life. Besides, I like being part of yours."

Penny smiled and put away her phone. Life was more interesting than her cyberlife at the moment.

They turned the corner and Penny was faced with the hill that led up to Quade's farm. She stopped and let out a groan. "Oh no. I wish we had taken the lift from Mr. Finch now. I just thought it would be nice to walk together."

Before she could say a word, Quade lifted Penny into her arms. "You should have said. I'll carry you home—well, to my home."

Far from annoying Penny as it used to, finding herself in Quade's arms made her smile. She wrapped her arms around Quade's neck and kissed her. "I'm too heavy."

"Don't be silly. I lift calves, bales of hay, fence posts—you're not heavy," Quade said.

Penny's eyebrows rose. "It's not very flattering to be compared to calves, fence posts, and bales of hay."

Quade kissed her nose. "You know what I mean. I'm strong enough for you."

Penny laid her head on Quade's shoulder. "Oh I know. You're a girl's dream."

Quade noticed Penny rubbing her temples. "Are you okay?"

"Yes, just a headache. It's all the crying I did today. I always cry at weddings and crying always gives me a headache."

"Getting hit in the head with Bridge's bouquet didn't help," Quade joked.

"God, I know."

When Bridge and Finn were leaving, all the guests went outside to wave them off and for the throwing of the bouquet. "Bridge isn't the best at throwing. It hit me on the head and fell into Mrs. Peters's hands," Penny said.

"I heard her tell Mr. Peters she was leaving him when this new suitor arrived."

"From the way Annie was lining Bridge up, I think she was meant to be aiming at me."

Quade loved the feel of Penny in her arms. It felt like that was how it was meant to be. Today had been a dream. Having someone like Penny as her partner at her friend's wedding would have seemed like fantasy a few months ago, and yet here she was, carrying the woman she loved back to her farmhouse.

Finn had told her to make sure Penny knew how much she cared, how serious she was about her, but if she said those words and frightened Penny off, Quade's heart would be broken. She needed to gauge how long Penny saw herself staying.

"How's the cookbook going?"

Penny yawned and nuzzled into her neck. "Great, I've got too many recipes for the book now that Mrs. Castle gave me her recipe notebooks. They're like gold, you know. She's written down recipes since she was just a girl, and kitchen maid at Axedale. I'll need to work with my editor to chop it down."

"And can you adapt them to your…" Quade wasn't quite sure how to describe it.

"My clean eating philosophy? Oh yes. I pride myself on being able to make any traditional recipe work."

"And what vegetable delights have I got to look forward to this week?" Quade asked.

She always pretended Penny's vegetable creations were a trial, but secretly she loved her dinners each night with her. All except the cauliflower rice. That was a step too far.

Penny smirked at her. "I'm not telling just now, because you might drop me on the road and run."

"Don't think I haven't noticed you putting more vegetables on my plate each day. You started with just a tablespoon, and now they cover half the plate."

Penny laughed and softly hit Quade on the chest. "They do not. Stop complaining. I wonder how our babies are?"

Our babies? That was new. It gave Quade a look into her perfect future, but did Penny really mean that? Since Quade started having dinner with Penny every night, she couldn't help but think of the two of them and Princess and Dougal as a family. That was her wish, her dream.

They got to the door of the farm and Quade let Penny slide down her body. Quade gulped. Their loving slow dances at the wedding reception had left her body aching for Penny's touch.

"Thank you for carrying me," Penny said.

"It's part of the courting service, Ms. Huntingdon-Stewart. Are you staying tonight? Or do you want me to drive you to the cottage?"

Penny grasped Quade's tie and pulled her forward into a kiss. "What do you think?"

Quade hoped she wasn't getting this spectacularly wrong. "Staying?"

"Of course. I'm happier than I could ever have imagined, sleeping snuggled up to you, Sammy."

I need to tell her how I feel. I need this woman in my life.

"You go and get ready for bed and I'll slip Tom a few quid for babysitting."

"Okay." Penny kissed her cheek. "Don't be long."

CHAPTER TWENTY

When Quade went in, the dogs made a big fuss over her, then ran upstairs to see Penny. Quade thanked Tom, locked up, and went into the spare bedroom to get changed for bed. Even though they were getting closer and closer, Quade liked to give Penny her space and privacy.

When she was changed, she knocked on the bedroom door.

Penny's response came quickly. "Get in here, Sammy. You don't have to knock."

Quade walked in and groaned internally. Penny was sitting at the dressing table taking off her make-up, but still in her dress. There was just something about watching Penny put on or take off her make-up that turned Quade on.

She sat on the bed and gazed at her using all the pots and potions and creams that Quade never understood. Penny finished and sprayed more of her gorgeous perfume onto her neck. Quade just wanted to bury her face in Penny's neck and kiss her way down her beautiful throat.

"Can you unzip me, Sammy?"

Penny stood and waited. She had needed help getting into her dress, and needed it getting out.

When Quade didn't move from the bed, Penny turned around to look at her. "Sammy?"

Quade rubbed her hands together nervously. "You want me to…uh…?"

"Yes, please."

But Penny began to see the problem when she felt Quade's fingers on her neck. She had taken another step to a deeper intimacy without even noticing. Penny felt goosebumps erupt all down her arms as Quade's fingers traced her skin while the zip lowered.

Penny's heart started to thud and mirrored the familiar beat that began lower down. Quade's fingers lingered at the bottom of Penny's spine, and Penny stopped breathing.

Quade took a step closer and Penny felt her breath on her neck. "Shall I go and let you get changed?"

Quade was asking more than her words conveyed. She was giving Penny the choice without any pressure. Penny closed her eyes and allowed herself to enjoy the sensation of Quade's fingers caressing her back. She imagined turning around and letting her dress fall to her feet, and Quade's fingers touching her.

Was she ready?

She knew she would have her answer when she turned around and looked in Quade's eyes.

Penny turned and saw a mixture of love, adoration, and hunger in Quade's eyes.

Quade had courted her so slowly and simply, until Penny wasn't worried any more. She wanted Quade. She was ready.

Penny let her dress slip off as she'd imagined and said, "No, I don't want you to leave. I want you to stay."

Quade's eyes caressed her body, making her hot. Penny slipped off her tights, leaving her only in her bra and knickers.

She lifted Quade's hand and placed it on her chest. Quade still looked uncertain.

She's worried she might scare me off.

Penny never imagined she would be the one to initiate sex, but this was the way it had to be, to show Quade she wanted this.

She took Quade's hand and said, "Come to bed, Sammy."

They slipped under the covers and turned to face each other. Quade stroked the hair back from Penny's face.

"You know you don't need to do this, don't you?"

"Sammy, if I felt I had to do this, we wouldn't be in bed together. We're here because I trust you, because you respect me and never push me," Penny said.

"I just don't ever want you to feel worried when you're with me. You will tell me if you want to stop—"

Penny surprised herself by kissing Quade. She could think of no better way to show Quade what she wanted, and to make Quade relax. It was strange. After all this time of being afraid to let anyone in, now that she had built this trust, this secure feeling with Quade, she wasn't in the least bit worried. This was the moment she'd been waiting for her whole life.

Quade felt so tense that Penny stopped kissing her and said, "Tell me what you're thinking?"

She wanted to pinch herself to make sure this was really happening, and not just one of her many fantasies.

"Sammy, tell me," Penny repeated.

Quade took Penny's hand and kissed it. "I'm thinking that I've never felt so terrified, but never wanted something as much in my life."

"It's okay to feel that way. That's what you've told me the whole time you've courted me."

Quade stroked the hair from Penny's face. "Yeah, but I'm the one supposed to be confident for you. To make you feel safe."

"I always feel safe with you. Just touch me," Penny said.

When Penny kissed her again, Quade lost her anxiety. She rolled Penny onto her back and took control of the kiss.

Penny's hands grabbed for her T-shirt and pulled it off. "Let me feel you."

Quade pushed her head into the crook of Penny's neck as she had longed to and moaned when she inhaled Penny's perfume.

Was this really happening? Was she really touching and kissing the woman of her dreams? She enjoyed the sensation of

Penny sweeping her hands across her shoulders and teasing her by scratching her skin with those sexy nails of hers.

Quade was throbbing and wet already but her arousal grew when she felt Penny's hips rock against her thigh and heard her moan.

"Sammy? Wait," Penny said breathily.

Quade stopped, worried that she had upset Penny in some way. "I'm sorry. Did I—"

Penny took Quade's hand and brought it to her lips. "I had fantasies about these hands."

Quade was relieved she hadn't done something wrong. "You did? But they're rough, not soft like yours."

Penny took Quade's hand and placed it on her lace-covered breast.

"Oh God," Quade moaned. Quade's dreams never made her feel what this moment of reality did.

"I love them because they are rough, so different from me. I fantasized about your rough hands touching my breasts."

Quade just had to give Penny what she wanted. She reached around and, with some fumbling, unhooked Penny's bra.

Penny eased her arms out and Quade saw the breasts that she'd only imagined, that had teased her in those little tight T-shirts and low-necklined dresses.

Quade must have been taking too long because Penny grabbed Quade's hand and pushed it onto her breast.

She grasped it, and Penny arched her back and moaned. Quade paused and licked her lips. Her mouth watered at the sight of Penny's puckered hard nipples.

"God," Quade said as she closed her eyes and just allowed herself to feel. She was overwhelmed with the softness of Penny's breasts, such a contrast to her own hands.

Quade opened her eyes and saw pure lust in Penny's eyes. The realization that she could make Penny feel like this gave her a shot of confidence.

She lowered her lips to just inches from Penny's nipple and whispered, "You're so beautiful."

Penny moaned, then pushed Quade's lips onto her breast. Her first taste of Penny didn't sate her hunger but made her crave for more. She ran her tongue all around Penny's nipple, teasing and enjoying her first taste slowly.

"Suck it," Penny groaned.

It turned Quade on so much to hear Penny say something so sexual, so needy. Penny needed her, and she would give her exactly what she needed.

She sucked in Penny's hard nipple and rolled her tongue around it, while squeezing her other breast. Penny's hips started to move and thrust in response.

Quade was so wet and throbbing. Nothing had ever felt like this.

"Sammy"—Penny pushed down the band of Quade's boxers—"take them off."

Quade wriggled out of her boxers, and Penny kissed her deeply before saying, "Take mine off."

Quade smiled at her and kissed her way down her chest and stomach. She took her time to place lots of soft kisses on Penny's abdomen. She could feel Penny's muscles tense and Penny's thighs tightened around her upper body.

"Sammy?" Penny said desperately.

"I know." Quade understood her need and moved lower.

She kissed and softly bit Penny's sex through her panties. Quade saw how wet she was and groaned. She felt her own hips start to move and thrust into the bed below.

Penny raised up on her elbows and looked down at the erotic sight of Quade pulling off her underwear. She thought she might come as soon as Quade's tongue touched her if the feeling of her hands on her body was anything to go by.

Quade looked up at her and smiled before lowering her mouth on her sex. Penny slammed her head back on the pillow and groaned, "Jesus Christ," as Quade licked all around her clit.

She wondered why they hadn't been doing this for weeks. What a lot of time they had wasted, but then if they had, she wouldn't have this trust, this intimacy with Quade.

As Quade sucked and licked her clit, building Penny's orgasm, she felt an ache deep inside her, an ache to be filled.

"Sammy? Go inside."

Quade kissed her way back up her body, then caressed her cheek. "Are you sure?"

Penny's heart was filled with love at that moment. Only her Sammy would ask her that. She recognized that it was the most intimate thing Penny could share and wanted to make sure she was ready to share it.

"Yes. I'm sure." Penny kissed Quade's lips and tasted herself. It was such a turn on, and she quickly pushed Quade's hand down to her sex.

Quade stroked her fingers through Penny's wetness, and they both moaned. Penny loved the feel of Quade's reassuring weight on top of her, kissing her, loving her.

She felt Quade's touch tease her opening, threatening to slip inside, but not. This made Penny ache for it even more. Penny was so desperate, so full of emotion, all because of Quade's touch.

Penny pushed her thigh between Quade's legs and felt how turned on she was.

Quade pulled away from their kiss and said again, "Are you sure?"

Penny cupped Quade's face and said, "I never even knew I needed this, but I do. No one else ever made me feel this way. I need you inside me. I need to give you everything."

Quade didn't hesitate. She kissed her and put one finger inside of Penny at first, then two.

She could feel Quade's hesitation at her tightness. Penny had to reassure her. "I've dreamed of you doing this, being inside of me. Make me yours, Sammy."

Quade filled her, then stilled her hand, and Penny held Quade tightly, getting used to the feeling.

"Are you okay, sweetheart?"

"Yes, just go slowly," Penny said.

And she did. Quade went achingly slowly, taking the time to tease her clit and fuck her slowly, until Penny felt herself start to tremor. Quade was moaning too, thrusting against her thigh and letting Penny feel how near she was to coming.

"It's too much, Sammy," Penny said desperately.

Quade didn't stop thrusting but raised her head and looked into her eyes. "You're always safe with me, Penny. I love you."

The words *I love you* sent Penny over the edge. She arched her whole body up as the wave of orgasm washed like a torrent over her body. Her body was shaking as it came back down to earth. She felt Quade thrust erratically against her and shout out as her orgasm hit her.

They both lay there, breathing hard, a mess of sweaty limbs, and Penny felt like she'd found her home. The words that Quade had been brave enough to say ran in circles across her mind.

I love you.

CHAPTER TWENTY-ONE

Quade became aware of a tickling sensation on her face and felt a weight on her chest. She opened her eyes and saw Penny wrapped around her, skin to skin. The tickling was from Penny's beautiful hair draped across her face. She stroked the hair away and whispered, "It wasn't a dream."

Last night had been everything she'd ever dreamed of, and to wake up skin to skin with the woman she loved was more than she could have hoped for. The trust Penny had shown her was something she would never forget or take lightly.

Quade looked over to the bottom of the bed and saw Princess and Dougal had sneaked up during the night. Happy that everyone was content, she closed her eyes again, allowing herself the luxury of a longer sleep than normal. After about ten minutes, Penny moaned and went stiff as a board. Quade realized what was about to happen.

She sat up quickly just as Penny's limbs began to flail. "No, no. It's okay, sweetheart."

Quade sat against the headboard, and as she had done the first time, rested Penny's head against her chest, held her arms, and used her legs to keep Penny's under control. The dogs had jumped up and Princess was barking.

"It's okay, Princess. I'll take care of your mummy."

Quade kissed Penny's forehead and talked, so she hoped Penny knew she wasn't alone. "You're safe, Penny. You're safe with me."

Quade kept an eye on the time. If this went on for thirty minutes or more she would have to call for help. Then a thought occurred to Quade. This was exactly what Penny had described as her worry about letting someone into her private world. Penny feared sharing herself with someone and having a fit when she was at her most vulnerable.

Would this freak Penny out? Her worst fears had come true. She had made love for the first time and now this. All Quade could do was show her love and hope it didn't make Penny retreat into her shell of protection.

Quade kept reassuring Penny with gentle words and kisses, until the jerking of Penny's limbs slowed and stilled. Penny's eyes started to flicker open, and Quade stroked her face gently.

Quade understood this part was the most frightening part of the condition for Penny. She was unable to move as yet, her mind fuzzy and slow, and so very vulnerable. She held Penny tightly against her skin and gazed lovingly into Penny's eyes.

"You don't need to be scared, sweetheart. I'm here, and you'll always be safe with me. Trust me to look after you."

"Safe?" Penny managed to say.

"Always. I love you, Penny. I don't want you to feel pressured, but I love you, and I'll not let any harm come to you—ever."

Penny hugged Quade's pillow, inhaling the reassuring scent of strength and calm. After Penny settled down from her attack, Quade had gone to let the dogs outside and make some tea. She was feeling such a maelstrom of emotions that she needed to hold Quade's pillow close and try to calm her mind.

Last night Penny had overcome her anxieties and made love with Quade. It had been perfect, gentle loving, and then the next thing she knew, she was waking up after her epilepsy struck. It was what she'd always feared, having a fit when she was vulnerable, naked, and out of control.

Contrary to how she had always pictured it happening, except for the initial fear and dread when she opened her eyes, when she looked in Quade's eyes, felt their closeness, skin to skin, Penny felt safer than she ever had.

It was a revelation. At her most vulnerable, she'd experienced safety, not fear, and that was all because of Quade and the strength she gave her. Quade had said something she wasn't expecting to hear, last night and this morning.

She told Penny she loved her.

Penny hadn't mentioned it, and she was frightened to. She knew she had been falling in love for a while, but as she lay unable to move, unable to speak, looking up into Quade's eyes, she realized she was completely in love, head over heels, and that was scary.

It was something that, if she admitted it, Penny knew would change her life. Change wasn't something she liked. With her health so unpredictable, Penny clung to things staying the same.

She heard Quade walking upstairs and the sound of paws following her. A feeling of warmth at the simple domesticity of it spread through Penny. The sensation of love and safety made her greedy for more, but she had to work out how she could make her business empire work with country life, because as Bridge had said, Quade wasn't going anywhere.

When she got that worked out, she could tell Quade about the love in her heart, bursting to get out.

"Here we are. A nice cuppa tea will make you feel better," Quade said as she came through the door.

Penny tried to push herself up in the bed with her one good hand. Quade put the tray down and frowned.

"Hang on a second."

Quade got out one of her T-shirts and brought it to the side of the bed. "Slip yourself out and I'll help you put this on." Again Quade recognized her feeling of vulnerability after one of her attacks.

Penny sat on the side of the bed and said, "Most women wouldn't be encouraging me to put clothes on."

Quade crouched down. "I'm not most women. Put one hand up."

She held the T-shirt over Penny's head and helped her put her numb arm through the sleeve.

"No, you're not, are you?" How could Penny even be hesitating about this?

"I want you to feel comfortable, and never exposed. What you shared with me last night was so special, and I'm honoured you shared it with me, but this morning I have to take care of you."

"When I had my fit on that TV show, I'd never been more terrified in my life. It's one thing having your schoolmates pointing and laughing, but to have the whole world doing it is another thing altogether. I'd never felt so exposed, and after that I thought I had no chance of ever conquering my fears. But this morning when I woke from my fit, I wasn't scared. I've never felt so safe in my life feeling your body against mine," Penny said.

Quade cupped Penny's cheeks and smiled at her. "That means more to me than anything. I will always keep you safe, sweetheart. I love you."

Penny gulped hard. There it was again. *I love you.* But could Penny say it back?

She opened her mouth—then leaned in for a kiss instead.

CHAPTER TWENTY-TWO

A week later Penny was feeling herself again. She and Quade had spent all their time together but hadn't made love again because Penny was recovering, but Penny hoped they could explore more on this weekend away together.

Penny was waiting with Princess and her bags at the front door of the cottage. Quade had teased her she wouldn't be ready to leave on time, so she had to prove her wrong.

Penny took out her phone and pressed record. "Hi, friends. I'm heading back to London today for a book signing on Monday. I'll put the details below and hope to see you there. Oh, and guess who's coming with Princess and me?" Penny winked at the camera and stopped it.

"That should make them excited, poppet."

Quade's Land Rover drove in and Penny felt butterflies in her stomach. A whole weekend with just Quade. Her parents were going to love her.

Penny walked over with Princess to meet Quade as she got out of the car. Princess jumped all over Quade.

"Hey," Penny said in mock annoyance. "I get my kisses first, Princess."

Quade laughed and pulled Penny into a kiss. "Don't worry, sweetheart. I've got more than enough for you."

Penny frowned and grasped Quade's red tie. "I thought I told you, you didn't have to wear a shirt and tie?"

Quade was wearing the same clothes she had the first time they had dinner together—a red tie, checked shirt, and brown suit jacket.

"I can't meet your parents looking like I've just come out of the fields," Quade said.

Penny had sensed Quade's nerves building up over the last few days. To Penny her family was normal, but she understood the gravitas the Huntingdon-Stewart name had to others.

Penny took Quade's hands. "Listen, Sammy. They are going to love you. Mum and Dad aren't grand—they are very ordinary people."

"I think they'd want you to bring home a banker, a politician, or a scientist."

"Mum was over the moon when I told her I was bringing you home. I've never brought anyone home before, and she'd be horrified if I brought a banker or a politician home. Remember, Mum is a campaigner for justice and equal rights. She's not some stuffy high society woman."

"Okay. I'm just nervous. It's not every day you meet a family you studied in history class at school," Quade said.

Penny smiled. "Were you nervous when you met me?"

"Amongst other things. We better get going. I dropped Dougal off with Riley on my way here."

"I still think we should have taken him with us. He'll miss Princess," Penny said.

"He'll have a great time with Riley and Caesar. I have enough to be nervous about without worrying about what Dougal's up to."

"Okay." Penny took the keys to her Ferrari out of her handbag. "Here you go. The keys to my other baby."

"Are you sure you trust me?" Quade joked.

"Of course I do, silly."

"You get in and I'll get the bags," Quade said.

Once they were packed up, Quade got in the driver's seat and simply gazed at the gorgeous interior. "This is a beautiful piece of machinery. Can I ask you something?"

"Anything," Penny said.

"Why do you have a car when you can't drive, and why a car like this?"

Penny let out a sigh and stroked Princess's ears. "I've never told anyone this, but when I found out I couldn't have a driving license, it felt like epilepsy was taking one more part of normal life from me. I vowed that one day I'd make enough money to buy my own car and have a driver. I wasn't going to let it beat me."

"I can understand that," Quade said.

"And why this car? It's a symbol of my success, or should I say *was* a symbol." Penny turned and smiled at Quade. "You've shown me there are a lot of better ways to live a successful life, but buying this car made me feel I'd made it. I could have bought it with the trust fund I got when I was twenty-one, but I wanted to make my own money and buy it. I didn't have advanced degrees like my brother and sister, but this to me showed I'd made my own way in life."

"You don't need things to show that you are a success, sweetheart, but I get it. Here's hoping I don't crash the bloody thing. I'm more used to tractors."

Penny laughed. "Let's get going."

"Okay, here goes." Quade turned on the engine.

Penny leaned over to put her bag in the back seat and saw a crate of vegetables.

"Why did you bring the vegetables?" Penny asked.

"A present for your parents. I thought they would like some farm-fresh veg."

Penny kissed her on the cheek. "That was a kind thought. They are really going to love you."

"Well, here we are," Penny said.

They'd arrived at Penny's family home in London. Quade had been quiet since they'd arrived. She felt more than overwhelmed as she drove into the area where the Huntingdon-Stewarts lived, but when she finally arrived outside their mansion, her stomach was tied in knots.

How could she ever fit in as Penny's partner? Would her parents think Quade was a gold-digger?

"It's very grand," Quade said.

"I've never really thought about it." Penny pointed up to the front door. "Look, Mrs. Parson is waiting for us."

Quade looked to the door and saw a tall, angular looking woman with bobbed hair, wearing a long black skirt and white blouse.

"Who's Mrs. Parson?"

"Our housekeeper since before I was born. She's like a second mother to me. Let's grab your veggie box and get inside."

Quade got out, straightened her tie, and buttoned her jacket. She felt like she should be using the servants' entrance to this place.

She got the box and followed Penny up the stairs to the front door. Penny fell into Mrs. Parson's arms.

"Ms. Pen, so good to see you. You look very healthy." Mrs. Parson kissed Penny's head.

"It's the country air. Let me introduce my—"

Quade held her breath while Penny paused, apparently considering the right word.

"My girlfriend, Sam McQuade."

Penny smiled at her, and Quade's heart soared. *My girlfriend.*

"Nice to meet you, Mrs. Parson," Quade said.

Mrs. Parson looked her up and down silently, and Quade wished she'd had something smarter to wear.

"Good morning, Ms. McQuade. I've heard good things about you and your farm."

"You have?" Quade looked at Penny.

"I do phone home, you know." Penny smiled, then pointed to Quade's veggie box. "Look what Quade brought from her farm, Mrs. Parson. Fresh organic vegetables."

Mrs. Parson smiled broadly. "Wonderful. Thank you, Ms. McQuade."

"Please, call me Quade or Sam."

"In you come then. I'll get Mr. Parson to get your bags," Mrs. Parson said.

What was Mr. Parson? A butler? She really was stepping into a different world.

When they walked into the entrance hallway, Quade was overawed. It was certainly not an Axedale Hall, but it was very grand indeed. A grand staircase faced her and led up to many floors of rooms, Quade suspected. Above her head was a large sparkling chandelier, and paintings of some very imposing figures hung on the walls.

"I'll take you up to your rooms. Your mother and father will be returning home shortly," Mrs. Parson said.

Penny gave Quade a panicked look and grasped Mrs. Parson's arm. "Two rooms? We had hoped that—"

Mrs. Parson smiled mischievously. "I didn't say that two rooms had to be occupied."

❖

Penny watched with happiness as her father and Quade engaged in relaxed conversation. She'd felt Quade's tension and nervousness all morning, but as soon as her parents got home and they met Quade, they immediately put her at her ease. They were enjoying tea and cakes in the drawing room, and her father was picking Quade's brain about his vegetable garden.

Penny's mother Lavinia sat beside her on the couch. "Sam is very nice, Pen. Guy seems to have taken to her right away."

"She's perfect, Mummy. Since I went to the country and met her, I've changed so much."

"In what way, Pen?" Lavinia asked.

Penny leaned her head on her mother's shoulder. "She makes me want to live my life in the real world, away from my online world, away from business."

"And could you make a life in Axedale? I presume Sam can't move to the city," Lavinia said.

"No, she can't. She has a lot of responsibilities in Axedale. I need to work out if I can make our two worlds mix," Penny said.

"I never thought I'd hear you talk like this. You're in love with her, aren't you?"

Penny sat up quickly. "How did you know?"

Lavinia smiled. "I know my Little Pen."

"Yes, I love her. She's so gentle, so old-fashioned, in a sweet way. She takes her time, never rushing me. I feel safe with her. Sammy made me feel safer than I ever have after…"

Penny's voice died away realizing she'd said too much.

Lavinia put her tea down on the side table. "Have you had any fits while you've been in the country? Tell me the truth, Pen."

Her father and Quade looked over after hearing Lavinia raise her voice.

Penny had to be honest. "I've had two incidents, but Quade was there for both and made me feel safe."

Quade smiled, and Penny gazed lovingly back at her. She had to tell Quade how much she loved her.

After a lovely dinner and evening with her parents, Penny and Quade went upstairs. Penny couldn't wait to get Quade on her own. She wanted to pick up where they left off the first time they made love and show Quade how much she loved her.

Quade had been a bit reticent to share a bed in her parents' house, but Penny sent her off to her room to get changed and told her she expected Quade back soon.

Penny looked through her nightwear, and her first instinct had been to wear the sheerest, sexiest lingerie she had, but then Penny remembered Quade's long-ago reaction to her little sleep shorts and unicorn pyjama top.

Penny picked up her pyjamas. "Cute and sexy it is."

She got changed and lay waiting on the bed for some time. Penny took her medications, then checked her social media accounts and her emails. They were going to have a busy day tomorrow. After some computer shopping, they were meeting Olivia for lunch, then having dinner themselves back here. Her mother and father had a dinner engagement, so they would enjoy some alone time.

Penny hoped Quade and Olivia would get on okay. Quade would be friendly to anyone, but Olivia could be a bit snooty.

After thirty minutes of waiting, Penny lost patience and texted Quade.

Get in here now, Sexy Farmer xx

A minute or so later she heard slow, creaking footsteps coming along the landing. Penny grinned and walked over to the door, so she'd be behind it when it opened.

The door opened slowly, and Quade popped her head in gingerly. Penny jumped out on her.

Quade jumped in shock. "Jesus Christ. Don't do that."

Penny laughed and put her arms around Quade's neck. "Did you think it would be my father with his shotgun?"

Quade shut the bedroom door and wrapped her arms around Penny's waist. "It makes me feel like a naughty teenager sneaking into my girlfriend's bedroom."

"Oh, exciting." Penny started kissing Quade's lips and face.

Quade had to say this before she got lost in a haze of lust. "Are you sure your parents won't mind me staying in your room?"

Penny stopped her kisses and sighed. "You really are old-fashioned, aren't you? My parents are very modern. Mummy comes to London Pride every year. I'm sure she wouldn't mind. Besides, they both love you."

"They do?" Quade said with surprise.

"Yes, Daddy really bonded with you when you went to see his vegetable garden, and Mummy loves you, because you've looked after me in Axedale, and they love the respect you've shown me. So can we get back to the kissing part? There's so much I want to explore with you."

Quade grinned and carried her over to the bed. "I think we've created a sex monster."

Penny laughed, snapped off the lamp, and began to pull off Quade's T-shirt. Quade lay back on the bed and pulled Penny with her. She gazed at Penny and ran her hands up and down Penny's thighs, each time getting higher underneath those little cute sleep shorts.

"You know, the first time I saw you wearing this, my tongue was hanging out, and my brain turned to mush."

Penny chuckled. "That's why I'm wearing it, silly." Quade groaned when Penny scratched her nails over her shoulders and over her chest. "I love your shoulders and arms. They're so strong."

"Why am I the only one half naked?" Quade said.

Penny smiled and pulled off her top. Quade's hands went immediately to her breasts, and Penny leaned over to kiss her. Quade deepened the kiss and tried to roll Penny over, but she sat up and said, "No, let me have some fun."

Penny's fun could only be good. "You can do whatever you want, as long as it's with me."

Penny gave her a lingering kiss. "Always." Then she began to kiss down her body until she reached her Jockey shorts.

"Oh God." Quade groaned when she realized where Penny was headed. Quade was so turned on, and throbbing for Penny's touch. The thought of Penny's mouth on her was overwhelming.

Penny pulled off her underwear and threw it to the side.

The very first sensation of Penny's gorgeous hair brushing against her inner thighs made Quade nearly come on the spot. Then she felt Penny's mouth sucking her in. "Fuck."

She put her hand on the back of Penny's head, holding her in place and encouraging her pace. There wasn't a sight like seeing Penny between her legs sucking her, her head bobbing up and down erotically.

It didn't take long before Quade's orgasm crashed over her, and she shouted into the pillow, hoping not to make too much noise.

Penny climbed up her body smiling. "Was that okay?"

"You're a naughty girl—you know it was. I think I blew a few blood vessels. Come here." Quade pulled Penny closer and kissed her.

Penny ran her tongue across Quade's lips, teasing her by dipping in and out of Quade's mouth. By the noises Quade was making now, like the ones she'd made when Penny was going down on her, Penny was sure she was enjoying it.

Quade pushed her back so she was sitting on her stomach. "I can feel how wet you are. How much you need to come."

Penny closed her eyes and groaned when Quade slipped her fingers into her sex and stroked her clit. This position was so good. She could thrust and move her hips as much as she wanted and have her hands free.

She thrust backward and forward over Quade's stomach and squeezed her own breasts. "You feel so good, baby," Penny moaned.

"You're so beautiful, Penny," Quade said.

Every time Penny thrust her hips, she tried to move Quade's fingers closer to her opening. She was beginning to understand her body and that she was really turned on by penetration and had a deep need to be filled by Quade.

"Baby, go inside," she pleaded.

"I love to be inside you, sweetheart." Quade pushed inside her and stilled, allowing her to get used to the feeling. It wasn't uncomfortable this time, and she loved the fact that she could control the pace and depth, as she lifted and lowered herself on Quade's fingers.

Penny lost herself in the feeling, thrusting on Quade's fingers. She got faster and faster, as her orgasm raced upon her. She felt Quade's other hand squeeze her breast, and her thumb graze her nipple.

She couldn't hold out any longer and as her orgasm hit, she leaned over and kissed Quade, so she wouldn't scream.

Penny collapsed on top of Quade, her breathing wildly out of control. "That was so good, Sammy."

Quade held her tight and kissed her head. "So good."

Once Penny had calmed, she lay beside Quade, drawing circles on Quade's stomach.

"I think we've definitely created a monster," Quade joked.

Penny chuckled. "I've repressed my sexual side so long, that now I've found you, I just can't get enough."

"I won't argue with that," Quade said.

Penny leaned up on her elbow and looked down at Quade with a smile. "There's so much I want to explore with you."

"Explore *A* to *Z*, no doubt?" Quade said.

Penny gave her a mischievous smile and said, "Let's start with *S*."

Quade scrunched up her eyebrows. "*S*? What does *S* stand for, apart from sex?"

"You'll see." Penny laughed.

Chapter Twenty-three

Penny couldn't think of a happier morning she'd had. She woke in Quade's arms and couldn't help but kiss and make love to Quade again. Now she had broken the icy walls that had blocked her all these years, she just couldn't get enough of Quade. She felt compelled to touch her, like an addiction.

After a nice breakfast with her parents, they went computer shopping, and Quade bought a laptop and a tablet. Penny was bringing Quade into the twenty-first century. It was such a liberating feeling to walk around the London shops holding Quade's hand, feeling proud that Quade was with her. Penny dragged her to a few more shops, one of which made Quade blush adorably.

As they spent more time together, Penny realized she didn't want to spend time apart from her lover. Ideas were constantly going around her head of how she could merge her business life with Axedale.

By lunchtime they were both ravenous for food. But Quade's heart sank when she realized Olivia had picked a clean eating vegan restaurant. She would have overlooked this if she had thought it was just to please Penny, but when she met Olivia and saw her false smile, and felt her forceful handshake, she was sure it was meant to annoy her, to annoy the cattle farmer.

Olivia was the complete opposite of her in a way. She could tell by her handshake and her stare that she had a strong alpha personality, but she wasn't butch in any sense of the word. She was feminine, with shoulder-length brown hair, wearing a designer business suit with a short skirt, but as hard as nails, Quade could tell.

Quade always tried to see the best in people, but the way Olivia looked at her, like she was so far beneath both Penny and Olivia, she was sure she didn't like her one bit. She felt awkward sitting eating lunch, so Quade decided to excuse herself and let the two friends talk. She had something in mind she wanted to buy anyway.

Once coffee had been served, Quade turned to Penny. "Why don't I go and get some of the things you wanted for dinner and let you two talk business?"

Penny looked unsure. "You don't have to."

"It's okay." Quade kissed her and said, "You talk, I'll have a look around the shops. Give me a text when you're ready to go."

"Okay then. We won't be long," Penny said holding on to her hand.

"I'll get the bill on the way out," Quade said.

"No need, Quade," Olivia said with a smirk. "It's my treat and already taken care of."

Quade didn't like the idea of someone else paying for her girlfriend's meal, but she just let it go. "Thank you. See you both later."

When Quade left the table, Olivia said, "So this is real?"

"What?" Penny said.

"This thing with Sexy Farmer."

Olivia managed to say *Sexy Farmer* with displeasure in her voice. "Her name is Quade, Olivia, and yes, it's real. We're together."

Olivia leaned across the table and said in a low voice, "I thought this kind of thing wasn't something you wanted. That's what you kept telling me, anyway."

Suddenly the penny dropped. She knew Olivia had a crush on her since they were at school, and Olivia had tried to make advances a few times, but when she'd explained a relationship wasn't something she wanted to explore, Olivia backed off. Now, Olivia was jealous.

"Quade helped me. She was kind and patient, and she really cares about me."

Olivia took her hand. "I could have been patient, Pen. You know how I've always felt about you. I know you've had your insecurities, but we could—"

Penny pulled her hand away. "I'm with Quade, Olivia. She makes me feel safe and loved, and I've fallen in love with her."

Olivia looked shocked. "You, in love? You've run from love your whole life, Pen."

Penny was getting angry at Olivia's assessment of her. "I obviously hadn't met the right person."

That comment appeared to sting Olivia. "I'm sure your parents aren't too pleased. I hardly think a farmer is an ideal addition to the Huntingdon-Stewart name, and if she were any more butch she'd be—"

"Don't even finish that sentence," Penny said angrily. "For your information, Olivia, Mummy and Daddy love her, and maybe I won't be a Huntingdon-Stewart forever."

Penny couldn't believe what she had just said out loud. It was intended to annoy Olivia but surprisingly the thought of becoming something other than a Huntingdon-Stewart was so attractive. How could she contemplate changing her life and being Penny McQuade when she couldn't even say I love you?

Olivia got out her briefcase, clearly still annoyed, and said, "Well this Sexy Farmer stuff has been good for business, and I have some good news for you."

"What good news?" Penny asked.

Olivia took out a folder and pushed it over the table. "Your dream."

"My dream?" Penny opened the folder and her heart nearly stopped when she saw a contract.

"The American TV deal. The Foodie channel want twenty-two episodes of *Penny's American Kitchen,* and they'll tie in a distribution deal with the large supermarkets for your food range. Penny's Kitchen will be truly international. Congratulations."

Penny's hands shook holding the contract. It was what her whole life had been leading up to. If she signed this contract, she would have made it despite all her physical problems.

Her elation then sank like a stone when Olivia said, "They want you in the States in a month's time for preproduction meetings."

Sammy. She'd never imagined her dream being offered to her on a plate would cause her such dread.

Quade finished her last few bites and put her cutlery down on her plate. She and Penny were enjoying a quiet meal together in the kitchen. Penny's mother and father were out for the evening, giving them time on their own.

"You know, I think I'm actually getting used to these weird vegetables. What was this?"

"What, sorry?" Penny said.

"The vegetables. What were they?"

"Oh, pan-fried Brussels sprouts with chilli and garlic," Penny said.

Quade felt there was something wrong. Something was worrying Penny. "Are you okay, sweetheart? You've been a bit distracted since we got back here."

Penny smiled. "I'm fine. I miss Axedale. I miss Dougal and our friends."

"That's nice to know." Quade was delighted to hear Penny was feeling so fond of Axedale. Her fear had been that coming back to London would remind her of her exciting city life.

Quade looked to the small basket in the corner of the kitchen and saw Princess sleeping quietly. She missed Dougal a lot, and so did Quade.

Penny got up and cleared the table and put all the dishes in the dishwasher.

"What are you going to call her?" Quade indicated the large stuffed unicorn sitting in one of the dining chairs. That was what she wanted to buy while Penny and Olivia were talking business. She tracked one down in a large toyshop. She felt a bit daft buying it but if it made Penny smile, it was worth it, and it had, and got her lots of kisses.

"Hmm...Truffle." Penny smiled.

Truffle the unicorn? Quade hoped no one found out about this, but she just said, "Great name."

Penny walked over to Quade and sat astride her lap. Quade slipped her hand under Penny's skirt and gently stroked her thigh. She felt Penny shiver and goosebumps erupt on her skin. She was amazed that she could have this effect on someone as beautiful as Penny.

Penny cupped Quade's face with her hands. "I miss being with you in Axedale, with no business to do, no fans to meet, just you, me, and only what we choose to share online."

"We're going back on Monday night. We'll be alone again soon." Penny studied her eyes, as if there was a lot going through her mind. "Penny, are you sure—"

Penny silenced her with a kiss, then pulled back quickly. "You wore it?"

Penny was talking about the strap-on they had bought earlier today. Quade had been so embarrassed even walking into the shop, but Penny took it in her stride, dragged her in by the hand, and was comfortable looking around and talking about the different kinds at length to the shop assistant. For someone who was new to sex, Penny was doing really well.

Quade was so sheltered in her closed country world, she'd had no idea these things even existed. She liked the idea when Penny suggested it, and when she had put it on earlier, she really got to like it. It made her feel sexy, confident, and ready for whatever Penny had in mind.

"You told me to. Isn't it what you want?" Quade asked.

Penny cupped her cheeks and breathed, "I want you to touch me, Sammy."

Their lips came together and Penny dug her nails into the back of Quade's neck. The kisses soon became frantic, and Quade stood, lifting Penny with her. Penny let her legs fall and she stood by the table, pulling Quade to her.

"Let's not go upstairs. Let's stay here."

Penny didn't give her a chance to reply. She kissed her frantically and pushed her hands under her T-shirt, scratching her with those nails that drove her crazy.

Quade loved this woman so much. She seemed to instinctively know how to touch her, make her feel good about herself, which was proven when Penny rubbed her strap-on. Quade could have never imagined that something not part of her could feel connected to her, but it did, and when Penny touched her there, it was like she was touching her clit.

She was on fire and pushed Penny back onto the table and pushed up her dress. She went straight to Penny's sex and found she was so ready for her.

"You're dripping wet." Quade groaned.

"For you, baby. You're all I've ever wanted," Penny said.

Quade was about to question again if Penny was okay. She'd seemed to have something on her mind all night, but Penny kissed her and started to unbutton her jeans and pushed them down her hips. She couldn't think any more, so she just went along with what Penny wanted.

She pulled off Penny's underwear, and Penny released her strap-on. Penny looked at her like she wanted to devour her. She rubbed and squeezed the strap-on for a minute, and Quade loved the feel of her touching it.

"I want you, baby," Penny said. "I just want to be as close to you as I can."

Quade nodded and pulled Penny closer to the edge of the table. She held the head of the cock at her entrance and said, "Yes?"

Penny rested her forehead against Quade's. "Yes."

Quade eased the tip in and Penny gasped. "Are you all right?"

"Yes, it's big, but it feels good," Penny said.

Quade rocked her hips and eased in a little bit more each time, so as not to hurt her lover. Penny held tight around her neck, and rested her forehead against Quade's, keeping them connected.

Soon she was in all the way, and they both gasped. Penny hooked her legs around hers, locking them in a tight embrace. Quade rocked slowly, in no hurry to get to their destination. This felt like nothing else. Being inside Penny like this was closer than she had ever felt to another human being. She felt so connected, emotionally as well as physically.

Quade fucked Penny slowly for the longest time, giving her what she needed, but as Penny's gasps and moans got louder, Quade's thrusts got faster, until Penny looked right into her eyes and said four words that nearly made Quade's heart explode.

"I love you, Sammy."

Penny dug her nails into her neck and Quade pushed her head into Penny's neck, thrusting wildly as she came.

"I love you, I'll love you always," Quade shouted out.

Penny loved her. Penny actually loved her. She was the luckiest person in the world.

Chapter Twenty-four

The next morning a limousine was sent to pick Penny up for the book signing. As soon as Quade got into the car with Penny, she felt out of place. Flash cars and book signings weren't her.

"Are you sure I should be going to this, Penny? I'll get in the way," Quade said.

"Of course you won't be in the way. You'll be there for me. I need you."

Quade had noticed Penny had been very tactile since they got back yesterday. As if she was frightened she would disappear. Perhaps it was because she told Quade she loved her.

Quade got a warm glow every time she thought about what Penny had said for the first time last night. To have someone who actually loved her was a dream come true, but to have Penny, her perfect woman, the woman she loved with all her heart, return that love was more than a dream. She was the luckiest person alive.

"I'm sure Olivia doesn't want me there," Quade said.

"Olivia doesn't get a say in my life." Penny was serious all of a sudden.

Quade turned around to face her girlfriend. "Penny, Olivia—"

"Besides," Penny interrupted her, "my fans will get such a kick out of seeing you."

They arrived at the bookshop and Quade saw a line of people from the front door, right along the building, and around the corner.

"Wow, you really are popular," Quade said.

Penny smiled and kissed her on the cheek. "I think some of them are here to see you too."

Quade stood behind Penny as she signed books. She had offered to get out of the way, but Penny insisted she stay right by her side. Quade didn't mind, but she felt particularly embarrassed when women looked at her, giggled, and asked for a selfie with her.

It was strange as well to watch her Penny be Penelope Huntingdon-Stewart. She was very different to the woman who said she loved her.

Penny turned to Quade and said, "Baby, could you ask Olivia to have some more books put out?"

"Okay."

Quade looked around the shop floor and saw Olivia talking to a member of staff by a book display on the other side of the room. Lots of eyes followed her as she walked past the line of fans.

"Hey, Sexy Farmer. If Penny's not enough for you, come and see me," one woman said, and then the others next to her giggled.

Quade felt the heat spread across her cheeks. She wasn't used to being the centre of attention—or female attention, more to the point.

As she got closer, Olivia put on what was clearly a false smile. Probably because of who she was—just a farmer. It became clearer every day how different Penny's life was to hers. Penny's family had been so welcoming, but it was hard to forget the social differences between them.

Olivia's false smile was testament to that. "Olivia, Penny thinks she's going to need some more books shortly."

Olivia turned to the bookshop staff member beside her. "Could you take care of that for us, Jamie?"

Once he left Olivia said, "I was hoping I'd get a chance to talk to you on our own. A bit of a chin wag, you know?"

Why Olivia wanted to talk to her she could not imagine. "Oh, okay."

"I wanted to thank you for coming along today. This whole Sexy Farmer thing has really magnified the interest in Penny at the moment, and she really needed it after the live TV debacle. Fitting on live TV did terrible things to her brand."

Quade liked Olivia even less now. To reduce Penny's suffering and embarrassment to a debacle, to something hurting Penny's brand, made Quade really angry.

"Olivia, I don't think—"

"Yes, that's why Pen went to the country, to repair the damage that had been caused. When she first posted that video of you showing her how to make a fire, the IT team saw a huge spike in interest. I said to Pen, get this new friend of yours into as many of your pictures, blogs, and videos as you can. It's a good gimmick."

"Gimmick?" Quade couldn't believe what she was hearing. Quade's mind was racing. This couldn't be right. Olivia had advised Penny to get close to her? Not Penny, she wouldn't do that. But the seeds of doubt were sown.

She looked over to the table where Penny was signing books. She wasn't the Penny that Quade knew in front of these people. Could what they had really be an illusion? When Quade thought back to when they first got closer as friends, Penny had seemed to change overnight from hostile to friendly.

When Quade didn't continue, Olivia said, "Oh, I'm sorry. Have I said something wrong? You didn't really think that you and Penny had something between you, did you?" Olivia laughed. "Oh dear, oh dear. She has gotten you to believe, hasn't she? Pen would do anything for business, honestly."

Quade rounded angrily on Olivia. "You have no idea of what we've shared with each other. I don't believe you."

Olivia sighed and opened her briefcase. "Quade, don't be a fool all your life. Read this."

Quade read over the front page of a contract for a TV show in America. She felt like she had been kicked in the guts.

"Preproduction starts in one month. She'll be over there for at least two years to get her brand going."

Quade looked up from the contract and looked again at Penny. "When did Penny find out about this?"

"Yesterday when you left us at lunch. You were a means to an end, Quade. Nothing more."

Penny knew this when they made love last night, when Penny told her she loved her. Everything fell into place. It was all a lie. Quade's heart shattered into a million little pieces, and all the air was stolen from her lungs.

Olivia patted her on the shoulder and said, "Did you ever really think, deep down, that you were in her league?"

"No," Quade said honestly.

She couldn't breathe. She had to get out of here. Quade slammed the contract in Olivia's chest and left.

A few hours later Penny finally got down to the last person in the line. She signed the book and said, "Thank you. I hope you enjoy it."

Olivia approached her with a big smile on her face. "Well done. Everyone had a great time."

Penny stretched her arms and yawned. She couldn't wait to get back to Axedale with Quade and have a quiet night.

"Have you seen Quade?" After sending her to talk to Olivia, she hadn't seen her since.

"No, she just went out for a breath of air and I haven't seen her since."

She got out her mobile and called Quade's phone, but it just went to voicemail. Penny started to have a bad feeling inside.

She called her parents' house and Mrs. Parson answered. "Hello? It's Penny. Is Quade back at the house, Mrs. Parson?"

"She is, but she's packing up her belongings. She looks upset."

Penny's eyes sought out Olivia who was talking to someone a few yards away. *What have you done, Olivia?*

"Thanks, Mrs. Parson. I'll see you later."

She hung up and walked over to Olivia. "Could I have a moment with my business partner?" They were soon left alone. "What did you say to Quade?"

Olivia furrowed her brow. "What are you talking about? She went out to get a breath of air, I told you."

"But why did she leave, Olivia? Mrs. Parson says that she's at my parents' house packing. She isn't doing that for nothing. I asked her to find you, and the next thing I know, she's left me. So tell me what you said. Now," Penny demanded.

Olivia sighed. "Just a few home truths."

"And what were those?"

"That she was very good to help rebuild your brand after everything that happened, and that I advised you to get close to her, to exploit the interest in you both, and you did. Also that you were going to America. I showed her the contract and told her I told you about it yesterday. It was only fair to put her out of her misery. It was never going to be the romance of the century. Not with you in America and her farming cows in Kent."

Penny clasped her hands to her mouth. *Sammy knows I knew last night, when I told her I loved her.* Oh my God. What had she done? Penny shook her head in shock.

"It's only business, Pen. You're leaving, and this little fling was in the way," Olivia tried to explain.

"This wasn't business, Olivia. This was jealousy. I have waited all these years to find someone who I could love and enjoy a normal relationship with, and you have destroyed my chance."

Olivia looked very worried all of a sudden and reached out to touch her. "Pen, I—"

"Don't touch me. Even if you were the last woman on earth, Olivia, I wouldn't be with you. You're not my type. You never, ever were, and I've tried to tell you that gently over the years, but now the gloves are off. I will never, ever forgive you for this."

Penny grabbed her bag and ran out into the street, tears flowing down her cheeks. She was in a panic. Some of her fans were gathered outside and pulled their phones out to video her. Yet again she had made a public spectacle of herself, and maybe lost the love of her life.

People were right to laugh at her. She was a joke.

Penny flagged down a taxi and headed back to her parents' as quickly as she could.

❖

Mrs. Parson told Penny that Quade was in the garden. She ran out and found her by her father's vegetable garden.

In the taxi on the way home she thought of lots of things she wanted to say, but now that she was here standing just behind her, everything vanished, and her mouth dried up.

Quade must have sensed her presence because she said, "Your father will need to get his gardener to separate this mint plant or it'll take over."

"I don't want to talk about mint, Sammy. What Olivia told you, Sammy—she's just jealous. She's been interested in me since school, but I never took her interest seriously. It's all lies, you have to believe me."

Quade stood and brushed her hands on her jeans. "I know she's jealous. I knew as soon as we met at the restaurant."

"You believe me then? I promise all that rubbish about using you for publicity—it's not true, it's all lies."

Quade turned and said, "It hurt so much to hear someone telling me those things. I was angry and hurt, but by the time I got back here, my head cleared. I knew it wasn't all true."

"What do you mean not *all* true? None of it is. I love you, Sammy."

"Really? What about America?" Quade said.

Penny's heart sank. She lowered her head, unsure how to explain herself.

"You knew about that for a while. You knew when we made love last night, when you told me you loved me. Why didn't you tell me?" Quade said.

Penny knew she had been wrong. It was true, but how could she explain? "I wanted to gather my thoughts, process it before I talked to you about it."

"You thought about it, Penny, and that means you are considering it, which means you were never committed enough to our relationship."

Penny was panicking now. "No, I wasn't, Sammy—"

Quade touched Penny's cheek and wiped away a tear. "Listen, Penny, I realize now that this relationship was always doomed to fail. Your heart would never quite be fully in Axedale, and I'd be holding you back to expect that. Penelope Huntingdon-Stewart was never going to be a farmer's wife."

This couldn't be happening. But she could see Quade's shutters had gone up. She was going to walk away from her.

"That's not true. Give me a chance to explain, Sammy."

Quade gulped hard, then gave her a forced smile. "You don't need to. Olivia was right about one thing—I was never in your league. Go and chase your dreams, Penny. Good luck in America."

She gave her a chaste kiss on the lips, then walked back towards the house.

What have I done. I can't lose the love of my life without a fight.

How could she prove to Quade what Olivia had told her about their relationship wasn't true, and that her heart was in Axedale?

"Think, Penny. Think."

Penny's phone beeped with an email from her IT team about her website, and then the answer hit her. Business had always driven her, and business could make her dreams come true.

CHAPTER TWENTY-FIVE

The gloom of the evening was settling on the grounds of the Axedale estate as Quade leaned on the fence, looking over the alpaca pen. Knowing her farm was being taken care of, she walked straight from the train station to Axedale to pick up Dougal from Riley. She managed to avoid questions from Harry and Annie since Riley was there, and went on her way, but as she walked away from the front entrance, going back to her farmhouse lost its appeal.

Her farmhouse had gone from a lonely place to one full of laughter and love since Penny had come into her life, and now all of that was gone. It had all been an unattainable dream. So she found herself walking over to the alpaca pen, while Dougal trotted around.

One of the friendliest alpacas, who Riley had annoyingly called Doris, came over to the fence for some attention. When she was feeding them, Quade didn't half feel a fool shouting for Doris. She patted her nose.

"Evening, Doris. I wish all I had to worry about was when my next feed was coming."

"Talking to the animals now, Quade?" a voice said behind her. It was Annie.

Quade tried her best to smile. "Sometimes animals make more sense to me than humans."

Annie leaned against the fence and said, "Harry and Riley are planning medieval day for the millionth time, so I thought I'd come out and visit the girls."

Annie didn't ask, but Quade knew she wanted her to talk about Penny. "I don't really want to talk, Annie."

"Would you rather talk to Harry or Finn?" Annie asked.

"No, I feel like enough of a fool as it is," Quade said.

"Surely it's something that can be fixed. I know how much Penny cares about you."

"Do you really?" Quade said sharply. "I'm sorry, I'm sorry. I don't mean that."

"That's all right. Quade, whatever's happened between you two, let Penny have a chance to talk to you. I nearly lost Harry because I wouldn't give her another chance."

"Penny's going to America. She's leaving and I'm not going to stand in her way."

She saw realization hit Annie. "I'm sorry, Quade."

"Yeah, well. She was never going to be a farmer's wife, was she?" Quade pushed herself back from the fence. "I'll be off."

Back to reality. Back to the loneliness of the farmhouse.

Two days later Penny's driver drove her back to Axedale. It had been torture staying away so long, leaving Quade thinking the worst of her, but if she wanted to convince Quade where her heart truly lay, she needed time.

By the time she arrived at Quade's farm, it was five o'clock. Quade would probably be back in the cottage by now. Her driver stopped at the bottom of Quade's drive and said, "Are you sure you don't want me to leave the car, Ms. Penny? I can get the train back."

Penny let Princess out of the car and gathered up her briefcase. "That's okay. Just drop my bags off at the cottage and take it back to my parents' house. I won't be needing it again—I hope."

She walked up the drive, and as she breathed in the country air she began to relax. Axedale was the home she'd always been looking for, and she hadn't even known it.

When she arrived at the farmhouse door, she took a breath and knocked at the door, but nobody answered.

"Maybe she's out in the fields, Princess."

But then she heard a bark and saw Dougal coming out of the barn. He ran straight for her and jumped up excitedly, giving both her and Princess lots of kisses. "Hi, Dougal. Is Sammy in the barn? Let's go and see."

The dogs played and tussled with each other as she walked up to the barn. Penny pushed open the barn door and walked in. She stopped breathing when she saw Quade lifting and stacking bales of hay. Quade was wearing a tight T-shirt and her muscles looked gorgeous as she flexed and carried the heavy bales.

This was like a scene from one of her fantasies. Quade with bales of hale, in a barn, with delicious muscles, but this was real life, and in real life Quade didn't want anything to do with her.

Quade must have heard the door, as she turned around quickly. "Penny?"

"Yes. Here I am." Penny smiled but Quade's face remained stony. This was going to be hard.

"What are you doing here? I thought you'd be packing for America."

"Let me explain—"

"Explain? That what we had wasn't real?" Quade had convinced herself Penny would never come back to Axedale, that way she wouldn't have to face her, and she could ignore the pain. But seeing Penny now made the pain inside her chest multiply tenfold.

How could she ever get over this?

Penny walked up to her and said with an edge to her voice, "Of course it was real, and if you had stayed and talked to me, instead of running away, you would have known that too."

"What? Stay so you could deny what your good friend showed me?" Quade said.

"I love you, Sammy."

Quade couldn't believe her ears, and she snorted, "Yeah, so in love that you're going to America? I saw the contract, Penny."

"Did you see my signature on the contract?"

That stopped Quade in her tracks. "What? Um…no."

"Sammy, Olivia is jealous. She's had a thing for me since we were at school. I always made it clear that a relationship wasn't going to happen, but when she knew we were together…anyway she wanted to break us up."

Quade rubbed her forehead with her palm. She was extremely confused. "Are you saying that contract was a fake?"

"No, it was real, is real, but I'm not signing it."

"But that was your dream," Quade said. "You told me that from the beginning."

Penny smiled. "I have a new dream now, and I've already started working on it. Look."

Penny took her iPad out of her briefcase and opened her website. "Tell me what you see."

Quade scanned the page carefully, but her heart was beating so fast she could hardly take anything in.

Penny pointed to the homepage header. "It used to say *Penny's Kitchen*, but it now says *Penny's Country Kitchen*."

Quade looked up at Penny quickly. She couldn't even dare to let herself think what this implied. "Penny's Country Kitchen?"

"Axedale is where I want my new dream to be, my new business, my new life," Penny said.

Quade was overwhelmed. She could feel the tiny pieces of her smashed heart starting to rebuild with every word and loving glance from Penny.

"Really? Is this really what you want, because I couldn't take the pain again like I've felt for the last few days. You live for your business."

"Not any more, but I've one more thing to show you." Penny opened up her email and brought up a contract, signed this time by Penny and Harry.

"What is this?" Quade asked.

"It's a long-term lease for a huge area of land behind the farm. My new dream is to live here with you and run a business that is true to what I believe in, what you believe in—organic farming. I want to grow the vegetables I use in my cookbooks and recipes, on a large scale, and sell them to farmers' markets and supermarkets. I want us to be partners in life and in business."

Penny handed Quade the iPad and said, "All that's missing is your signature. I can be a farmer's wife *and* a businesswoman."

Quade took the iPad, set it down on a bale of hay beside her, and pulled Penny close. "Is that what you want? To be a farmer's wife?"

Penny rested her forehead against Quade's. "Yes, I want that more than anything."

"Oh God. I didn't think you would come back. I didn't think what we had could work," Quade said.

Penny threaded her fingers through Quade's short hair. "I'm so sorry Olivia hurt you, but she's gone from the company. I bought her out." Penny took Quade's hand and placed it on her chest. "I want you, I want to be a family with Dougal and Princess, and I want Axedale to be our home. I love you, Sammy."

Quade was overwhelmed with emotion. All the hurt and pain she'd felt for the last few days needed more than words to be banished. She needed to feel Penny.

She pulled Penny to her and leaned her forehead against hers. "I thought I'd lost you, Penny. I love you with all my heart. If you'll be my wife, I'll promise to always make you the happiest I can."

"It that a proposal?"

"It is," Quade said.

"Yes," Penny replied.

"Is that a yes, you will marry me?" Quade wanted to make sure before making any assumptions.

Penny gazed into her eyes and smiled. "It's a yes."

Quade kissed Penny and soon their kisses became frantic, the emotion and difficulty of the last few days taking over.

Quade pulled up the side of Penny's dress and grasped her thigh. Penny moaned into their kiss, and Quade pulled back. "I think we better go back to the farmhouse and talk about this some more."

Penny gave her the sexiest smile. "No, I think we should stay right here."

After a couple of seconds, Quade got her meaning. Penny's fantasy. "Here?"

Penny took her hand and led her over to the ladder that led to the hayloft. "I think in order to be a true farmer's wife, you need to make love to me in the barn."

Quade didn't need to be asked twice. Still holding Penny's hand, they both climbed up.

Penny looked around at the bales and giggled. "It's my fantasy come true."

Quade took a step to her. "What is your fantasy? Just the hay bales?"

Penny swept her hand over Quade's shoulder muscles. "It's not just the hay. It's you and the hay, dressed like this, so I can ogle your muscles, and"—Penny lifted Quade's hand and caressed her palm—"these hands on my body."

"I had no idea working hands could be considered a turn on," Quade said.

"They are to city girls." Penny slipped off her jacket and pulled off her sparkly T-shirt.

Quade was starting to see the attraction of barns, seeing her lover standing there in just her jeans and lacy black bra. The pain she had felt over the past few days was melting away, to be replaced by want and hunger.

She lifted Penny in her arms and carried her over to the back of the hayloft. When she laid her down, Penny said, "I love it when you carry me."

Quade lay down and leaned over her. "You didn't think that the first time I carried you."

"That's before the benefits of carrying were fully explained to me." Penny cocked her finger and beckoned Quade. "Come and show me how sexy farmers make love."

Quade smiled and then said seriously, "You're really sure about this? You're the love of my life, Penny. There'll be no one else for me."

Penny put her hands around Quade's neck. "You're the only love of my life, the only one I've ever trusted to touch me. There will never be anyone else. I love you, baby."

Looking into Penny's eyes, Quade saw the truth. Penny was hers. She'd found her farmer's wife.

Penny pulled her down into a kiss. She moaned when she felt Penny's nails dig in to her neck. She swept her hand over Penny's bare stomach, and she could feel Penny shiver at her touch. Quade pushed her hand under Penny's bra and grasped her breast. Penny's nipple hardened under her touch.

"Yes, baby."

She never thought she would feel Penny ever again, and here she was touching her, loving her. Quade wanted to never let go of her, and she had to make her come to erase the past few days of pain.

Quade pulled out of the kiss and took her hand from Penny's breast. She slid down to the button of Penny's jeans. "I want to make you come, sweetheart."

Penny put her hand over Quade's and pushed it, encouraging Quade. "Please? Give me my fantasy, Sexy Farmer."

Quade unbuttoned her jeans and pushed her hand straight in Penny's sex. She groaned when she felt how wet Penny was. "Jesus. This really is your fantasy, isn't it?"

"Yes." Penny gasped as she thrust her hips against Quade's fingers.

"I love you," Quade said before kissing Penny again.

Her fingers stroked Penny, tenderly at first, and then faster as Penny started to lose control.

Penny gripped her neck tightly, went taut, and Quade swallowed her cries of pleasure.

"I love you, I love you, baby," Penny said, catching her breath.

"I think I see your attraction to barns," Quade joked.

Penny rolled onto Quade and placed her head on Quade's chest. "You will when I get my breath back. You know, I've had to hug Truffle every night since we've been apart?" Truffle, the stuffed unicorn Quade bought her in London was very special and had reminded her of Quade and their love. Quade knew what she liked, and it had melted Penny's heart.

"Now you can hug me, Truffle, Princess, and Dougal," Quade said with a smile. "Our little family."

Penny kissed Quade's nose and said, "Our little family."

EPILOGUE

Penny checked her camera and turned it towards herself. "Hello, friends, welcome to what is truly the first day of *Penny's Country Kitchen*. After a lot of preparation of the soil and choosing what vegetables we are going to plant, we are going into production."

She turned the camera away and walked into one of the large greenhouses they'd had constructed on the land they had leased from Harry.

"This is just one of the two huge greenhouses we've built. We are going to grow tomatoes, lots of delicious greens, and micro veg—by the way, I've given up trying to explain micro veg to Sexy Farmer," Penny joked.

"I hope that one day soon, Penny's Country Kitchen veg will be in a supermarket near you."

Penny heard the honk of a horn and smiled. "My carriage awaits."

She hurried out of the greenhouse and saw the sight that made her heart flutter, her little family. Sammy was sitting in the driver's seat of the quad, Princess in the passenger seat, and Dougal in the back.

But the nicest sight of all was the thick gold band on Quade's wedding finger. She looked down at her own engagement and wedding rings, as she did often, just to make sure her dream was real. They had only just returned from their honeymoon the day before, a long wonderful honeymoon, with no cameras, no internet, and no distractions.

"We'll be late for Riley's medieval day, sweetheart."

"Coming. I was just admiring you from afar," Penny said as she walked over.

Penny lifted Princess up, so she could sit in the passenger seat. "I don't think I've got a dog any more. She's been glued to you since we picked them up last night."

Riley had looked after Dougal and Princess at Axedale while Penny and Quade were on honeymoon. The only other time Penny had been without Princess was her stay in hospital, and that had been hard on them both, but here in Axedale, everything was different for them.

Princess had Quade and Dougal, whom she adored, she had new friends in Riley and Caesar, and she knew she was loved and protected, no matter what. Just the way Penny felt.

Quade ruffled Princess's fur and gave Penny a lingering kiss. "She's just happy to have lots of people to love her. Now let's go before we miss all the roasted boar."

Penny laughed. A true carnivore, Quade had been particularly excited by the thought of eating roasted boar at the medieval day celebrations.

"I'm sure there'll be more than enough for you." Penny leaned over and ran her hand up and down Quade's thigh and whispered, "And if not, then I can satisfy you when we get home."

Quade shivered. "Don't say things like that or we won't make it to medieval day."

Since they had discovered each other and the joys of physical pleasure, Penny and Quade had been like a pair of horny teenagers.

"Hmm. I've missed our barn," Penny said.

Quade gripped the steering wheel tightly. "Me too. Who knew I was missing out on all this exciting barn activity before I met you."

"Now you've got me, and I'm going to show you just how much fun it can be." Penny winked.

❖

The noise of children's laughter reverberated around the grounds of Axedale Hall. The space at the front of the house had been given over to a medieval festival, planned by Riley and Harry.

Annie and Bridge leaned on the fence around the field set out for the pony tournament. Annie sighed with contentment. Everything had come together perfectly. After long planning, the Axedale grounds were full of visitors who had come from all over the country, vendors from the farmers' market selling their goods, as well as booths promoting local businesses. It was a great boost for local tourism, but what Riley had been most excited about were the medieval re-enactors. Knights in shining armour having sword fights and fair maidens were all over the place.

Bridge said, "Aren't they sweet?"

Annie followed her gaze over to the two loves in her life, Harry and Riley. Both were dressed in armour, and Harry was helping Riley get her pony ready for competition.

A mini-course had been set up for the children to ride around, with targets for them to hit with jousting poles. It had been what Riley had been most excited about.

"They really are, Bridge," Annie replied.

Bridge nudged her and said, "Who would have thought Harry would be a great parent?"

"I did." Annie smiled. "I've always had complete faith in her."

Bridge rolled her eyes.

Annie chuckled and pointed to Finn, who was a few yards away from them with a group of young children gathered around her, showing them magic tricks. "Anyway, who'd have thought you would have your own little miracle love story."

"Certainly not me. She really is achingly adorable, isn't she?"

"Who is?" Harry had walked over and put her arm around Annie.

"Hello, Sir Knight," Annie said. "Finn is adorable."

Harry frowned and said, "Buss me, my Lady Annie."

"What?" Annie said in confusion.

Harry smiled. "It means, give me a kiss."

"Oh, gladly." Annie gave her a soft kiss on the lips, and Harry's hand went to the growing swell of her stomach.

"Are you feeling all right? Not too tired?"

"I'm fine. Just make sure baby number one doesn't break something," Annie said, pointing to Riley brushing her horse Willow.

"Don't worry," Harry said. "Riley is worried about impressing Sophie."

Finn joined them and Bridge grasped her chin to give her a kiss. "Done with all your little tricks, Magician?"

"For the time being, M—Bridge," Finn said with a smile.

Annie heard her name called. She turned around and saw her other favourite couple, Penny and Quade. Penny waved, and their two dogs ran by their side. Penny was the only woman she knew who could pull off a dress and wellington boots.

As they got nearer Bridge said, "Oh, look. It's Mrs. Sexy Farmer."

Penny laughed, and Quade gave her lopsided smile. "Thanks, Bridge."

"Good honeymoon?" Finn asked with a smirk.

"Fabulous," Penny said.

Harry chimed in, "Somehow I couldn't quite picture you in Barbados, Quade."

Quade pulled Penny to her and kissed her head. "Penny is broadening my horizons."

"I bet." Harry winked.

Annie was so happy for Quade and Penny, and Bridge and Finn. Harry once described Axedale as the gloomy, loveless place where she grew up. Until Annie arrived with her cakes, bread, hot choco surprise, and fudgie-wudgies—then love had won out as it always did. Love had brought Axedale Hall and its village to life.

It gave Annie so much satisfaction to see her friends as happy as she was. Whether it was someone up in the sky or destiny that had brought Annie here, she was exceptionally grateful, because now she had a home, and she and her friends had love, and nothing had greater power than love.

"Riley's up next, darling," Harry said.

Annie hugged Harry and watched Willow and Riley trot to the start of the course.

"Yes, she is," Annie said.

About the Author

Jenny Frame is from the small town of Motherwell in Scotland, where she lives with her partner, Lou, and their well-loved and very spoiled dog.

She has a diverse range of qualifications, including a BA in public management and a diploma in acting and performance. Nowadays, she likes to put her creative energies into writing rather than treading the boards.

When not writing or reading, Jenny loves cheering on her local football team, cooking, and spending time with her family.

Jenny can be contacted at www.jennyframe.com.

Books Available from Bold Strokes Books

Comrade Cowgirl by Yolanda Wallace. When cattle rancher Laramie Bowman accepts a lucrative job offer far from home, will her heart end up getting lost in translation? (978-1-63555-375-8)

Double Vision by Ellie Hart. When her cell phone rings, Giselle Cutler answers it—and finds herself speaking to a dead woman. (978-1-63555-385-7)

Inheritors of Chaos by Barbara Ann Wright. As factions splinter and reunite, will anyone survive the final showdown between gods and mortals on an alien world? (978-1-63555-294-2)

Love on Lavender Lane by Karis Walsh. Accompanied by the buzz of honeybees and the scent of lavender, Paige and Kassidy must find a way to compromise on their approach to business if they want to save Lavender Lane Farm—and find a way to make room for love along the way. (978-1-63555-286-7)

Spinning Tales by Brey Willows. When the fairy tale begins to unravel and villains are on the loose, will Maggie and Kody be able to spin a new tale? (978-1-63555-314-7)

The Do-Over by Georgia Beers. Bella Hunt has made a good life for herself and put the past behind her. But when the bane of her high school existence shows up for Bella's class on conflict resolution, the last thing they expect is to fall in love. (978-1-63555-393-2)

What Happens When by Samantha Boyette. For Molly Kennan, senior year is already an epic disaster, and falling for mysterious waitress Zia is about to make life a whole lot worse. (978-1-63555-408-3)

Wooing the Farmer by Jenny Frame. When fiercely independent modern socialite Penelope Huntingdon-Stewart and traditional country farmer Sam McQuade meet, trusting their hearts is harder than it looks. (978-1-63555-381-9)

A Chapter on Love by Laney Webber. When Jannika and Lee reunite, their instant connection feels like a gift, but neither is ready for a second chance at love. Will they finally get on the same page when it comes to love? (978-1-63555-366-6)

Drawing Down the Mist by Sheri Lewis Wohl. Everyone thinks Grand Duchess Maria Romanova died in 1918. They were almost right. (978-1-63555-341-3)

Listen by Kris Bryant. Lily Croft is inexplicably drawn to Hope D'Marco but will she have the courage to confront the consequences of her past and present colliding? (978-1-63555-318-5)

Perfect Partners by Maggie Cummings. Elite police dog trainer Sara Wright has no intention of falling in love with a coworker, until Isabel Marquez arrives at Homeland Security's Northeast Regional Training facility and Sara's good intentions start to falter. (978-1-63555-363-5)

Shut Up and Kiss Me by Julie Cannon. What better way to spend two weeks of hell in paradise than in the company of a hot, sexy woman? (978-1-63555-343-7)

Spencer's Cove by Missouri Vaun. When Foster Owen and Abigail Spencer meet they uncover a story of lives adrift, loves lost, and true love found. (978-1-63555-171-6)

Without Pretense by TJ Thomas. After living for decades hiding from the truth, can Ava learn to trust Bianca with her secrets and her heart? (978-1-63555-173-0)

Unexpected Lightning by Cass Sellars. Lightning strikes once more when Sydney and Parker fight a dangerous stranger who threatens the peace they both desperately want. (978-1-163555-276-8)

Emily's Art and Soul by Joy Argento. When Emily meets Andi Marino she thinks she's found a new best friend but Emily doesn't know that Andi is fast falling in love with her. Caught up in exploring her sexuality, will Emily see the only woman she needs is right in front of her? (978-1-63555-355-0)

Escape to Pleasure: Lesbian Travel Erotica edited by Sandy Lowe and Victoria Villasenor. Join these award-winning authors as they explore the sensual side of erotic lesbian travel. (978-1-63555-339-0)

Music City Dreamers by Robyn Nyx. Music can bring lovers together. In Music City, it can tear them apart. (978-1-63555-207-2)

Ordinary is Perfect by D. Jackson Leigh. Atlanta marketing superstar Autumn Swan's life derails when she inherits a country home, a child, and a very interesting neighbor. (978-1-63555-280-5)

Royal Court by Jenny Frame. When royal dresser Holly Weaver's passionate personality begins to melt Royal Marine Captain Quincy's icy heart, will Holly be ready for what she exposes beneath? (978-1-63555-290-4)

Strings Attached by Holly Stratimore. Success. Riches. Music. Passion. It's a life most can only dream of, but stardom comes at a cost. (978-1-63555-347-5)

The Ashford Place by Jean Copeland. When Isabelle Ashford inherits an old house in small-town Connecticut, family secrets, a shocking discovery, and an unexpected romance complicate her plan for a fast profit and a temporary stay. (978-1-63555-316-1)

Treason by Gun Brooke. Zoem Malderyn's existence is a deadly threat to everyone on Gemocon and Commander Neenja KahSandra must find a way to save the woman she loves from having to commit the ultimate sacrifice. (978-1-63555-244-7)

A Wish Upon a Star by Jeannie Levig. Erica Cooper has learned to depend on only herself, but when her new neighbor, Leslie Raymond, befriends Erica's special needs daughter, the walls protecting her heart threaten to crumble. (978-1-63555-274-4)

Answering the Call by Ali Vali. Detective Sept Savoie returns to the streets of New Orleans, as do the dead bodies from ritualistic killings, and she does everything in her power to bring them to justice while trying to keep her partner, Keegan Blanchard, safe. (978-1-63555-050-4)

Breaking Down Her Walls by Erin Zak. Could a love worth staying for be the key to breaking down Julia Finch's walls? (978-1-63555-369-7)

Exit Plans for Teenage Freaks by 'Nathan Burgoine. Cole always has a plan—especially for escaping his small-town reputation as "that kid who was kidnapped when he was four"—but when he teleports to a museum, it's time to face facts: it's possible he's a total freak after all. (978-1-63555-098-6)

Friends Without Benefits by Dena Blake. When Dex Putman gets the woman she thought she always wanted, she soon wonders if it's really love after all. (978-1-63555-349-9)

Invalid Evidence by Stevie Mikayne. Private Investigator Jil Kidd is called away to investigate a possible killer whale, just when her partner Jess needs her most. (978-1-63555-307-9)

Pursuit of Happiness by Carsen Taite. When attorney Stevie Palmer's client reveals a scandal that could derail Senator Meredith Mitchell's presidential bid, their chance at love may be collateral damage. (978-1-63555-044-3)

Seascape by Karis Walsh. Marine biologist Tess Hansen returns to Washington's isolated northern coast where she struggles to adjust to small-town living while courting an endowment for her orca research center from Brittany James. (978-1-63555-079-5)

Second in Command by VK Powell. Jazz Perry's life is disrupted and her career jeopardized when she becomes personally involved with the case of an abandoned child and the child's competent but strict social worker, Emory Blake. (978-1-63555-185-3)

Taking Chances by Erin McKenzie. When Valerie Cruz and Paige Wellington clash over what's in the best interest of the children in Valerie's care, the children may be the ones who teach them it's worth taking chances for love. (978-1-63555-209-6)

All of Me by Emily Smith. When chief surgical resident Galen Burgess meets her new intern, Rowan Duncan, she may finally discover that doing what you've always done will only give you what you've always had. (978-1-63555-321-5)

As the Crow Flies by Karen F. Williams. Romance seems to be blooming all around, but problems arise when a restless ghost emerges from the ether to roam the dark corners of this haunting tale. (978-1-63555-285-0)

Both Ways by Ileandra Young. SPEAR agent Danika Karson races to protect the city from a supernatural threat and must rely on the woman she's trained to despise: Rayne, an achingly beautiful vampire. (978-1-63555-298-0)

Calendar Girl by Georgia Beers. Forced to work together, Addison Fairchild and Kate Cooper discover that opposites really do attract. (978-1-63555-333-8)

Lovebirds by Lisa Moreau. Two women from different worlds collide in a small California mountain town, each with a mission that doesn't include falling in love. (978-1-63555-213-3)

Media Darling by Fiona Riley. Can Hollywood bad girl Emerson and reluctant celebrity gossip reporter Hayley work together to make each other's dreams come true? Or will Emerson's secrets ruin not one career, but two? (978-1-63555-278-2)

Stroke of Fate by Renee Roman. Can Sean Moore live up to her reputation and save Jade Rivers from the stalker determined to end Jade's career and, ultimately, her life? (978-1-63555-62-4)

The Rise of the Resistance by Jackie D. The soul of America has been lost for almost a century. A few people may be the difference between a phoenix rising to save the masses or permanent destruction. (978-1-63555-259-1)

The Sex Therapist Next Door by Meghan O'Brien. At the intersection of sex and intimacy, anything is possible. Even love. (978-1-63555-296-6)

Unforgettable by Elle Spencer. When one night changes a lifetime... Two romance novellas from best-selling author Elle Spencer. (978-1-63555-429-8)

BOLDSTROKESBOOKS.COM

Looking for your next great read?

Visit BOLDSTROKESBOOKS.COM
to browse our entire catalog of paperbacks, ebooks,
and audiobooks.

**Want the first word on what's new?
Visit our website for event info,
author interviews, and blogs.**

Subscribe to our free newsletter for sneak peeks,
new releases, plus first notice of promos
and daily bargains.

SIGN UP AT
BOLDSTROKESBOOKS.COM/signup

Quality and Diversity in LGBTQ Literature

*Bold Strokes Books is an award-winning publisher
committed to quality and diversity in LGBTQ fiction.*